OUTLIERS

OUTLIERS

S.M. PEARCE

Audbade Publishing

ISBN: 978-1-7753439-0-5 (Paperback)
ISBN: 978-1-7753439-1-2 (Hardcover)

Any reference to historical events, real people, or real places are used fictitiously. Names, characters, and places are products of the author's imagination.

Cover Design by Anita B. Carroll
Book Design by Erin Rhew

Printed by Ingram Spark, Inc., in Canada.

First printing edition 2018.

Aubade Publishing
1344 Augustine Dr.
Burlington, Ontario, L7P2M8

www.smpearce.com

For my little brother, whose adventure knows no bounds.

Part 1

ONCE UPON A TIME...
IT ALL STARTED WHEN...
THIS IS NOW MY LIFE,
RUNNING FROM THE END.

THEY TOOK IT ALL FROM US,
OUR HOMES, FAMILIES, LIVES,
AND NOW THEY WANT US TOO,
WHAT CAN WE DO BUT HIDE?

IT'S ONLY BIDING TIME,
THIS KEEPING HEADS DOWN LOW,
BUT THERE IS NOTHING LEFT FOR US,
NOT A SINGLE PLACE TO GO.

Chapter 1: Dying

I was having dinner at the round table on my backyard patio. Moon-lights surrounded us and warded off the dark. The air was cool, but it was never too cold—the government made sure of that. It never rained, snowed, or got too hot or cold. My older brother, Damion, and I stepped on each other's feet under the table but were careful to pause whenever our parents looked our way. He was decked out in his usual black, his dark bangs covering one of his eyes.

On his other side, Ariana rolled her eyes. She'd been living with us for about a year, ever since her family threw her out. "You guys are so mature," she said, her voice dripping with sarcasm.

"Thanks," I said, giving her a quick, overly wide grin. She rolled her eyes again and turned back to her food.

Xavier nudged me with his elbow. "Can you pass the salt, Renee?"

"Sure," I slid it over. Xavier and his mother, Ms. Cage, only lived a few houses down the street, so they came over a lot. She was sitting next to my parents, chatting about our school.

"Thanks," Xavier said as he sprinkled the salt over his potatoes.

"Fifty creds," I said, motioning like I was tapping a cred-stick on my holo-watch.

"Yeah," he said with a laugh. "Okay."

My brother stepped on my foot again, restarting the foot war.

"Well." I shrugged as I stomped on Damion's foot. "It was worth a try."

Chatter floated around the table, as well as the harsh scraping of knives and forks on plates. The smell of chicken and steamed carrots drifted through the air. Just another normal night.

Until a black van pulled up in front of our back gate.

"Who's that?" I peered out the gate. Nobody we knew owned anything that big, and certainly not without a special work permit.

My parents turned around in their chairs, and the plastic scraped against our faux-stone patio. Everyone followed my gaze to the now parked vehicle.

"I...don't know," my mother said. Her light, calm tone had been replaced by an unusual, guarded one. Her light-brown eyes flicked over to my father, and she spoke to him in a low voice. "We didn't order anything, did we?"

"No." He shook his head, and his dark eyebrows dipped down.

"Prob'ly got the wrong house," Ariana said. She lifted a forkful of Chicken-Sub to her mouth, careful not to smudge her pale-pink lipstick. I didn't know how she could eat those gross meat substitutes, but she insisted on being vegetarian.

The doors of the van clicked open, and three people stepped out. They were dressed in some sort of padded fighting gear that matched the tar black of their van.

Hey, Damion, I thought to my brother. *Maybe it's the Black Clothes Club coming to recruit you.* Although, Damion's fashion sense was hardly the strangest thing about him.

My brother, my friends, and I were all normal in most regards, except for the abilities we'd each developed over the years. I was the first, discovering my telepathy when I was about eight. Only my parents were in on the secret.

The doors of the van slammed closed, and the strangers headed towards our backyard. They moved with an unnerving confidence, an authority to their step that proved they hadn't gotten lost and turned up at the wrong house.

"I'll go see who it is," Damion said, pushing his chair back to stand.

"Don't," my father said, his tone sharp with warning. His already fair face had lost its colour, as had my mother's. Did they know what was going on?

The woman and two men heading towards us each had a weapon belt strapped around their waist. There were guns, skinny rods, and knives, but the handcuffs sent terror shaking through my body. The cuffs emitted a pale, green glow, and they swung towards us in an ominous warning.

Are those for us?

"Are those *guns*?" Xavier asked, squinting to see.

"What?" Ms. Cage asked, alarmed. It was illegal for civilians to own guns. She shot up from her chair and stepped forward for a better look.

My mother nodded to my father, a silent communication that I couldn't understand. Their expressions were grim. My heart started to beat harder in my chest. Whatever was happening, it couldn't be good. Why did those people have weapons? Why were they here?

My father pulled something out of his pocket. "Take this," he said to Damion and placed a small white cube in my brother's hand.

"What—" Damion started.

"Go with them," my father instructed, gesturing to Ariana, Xavier, and me. I'd never seen him so afraid. "It's a teleport. Press the button on the bottom—"

"What're you talking about?" I asked, looking between my parents. Blood pounded in my ears.

The strangers yanked open our gate.

"Go," my father said. It was an order, not a request. "We'll come if there's time."

Unable to take it any more, I listened in on his thoughts. This definitely qualified as a special circumstance. *We have to hold them off long enough for the kids to get away. We were so careful…*

My parents definitely knew something. What did my father mean by "careful?"

Ms. Cage looked as confused as the rest of us. She stood uncertainly beside my parents and turned to Xavier. "I don't know what's going on." She took a large breath. Her eyes flicked to the fast-approaching strangers. "But it can't be good. Go."

Xavier opened his mouth, likely to protest.

"There's no time," my mother said. Her voice held urgency but was unwavering and authoritative at the same time. My brother inhaled sharply and nodded. He backed away from the table.

Renee, go, my father thought, looking at me. He must have assumed I would be reading his mind. His dark-blue eyes, mirrors to my own, pleaded with me to leave. I stood up with a jolt, almost knocking my chair over. *Remember,* he added, *you make your own happiness.* He was always saying that, but why now?

Damion set the white cube on the grass. I widened my eyes as the cube unfolded its sides so that it lay flat, revealing what looked like a large circuit board.

My friends and I ran towards my brother. A hologram of some alley projected from the unfolded cube. The strangers who had invaded our home charged at the table. My mother punched one in the face.

Damion shoved Ariana into the hologram. But it wasn't a hologram. Ariana appeared in the street, holding her hands out to catch her balance. A teleport, that's what my father had said. Government workers used them for important jobs, but regular citizens weren't allowed to have them because they couldn't be tracked. How did we have one? Why? Were my parents criminals?

"Wait—" Xavier said. He tried to get a look at our parents.

"I'm sorry." Damion pushed Xavier through as a loud cry rang through the air. I whipped my head around to see Ms. Cage on the ground. My father had those glowing handcuffs on, and his face was twisted in pain. He was being held back by one of the strangers. My mother struggled against another.

Damion started to tug me towards the teleport.

"No!" I shook my head wildly, my dark brown hair whipping around, and tried to jerk out of his grasp. Our parents were in trouble. We couldn't just leave them. Two of the thugs left my father and Ms. Cage on the ground and ran towards us. The third secured cuffs onto my mother's wrists.

"I'm right behind you," Damion said.

I'd given up fighting his hold. Tears cascaded down my face. He kissed me on the top of the head and started to push me into the teleport. The two strangers were only a couple feet away.

"Be brave," he breathed. A tear fell from his eye. I'd never seen Damion cry. Not even when we were little.

I fell through the teleport, landing on the hard, grey pavement. Xavier helped me to my feet as the bulky man and woman reached my brother. They yanked him backwards by the shoulders.

"Damion!" I screamed. I lunged at the teleport. My brother, unable to break free, gave me a pain-filled look as he crashed his foot down on the teleportation device. Overcome with grief, I dropped to my knees. They slammed into the pavement, rattling my teeth, as the image of my backyard disappeared, replaced with the solid black wall at the back of the alley.

My brother was gone.

My parents were gone.

I was in a dark alley. The memory of my brother's tear-stained cheek and his foot coming down played on a loop in my mind. Damion *never* cried. He'd known he wouldn't be coming with us.

The strangers had had guns. My family was probably dead or, at the very least, unreachable. I wouldn't see him or my parents again.

I put my hand to my mouth as a squeak-like noise escaped it.

"I...I don't understand," Ariana said, nearly sobbing. Her breathing was shaky at best, and she stammered when she spoke. "Those people..."

My breathing was uneven too. With watery eyes, I stared at the spot where the teleport had been only moments ago.

"What was that?" Xavier asked, panicked. His feet slapped against the pavement as he got closer. "We have to get back—"

"How?" I asked. My voice carried a bit of an edge to it. "The teleport thing is gone, and they had *guns*." Only the police had guns. But weren't the police supposed to help people?

"Do you think they're..." Ariana broke out in a fresh round of sobbing. She didn't need to finish her sentence. We knew how it ended.

"Where are we?" Though I tried to wipe the tears from my face, they just kept coming. I wanted to focus on something else. Anything else. I turned around, but my view of the alley was blurred.

Xavier and Ariana looked around too.

"Are we in Brampton?" Xavier asked. I followed his gaze, still wiping tears from my face.

There was a plaza across the road from the alley, and one of the stores had a sign that read Brampton Solar. Everything ran on solar energy. Cars, houses, holo-watches. That was the store where people would go to replace broken panels.

"That's pretty far." Brampton was about an hour's drive away from my house. The rest of the small white buildings in the area were the same for the most part—probably mass printed. It was a Service neighbourhood.

"We're in the ghetto?" Ariana asked, sniffling.

That was another way to put it. When careers were selected each year for the eleventh graders, those unfit for "real" work were placed in the Services—cleaning, running stores, doing labour that machines couldn't, and performing whatever else nobody really wanted to do. They didn't make much money and usually lived in poor cities like Brampton because it was all they could afford. "Isn't...Isn't that dangerous?" Ariana's light-purple eyes flicked from left to right.

"You're seriously worried about that after what just happened?" Xavier asked. "Apparently *our* houses weren't all that safe."

We'd lived in a wealthy enough neighbourhood. My mother was one of the genetic scientists that helped design children before they were born, specializing in immunizations and healing efficiency. My father was a marine biologist, working with the few marine species left to preserve and care for them. I'd always wanted to follow in his footsteps. Would that even be possible now?

"We need to go to the cops or something." Ariana tripped and stumbled over her words. Her lips were quivering, and her long black ponytail—which she never allowed to be messy—was frizzed and coming undone. Black mascara lines trailed down her mocha-coloured cheeks, and she sniffled every few seconds, wiggling her small nose. She looked...unraveled. "Get help... We can tell them wh...what happened, and they can find—"

"We can't." I shook my head. The idea of going to the police set off a bad feeling in my gut. Though it might have been that I wanted to puke after what had just happened.

"Why?" she asked.

"I just—" I pressed my lips together. "I have a bad feeling. They had guns, and those handcuff things... Where would they have got that stuff?" Someone would be lucky to steal a meal bar and not get caught, let alone weapons.

All that was left of the human race lived on the sort-of-spaceship-but-really-not that was Mozaan. We called it home. We'd all been taught it was a healthy chunk taken from Earth, all that was left after the planet started dying almost two centuries ago. They had suspended it above Earth, using something that manipulated Earth's magnetic field. A dome surrounding Mozaan allowed the government to control the atmosphere, air pressure, and other technical stuff I didn't understand. Between the dome, the small space, and the technology the government had, it was almost impossible to get away with anything.

"You think the cops did this?" Xavier asked. "That wasn't exactly a typical arrest." Normally the government would freeze people's accounts so they didn't try to go anywhere—not that it really mattered—and send a holo-message that told citizens when to be at a certain jail.

"I don't know," I said. "But what if it was? They were trying to get us too."

My parents had been terrified. But they hadn't been surprised. They'd had the teleport on them, ready to go. And my dad had known they wouldn't get away with us. What else had they known?

"Why?" Ariana asked. She wiped at her face, further smearing the mascara running across her cheeks. "We didn't do anything wrong."

"Well, they must think we did. I'm not saying we won't ever go to the police. I'm just saying let's not go right now when we don't even know what happened and what we're gonna do about it," I said.

The resolute look in Xavier's glassy eyes said he had a few ideas—all of which involved finding those people and beating them to the ground. Maybe setting them on fire with his ability. I'd seen similar looks on him before, when he'd gotten into fights with school bullies.

It was tempting, but as angry as I was, I also had the sense to be terrified. There was no way we could find those people, let alone do any damage to them. They probably had some sort of connection to the government, so we couldn't go to officials for help. How could we even survive? "It's dark, and we have nowhere to...go." I'd been about to say "sleep," but it wasn't likely any of us would sleep tonight.

"My aunt lives in Brampton," Xavier said. His eyes searched for a street sign. "On Fisher."

"She does?" Ariana asked. Her voice was cracked and broken but held onto a shard of hope.

"Yeah." He swallowed, giving a single somber nod.

"We...we should find her." Ariana said.

"It's too late." My tears had dried up, and the shock had settled in. "We can't be out on the streets."

"Honestly," Xavier said, "after that, I don't really think we need to worry about some cranked person on the street."

He had a point. What were the odds that any other terrible things could happen tonight? It still hadn't fully sunk in, what had happened and what we'd just lost.

"I don't know." Ariana said, biting her lip. "What if Renee's right? Something could happen."

I tore my gaze from the dark plaza and looked between my friends. "I think Xavier has a point," I told Ariana. "We need help. It might be just as dangerous to stay in an alley all night."

"But..." She glanced beyond the alley.

"We could crush anything we run into here anyway," Xavier said.

Of course, we hadn't been able to do a thing to stop those strangers. If they found us, we wouldn't be crushing anything.

Chapter 2: Gimme Shelter

S o, where's Fisher?" I asked Xavier. We were at the edge of the alley, ready to step onto the sidewalk. "Which way do we go?"

"Uh." He scratched the back of his head, disheveling some of his short, thick brown hair. "I don't know. It's not like I'm here a lot, and I've never been in this area."

I sighed, rubbing my hand over my face. "What are we gonna do now?" I asked, shoulders slumping. We couldn't just walk around the city for hours.

"What about that woman over there?" Ariana pointed down the street to a tall woman with a bounce in her step.

"What about her?" I asked, furrowing my eyebrows.

"We could ask to borrow her holo-watch and look up the street," Ariana said.

"Think she'll let us?" Xavier asked.

"Well," I sighed. The woman would be gone soon if we didn't approach her. "Only one way to find out."

We left the alley, walking briskly down the sidewalk. It was only a minute or so before we reached the woman.

"Sorry," I said as I tapped her on the shoulder.

She turned around to face the three of us. When I got a closer look at her, I realized she couldn't have been much older than we were. She had platinum blond hair and bold red lipstick. It was easy to believe she lived in Brampton. She wasn't designed well, if at all, with her crooked nose being the most obvious flaw. There were also the baggier, dark clothes that poorest people seemed to wear, due to the fact that they didn't cost as much or fade as quickly. She seemed to belong in Brampton.

"Could we borrow your holo-watch for a sec? We're totally lost, and ours are dead." I pointed to mine. The portal had done something to them, making them useless.

"Oh, um..." She looked us up and down. She twisted the ends of her hair around a couple of her fingers. Our ragged appearances probably didn't help. "I dunno..."

"We'll only be a sec," Xavier said. He smiled at her, keeping his tone light. "And what are we gonna do?"

She smiled, and I could've sworn she batted her mascara-coated lashes at him. How old was she anyway? Eighteen?

"Alright," she said. "Here." She tapped the watch to life and unlocked it with her thumbprint. She held out her wrist to Xavier.

"Uh...thanks," he said, awkwardly taking her wrist. She couldn't have just handed him the watch? She stared at him almost the entire time he searched. "Here." Xavier let go of her wrist, and she pulled her arm back, her face falling slightly.

"Oh, that *was* quick." She smiled at him again, and not in a way an eighteen-year-old stranger should smile at a fifteen-year-old.

Even I could admit Xavier was good-looking. He'd gotten lucky enough that it was barely noticeable that he wasn't designed much outside of the mandatory vaccines, the few freckles he had being the main giveaways. He had a strong, sharp jawline and was lightly tanned, with an athletic frame. He had almond-shaped dark chocolate eyes and matching hair, which had been cut just below his ears but frayed out at the sides. His lips were full, with a sharp Cupid's bow and narrow corners. Xavier ranked higher on the attractiveness scale than most guys, probably more than any of the guys the girl had seen in this Service area, but she didn't need to throw herself at him like that.

"Yep, thanks." I gave her a tight smile. "Bye."

Her eyebrows rose in surprise, but she turned around and continued on briskly to wherever she was headed.

"So." Ariana turned to Xavier. "Where're we going?"

He nodded in the other direction. "This way," he said, and we started walking.

"I was thinking," Ariana said, picking at her nail polish. "We...we need something to call *them*."

I'd already been calling them a few choice names in my head.

"What were you thinking?" Xavier asked.

"I dunno," she said. "Like, the *Takers?*"

"I like that," I said, and Xavier nodded. It was fitting. They had taken everything from us.

We walked for almost an hour before we found Fisher Avenue. A gloomy silence hovered over us.

"Fisher." I looked up at the sign, then to Xavier. "That's it, right?"

"Yeah," he said, and we turned down the street. "Looks familiar too."

"What number?" Ariana asked. She looked back and forth between the houses. There were a lot.

"Forty-three thirteen," he said. We were still in the three thousands.

"Great," I said.

We still had at least fifteen minutes to go. *Can I really make it that far?* I was exhausted, and what was the point of it all anyway? My parents and my brother were gone. *Can't I just collapse right here and never get up?*

The street never seemed to end. Small houses that all looked the same wound down it, and the faint smell of jasmine filled my nose. All we saw for over a kilometre were repetitions of the same solar-paneled house, each with a small garden and a neat lawn. I focused on trudging alongside my friends, just putting one foot in front of the other.

Ariana was the one who made us stop. "Hey," she said. There was a certain uplift to her voice that made me follow her gaze. "That's it, right?"

"Finally," Xavier said. I couldn't have agreed more.

The house looked like all the others, but with one small difference—a little, rainbow-coloured wind spinner was stuck in the front of the garden. We walked up to the front door, and Xavier rang the bell.

Xavier's aunt ushered us into her house seconds after opening the door. She brought us to her living room and seated us on her long grey couch. She sat down on the black coffee table in front of us, looking at us with wide and worried eyes.

"Xavier, what happened?" she asked. "Why are you here so late? And your clothes are all ripped up... Were you three in a fight?"

He cast his eyes down at his lap. "They're gone," he said, so low she leaned forward to hear him.

His words felt so final. Our families were gone. We were sitting on a stranger's couch. There was nobody left in the world to care about us, besides this lady I'd never met.

"Who's gone, hon?" his aunt asked. Xavier fiddled with his thumbs. "What happened to you?"

"They took them—our parents," Xavier said. "They took mom."

I had been staring at the ripped and dirty knees of my white pants, but I lifted my head up. Xavier's eyes were glassy, his voice broken. He wasn't going to say anything more.

"What?" she asked. Her worry had increased tenfold. "Who did? What d'you mean?"

I took a deep breath. "People came at night. We don't know who they were. Our parents got us away in time, but..." My voice was already cracking. I had to tell her if she was going to help us, but I didn't want to say it. Saying it made it real.

"They killed them," Ariana said in a stroke of bravery. Tears started to pour from her eyes. She stuttered again, but she continued, "Ms. Cage, the Strykers... They put us through a teleport thing, and we ended up in this alley, but they didn't make it."

"Elaena?" The woman's expression dropped, and her lip held the slightest tremble. "I don't understand. How could any of this happen?"

Good question.

After some more painful questioning and crying, Xavier's aunt offered us each a glass of water. As we sipped from the cups, she told us she'd decided we would stay there. Xavier offered to take the couch, leaving Ariana and me with the spare bedroom.

Aunt Liz, who had insisted we call her that, said we should get some rest. She couldn't have been more right. I barely made it up the stairs. Not bothering to pull back the covers, Ariana and I collapsed onto our own sides of the soft, cool bed.

~

"Shut up!" I yelled at my brother from atop a branch in our backyard tree. We were fighting about something stupid. I kept a tight grip on the tree with my small, ten-year-old fingers. "I'm staying up here forever, and I'm never talking to you again!"

"Promise?" He yelled back up at me, arms crossed over his chest. I plucked a thin stick from the tree and hurtled it towards him.

"Go away!"

A taunting smirk crept up onto his face. "Thought you weren't talking to me."

I scrunched my face up in anger and gripped the tree harder. He ruined everything! Under my fingers, the tree began to turn grey. I stared with wide eyes as it crumbled into ashes. I tried to scramble off of the branch, but it was too late. It disintegrated.

As I fell, a short, high scream erupted from my throat. I landed hard on the ground, one of my legs underneath me. A sharp and intense pain shot up my leg. I quickly shifted off of it, but the movement only sent harder bursts of pain through it. I held my hurt leg as best I could, tears spilling.

"Ow," I whimpered. I couldn't move my leg, and the pain was so bad it was all I could do not to scream again.

Damion was by my side in an instant. He grabbed me by the shoulder. "Renee," he said. "What... Are you okay?"

I shook my head, sniffing. "It hurts. A lot."

"Hey, it's okay." He wiped away my tears with his thumb. "It's alright." He took my hand, and I squeezed his hard.

"I...I think it's broken." My face tightened with the pain. The tears still pricked at my eyes. "It hurts so bad."

My brother's expression was heavy with concern. "I'm so sorry, Renee," he said. "This is all my fault. I was just being a jerk."

I'd never heard him sound so guilty. Then, the second impossible thing happened that day. The pain in my leg started to fade until, within a few seconds, it felt perfectly fine.

I squinted in confusion. "What?" I asked, lifting up my pant leg. There wasn't a scratch. I looked back up at Damion. "What did you do? How did you do that?"

"I..." He stared at me, perplexed. "I have no idea."

I had been wrong. Damion didn't ruin everything; he was the one who fixed everything.

I opened my eyes and blinked rapidly at the sudden light. I didn't get out of bed right away. I just breathed and lay there for a few minutes. *Damion.* Who would make things better now?

I sighed, slowly sitting up and rubbing my eyes. *Just get through today.* I forced myself out of bed.

Aunt Liz greeted us in the morning, her brown hair straightened and her clothes simple yet stylish. She made us breakfast and gave us fresh clothes from Xavier's cousins, who had long since left home for their Careers. We were being taken care of. I had to try and hope things could get better.

Having a shower almost convinced me. I let the hot water cascade over my skin for a while. Aunt Liz had said to help ourselves to the soaps and everything. I stayed in the shower as long as possible. It seemed almost symbolic, like washing away the fear of yesterday or something like that.

I slipped my new clothes on. They were a bit big, but I wasn't swimming in them. The shirt was dark blue, with some white curving around the hips, and the pants solid grey. Far from my usual look of form-fitting clothes in pastel colours. It didn't matter. They were clean.

Aunt Liz had to leave shortly after I came downstairs. She worked in the Green Industries, cleaning up plant waste and stuff. A pang went through my heart as I thought again of my father, who had been teaching me about marine life only days ago.

Aunt Liz grabbed a long violet coat from the silver hook on the front door. "You can make anything you want to eat for lunch," she said. "Stuff's in the kitchen. I'll be back soon. Be safe." She closed the door behind her. The locking system beeped, and the three of us were alone. Again.

We sat on the couch, unsure what else we could do. Until I saw the Screen in the wall. "Do you think your aunt would mind if we used that?" I asked Xavier.

"Don't think so," he said, turning his head towards me. "Why?"

"We should try to figure out what's going on. I mean, those...Takers looked so professional. They had all those weapons." Why would they have had all that just to target us? "Maybe there's more stuff like this going on."

"I think there is," Ariana said. "Like didn't Rebecca from school stop showing up all of a sudden?"

"Oh, yeah," Xavier said. "And she was like us, wasn't she?"

"Yeah," Ariana nodded. She was the girl that tried to get to know everyone. "She had, like, super speed or something."

We all huddled around the Screen as I turned it on.

The search bar was up on the Screen, and the keypad awaited my fingertips. "What should I look for?" I asked.

We spent over an hour searching. Maybe it had been a stupid idea. It didn't look like we were going to find anything.

"Just try one more thing," Ariana said, after I had suggested we give it up. "You never know."

"Alright," I covered my mouth as I yawned. I wasn't sure what good it would do. I typed in *People, Taken, Strange,* and *Different* into the search bar. Endless results came up. I scrolled down, looking for anything relevant.

"Doesn't look like there's anything, Ari," Xavier said, scanning the search results.

She sighed. "It was worth a shot."

I furrowed my brow. What did that link mean? "Guys," I said. "This one might be something." I pointed to the link.

"Outliers Being Subtracted," Ariana read. "What's that even mean?"

"It means the odd ones out are subtracted," Xavier explained. "Taken away. We're Outliers." We decided that it was a fitting name for people like us with abilities.

I clicked on the link. "Let's hope it's not just a math help site." It took a long time to load. Two full seconds.

You know who you are.
You are not safe.
Don't stand out.
Don't trust anyone.
They'll come for you next.

"Well," Xavier said. We were all staring at the screen. "I don't think it's a math help site."

"Don't stand out," Ariana read. "So, you think it's people like us being taken? With powers?"

"It has to be," I said. "Why else would Damion and the three of us, and that Rebecca girl, be targeted? There's no way that's a coincidence."

"But who could have the power to be tracking us and taking us?" Xavier asked.

"Not to mention covering it up," Ariana added. "I've never seen anything about it on the Media, and look how long it took us to find a site." The site flickered off. An error message came up saying the site had been shut down due to slander. "What?"

"It has to be the government," I said. I turned the Screen off. "Think about it. Why else would they care if people knew what was going on?" If it wasn't them, they would have wanted to help.

"But how do you think they even knew about our powers?" Ariana asked. "It's not like we advertise."

"Spies in the neighbourhood probably," Xavier said. I hummed in agreement. "The site's right. We can't tell anybody. Not even my aunt."

"But..." Ariana looked let down. "If the government's doing this, shouldn't we, like, expose them or whatever?"

"We can't." I shook my head. "They control all the Media. Nobody would believe us if we started talking, but the Takers might hear and come for us."

"She's right," Xavier said. He didn't sound happy about it. "If we wanna live, we keep a low profile."

There was nothing more to do. It wasn't safe to look for more on the Screen; the government could have been watching. So we did what everyone does after a shock; we got ourselves some food.

We cooked and ate our cheeseless Sub-Beef burgers in silence. The wave of purpose that had come from research was gone. There was nothing to do now but sit around and be sad.

We tried playing a virtual board game, but it only worsened how we felt. We'd always played with Damion. He'd always won, and I'd always joked that he must have found a way to cheat. It was wrong for anyone else to win. My friends agreed, so we gave up on the game ten minutes in.

We switched to a television program. The experience surrounded us, taking our senses to an alternate reality where the Mars colonists had survived a hundred or so years ago. Some were currently caught off base in a windstorm. It was a shameless distraction from real life. I was happy to have the distraction for a few hours. It liberated me from my thoughts.

We didn't speak or pause the program until I heard Aunt Liz talking with a neighbour at the front of the house. I waved my hand in front of me, shutting the program off, and turned to face the Window-Screen. It took up almost the entire wall beside the door. Light poured into my eyes, and I saw Aunt Liz was approaching the front door. The door beeped, and she strode inside.

"Hello," she called, her tone pleasant.

"Hey," we all replied, monotone. We strode over to greet her at the door.

"How was the day?" she asked. She hung up her long coat. "How are you feeling? Did you find everything okay?"

"Fine." Xavier said.

If numb counted as fine.

"Lot less tired," I said. I gave her the best smile I could. "Thanks."

"Oh, you're so welcome." Aunt Liz took the time to hug each of us. She smelled like a sweet perfume.

"How was your day?" Ariana asked. She had just been crying, leaving her eyes red and puffy and her hair disheveled.

"Oh, good." Aunt Liz's eyes crinkled. They were an extremely light brown. Much different than the solid, dark brown of Xavier's eyes. "Er, what would you three like for dinner? I've never really been a chef..."

It felt wrong to ask for anything specific. We were already staying in her home and eating her food. I would take whatever she gave me.

"We could do something simple." Xavier glanced at the cupboards. "Like Chicken-Sub and a vegetable."

Meat substitutes weren't just for those who didn't like meat. I was lucky my family could afford to get meat almost once every week, but Aunt Liz had probably never had it.

"That sounds good," Ariana said.

"Renee?" Aunt Liz turned to me. "Would you be okay with that?"

"Yeah." I tried to seem happy about it, but my voice still sounded like I was on the verge of crying. "That's great."

"I'll search up instructions then," she said. She lifted up her holo-watch and tapped it on. "One sec."

"I could cook it," Xavier said, semi-reluctantly. "If you want."

Ariana and I looked at him. "You can cook?" I asked. How had I not known this? We'd been friends our whole lives.

"A little," Xavier shrugged. "Had to. 'Cause of how late my mom works."

"Oh." What else could I say?

"But anyway." He turned to his aunt. "I can make dinner, if you want."

"Could you?" She slumped, and the worry lines disappeared from her face. "It's just I've never been good at cooking. I burn everything, so I mostly eat the packaged stuff."

"No problem," Xavier said. Soon, the kitchen was filled with the smell of fake chicken and steamed broccoli. The chicken smelled just like Ariana's had the night before. I closed my eyes for a few seconds, trying to get back to earlier that night, before the Takers showed up.

Due to a lack of chairs, we sat in the living room. Xavier had lied when he said he could only cook "a little." The food was simple, but everything was done perfectly. I made a mental note to ask him to cook in the future. Aunt Liz wouldn't stop praising him for it. He just waved off her compliments, saying it was nothing special.

It felt like a long time before we finished eating dinner. But then, the hours just seemed to go by slower in general. Since Ariana had asked, Aunt Liz was telling us all about her job in the Green Industries, cleaning up community gardens and the like. I tried not to listen. It reminded me too much of my father.

Every night after work, he used to tell me about all the plants and animals he'd seen and studied. It made me sad to think I'd never hear another story about Piper, the excitable dolphin. Or Bobby, the crab who was always trying to find a way out of his tank. I hurried to clear my plate and escape upstairs.

I changed into a random pair of pyjamas and crawled under the covers on my side of the bed. Ariana was still talking down-stairs. Maybe that was her way of taking her mind off things. I just wanted to sleep. I closed my eyes, sinking into the pillow.

Chapter 3: To Normal Or Not To Normal

Two weeks later, Aunt Liz had taken quite a liking to us. She registered as our guardian. Then, she registered us in school. She didn't believe it could be the government after us, and she needed the Caretaker Bonus if she was going to have enough money to feed us. Honestly, we were all too drained and depressed to care much.

But, how can we just go back? Like everything is normal? It was the least we could do though. Aunt Liz had taken us in without even knowing us that well. She had given us warm beds. Food. Clothes. Going to school was a small thing to ask by comparison.

I had always liked school. Damion hadn't. He'd been looking forward to the end of this year, when he would graduate from grade eleven into his Career Co-op. I didn't normally see him much during the day at school, but this morning still felt different as I put on my stiff, irritating uniform. We were in someone else's house. My and Damion's names weren't messily carved into the table. Only Ariana hogged the bathroom now. There were no parents to kiss me goodbye or make me wear a sweater. There was no strawberry jam for toast.

I closed my eyes and took a deep breath. I could do this. I held back any trace of the tears that wanted desperately to emerge and pulled on some black socks. I hated socks. Damion and my dad had loved them. They'd even wore them to bed.

Stop it. You have to get ready. I flipped down the collar of my navy shirt, smoothed it out, and headed downstairs to get my bag ready.

Ariana sat at the table, eating a yogurt and a small meal bar. It was hardly breakfast, but I didn't say anything. I'd given up on that fight some time after she'd started living with us.

Xavier was already there, ready to leave. I grabbed my plain black lunch bag and went out to join him. I'd chosen the lunch bag because it reminded me of Damion's fondness for dark apparel. I didn't tell Aunt Liz that. My friends might have guessed, but they didn't say anything.

I reached over and took my new sneakers from the shelf. As per school rules, they were solid black, below the ankle, and completely flat on the ground. I tied the laces tightly since I probably wouldn't do it again. I had a habit of just shoving my feet into shoes. My mom and brother had been the same.

By the time I was done with the laces, Ariana still hadn't joined us in the foyer. She always took a long time to eat and get ready. It wasn't as if she needed all the makeup or styling. She had always been beautiful, but she never believed people when they told her. I blamed her parents, who'd been awful to her.

When her royal highness finally came to join us, the school-car was already honking. We rushed out of the house.

I hastily swiped the keycard to lock the door behind us. The driver did not look happy. Ariana smiled sheepishly at Xavier and me as the silver door slid open.

The only seats left were at the back of the car. We awkwardly walked down the tiny aisle, forcing people to shift around so we could get through. Ariana and I took the seat together on the right. Xavier took the left, beside some guy who seemed to be sleeping.

"You suck," Xavier said to Ariana.

She stuck her tongue out at him. "Sorry, not sorry."

Each time the car turned, it took all my willpower not to fall into the aisle or smack into Ariana. I curled my foot around the leg of the seat to stop myself moving. Ariana didn't seem to mind smacking into me though.

It was a relief to finally exit the car ten minutes later. We headed with the herd of other teenagers into the building, but we split off from everyone else and headed towards the office to pick up our Drives with our timetables and coursework. It was not a welcoming office, with only a pristine white desk and a scowling man behind it.

"Can I help you?" he asked, staring at his holo-desk instead of us.

"We just transferred here," I said. "We were supposed to come and get our Drives."

"Names?" he drawled, finally looking up at us.

"Renee Stryker, Xavier Cage, and Ariana Colburn," I said.

He tapped away at his holo-desk. He looked back up at us after a minute with a tight smile. "Over there." He pointed to the tray underneath the printer. "Then you can go."

We grabbed the small, flat Drives from the tray and sorted out whose was whose by checking the projections of our timetables. We got to keep our old courses. That was nice at least.

We separated to find our classrooms. I got to mine just as the final bell rang. Everyone had already taken their seats. There was one left in the middle row, beside a girl with strawberry-blond hair. I took it quickly and inserted my Drive into the port. The holo-desk activated, bringing up the home screen.

"Um," the girl laughed. "I think you're in the wrong class. This is English."

"I'm a transfer," I said.

Her grey eyes widened. They were a faded colour and a bit too close together. It was weird seeing so many undesigned people. At my old school, most kids were designed almost without flaw. I probably looked different to them too because a few people were staring at me.

"Really?" she asked.

It was incredibly rare for someone to switch schools. Families were only permitted to move houses on occasion, and only if there was an excellent reason. Nobody owned property. They rented from the government or from a landlord the government had licensed. The government said it was to help with debt or something. Most people figured it was just so the authorities could keep an eye on everyone better. It was probably good since a person couldn't commit a crime and just run off. But it also meant the government could target people a lot easier if they wanted to, for whatever reason.

"Yeah," I said, not bothering to elaborate.

"How come?" she asked.

I sighed internally then recited the backstory we'd all practised the night before. Even Aunt Liz had agreed that it was best people didn't know what happened, that it might draw unwanted attention to us.

"My parents got D.R.D. a little while ago," I said. It wasn't hard, making myself look sad. It was basically my default expression now.

Dissociative Reality Disorder was a common disease that raged in Mozaan. It had only gotten worse over the years as the technologies such as VirtReel became more realistic. It blurred the lines of real and virtual life and often rendered people non-functional. There were treatments available, but with everyone on Mozaan so immersed in the virtual world all the time, it was impossible for patients to avoid it completely. "They couldn't take care of us any more, so we had to be moved." Other than design flaws, D.R.D. was the most common reason kids were given up for adoption.

"That's tough." She gave me a small, sympathetic smile. "I'm really sorry."

"Thanks," I said. The Artificial Teaching Intelligence, nicknamed by most as Ati, activated in the centre of the room and presented the image of a young woman, saving me from the conversation.

Ati's assignment didn't take me long, so I pulled up a math game on my holo-desk. All the game programs in the holo-desk were school related. As I was working my way through the factoring level, the girl beside me finished her work. She tapped me on the shoulder, and I paused my game.

"Yeah?" I asked.

"I was just wondering what courses you're taking," she asked. "Maybe we have another class together or something... I dunno."

"Oh," I said. I tried to appreciate that she was making an effort to be nice. "Well, I have art next. Then math. Then bio."

"I have art too." She curled her pale lips into a sweet smile. "I can show you where it is, if you want."

"Sure, thanks," I said, trying to be nice even if I didn't want to be there making small talk. How could I be in school, going to classes, like everything was normal? Things were far from normal.

"I'm Amelia, by the way," the girl said. She looked over at my game. "You got that far in fifteen minutes?"

"Yeah," I shrugged. "I'm good at math." Most people were, thanks to designing. But then, around here, that probably wasn't the case.

"I'm not too bad," she said. "But I take forever."

"Cool," I said. "What other courses are you taking?" It was only polite to ask.

"Chem and history."

"Is history any fun?" I asked, actually curious this time.

It was a mandatory course, but I'd always liked it. Not so much the history of Mozaan, but the animals that used to live on Earth. On Mozaan, we didn't get to see animals bigger than squirrels, unless people worked with them as part of their job. I could only imagine seeing a real-life dolphin, chimpanzee, or dog.

"No way." Amelia crinkled her nose. She saw my expression and laughed. "Oh my god. You're a history nerd."

"Kinda," I turned back to my game, hoping she might leave me alone.

"Blasted tattoo." She added a few seconds later, seemingly determined to keep the conversation going.

I looked down at it. My last name was printed in the centre in a cursive font. Four black lines curled around in a design and met at the ends, creating a full circle of ink on my wrist. My parents, Damion, and I each had one.

Just me now. It felt like a blow to the chest. The tattoos had connected us as a family. Now, it was only a reminder.

"Thanks." I made myself smile, though my throat felt tight. "I had it done when I was little."

"That's co—" she began. The bell rang.

"Guess we'd better go." I stood up from my chair, taking my Drive out from the desk.

"Oh, yeah." She got up.

I waited for her to get her Drive. I was tempted to ditch her and all the questions, but I kept my feet planted where they were.

"This way," she said, heading out into the hall.

At least Xavier would be in the art class with me. We were always a good creative team. We were always a good team in general. He was easy to work with because he understood me, without my having to explain.

We'd often have the same ideas when we were working on something, like we were in sync. And I liked art anyway. I had fresh a sketchbook tucked away in my dresser at Aunt Liz's. I'd always been good at drawing, but I hadn't drawn anything in this new book yet.

I was waiting to draw Damion. It was stupid, but I just wasn't ready to draw him yet. What if I messed it up? If I was going to draw him, I wanted it to be perfect.

~

Getting back to Aunt Liz's after school was a relief. I went straight to the room Ariana and I shared, tired from being around a bunch of nosy strangers. I would have liked school a lot better if I could just do my work and be left alone.

I didn't used to be so antisocial. I would usually have been happy to start meaningless conversations with random people to pass the time. But what if they weren't just random people? What if one of them was a Taker coming for us?

I just couldn't help going back to that idea. How could we be going to school, playing VirtReel, and acting normal after what had happened? We didn't know who these Takers were, and for all we knew, they *were* Earth-bent on tracking us down again. Even if they weren't, what was the point of it all? Why were we trying to act normal when our families were gone? Normal was gone.

Normal left when my father handed that stupid white box to Damion.

Tears pooled in my eyes. That also wasn't normal. Before all this, my friends had seen me cry maybe once in all our lives. Now I cried all the time. It was all I could do. I couldn't fix what happened. I couldn't even go to school without ending up a mess afterwards. I rubbed furiously at my eyes with the scratchy sleeve of my uniform.

I locked the bedroom door and yanked the irritating uniform shirt over my head. I threw it on the floor and grabbed a T-shirt from the small white dresser in the corner. I pulled the black-and-green fabric over my head. I changed next into some dark blue jeans that fit snugly against my skin. I let out a breath. That was better.

I sat down on the edge of my bed, wiping away the remaining tears. "It's gonna be fine," I whispered to myself. I picked up the uniform clothes and tossed them down the small laundry shoot in our closet. I just had to keep pushing forward.

"Renee?" Ariana knocked on the door. "I need to change." Right. Ariana had gone for an early shower.

"Sorry." I opened the door and stepped out of the room. "All yours."

"Thanks," she said. Her smile dropped. "You alright?"

"Yeah." I feigned a yawn. "I'm good. Bit tired."

"You sure?" she asked.

"I'm fine, Ari," I said and faked a chuckle. "Go get changed."

"Okay. See you downstairs." She walked into the room and closed the door behind her.

Xavier was already on the couch playing VirtReel when I got downstairs. "Hey," he said, pausing the game. "Playing baseball. You up for a game?"

"Sure," I said. "Sounds good."

I had to keep pushing forward. This used to be normal. We all had to try and get back to that, no matter how hard it would be. I flopped onto the couch beside him, and he started a new game.

"I call blue team." I rushed to select it.

"Fine," he grumbled, but there was no real bitterness in it. "I'll take red."

Xavier beat me 5–0. I'd known he would win, but that hadn't stopped the pregame trash talking that always took place. Nor the after-game gloating on his part. I would have done the same.

"I want food," I said suddenly, standing up. "You coming?"

"Definitely." We walked across the squishy green carpet of the living room and onto the cold grey tile of the kitchen.

We made some pasta, and Ariana joined in on the dinner a little while later. Aunt Liz was still at work. We ate until we were full and completely emptied the small pasta dish. Xavier and Ariana took over on the dishes, and I headed upstairs.

It was my turn to have a shower. I selected the temperature I wanted on the wall, and the shower started. The hot water and steam relaxed me. I hadn't realized how exhausted I was. I spent as long under the stream of water as I could before the timer ran out. Like it or not, we were allowed only thirteen minutes per shower. Only so much water could be produced at once on Mozaan, so it couldn't be wasted.

I picked a pair of cotton pyjamas from my drawer. They were soft against my skin, enticing me further to fall on my bed and sleep. The feeling of my head falling against the cold pillow, and the blanket draped over me, could only be described as bliss.

The next morning, we got ready and went to school. This would be our routine now. I went to English again. I talked with my inquisitive desk partner, Amelia. Then we walked over to art.

The teacher put us in groups for still-life studies. Xavier, four other kids, and I were in one group. Each group had a couple objects arranged on a spare desk to draw in their sketchbooks.

"What the hell is this thing?" Xavier whispered as the teacher walked away.

I looked at our main object. It was a sort of metal owl. It had solid, ketchup-red eyes with thick teal rims around them. Its yellow beak curved unnaturally into what was supposed to be a smile. The thing was terrifying.

"I have no idea," I whispered back. "I think we're being punished or something."

"This is cruel and unusual," he said.

I pressed my pencil to the paper and started sketching the feet. They were made of thin, metal tubes with wire curled around the exterior.

After circling around the room to see how everyone else was doing, the teacher reached our table. "How's it coming?" she asked.

I looked up at her and smiled. "Great," I lied.

I liked this teacher. She was older, with sandy-coloured straight hair and laugh lines surrounding her mouth. Art was considered too complicated and creative for the artificial intelligence to teach.

"Oh, I just love this little birdie," she said, tapping the metal abomination on the head. "Don't you?"

"Yeah," I said. "It's really interesting." If metal birds that looked like part of a horror simulation counted as interesting.

"He has a little family too, in the cupboard," she said. *Oh, joy.* "A student made three of them a few years ago. I'll go get them out to show you."

"That would be blas—" I was cut off by pounding at the door. My breathing quickened. The hair stood up on my arms. *I'm only being jumpy, right?* But Xavier was staring at the door too, his body tense.

The teacher opened the door, and two men in black suits and ties walked into the class. Surely it was nothing.

I tuned in to their thoughts, just in case. *Wasn't even hard to track them down. Look how young they are. Can't believe those idiots had trouble with them.*

It wasn't nothing.

Window, I thought to Xavier.

We sprinted over to it, catching the Takers off guard. *Run, Ari!* I screamed to her telepathically. *Takers are here.* Xavier and I broke the glass window as we jumped through.

Chapter 4: Running

Ilay on my back for a moment, trying to breathe. The whiplash made me feel like I was choking. We'd made sure to bend our knees when we fell, but the aftershock and the speedy tumble forward had left me motionless.

My legs ached, though I didn't think they were broken. Shards of glass poked into my flesh from various spots. My vision was spotted with the blood from a stinging cut above my right eye.

A few classmates were screaming above us. *Why won't the air go into my lungs?* I needed to breathe. All that noise. Someone was yelling.

Suddenly, I was hauled to my feet. Everything spun around me. I gripped one of the strong arms for balance. The air finally started to reach my lungs. I breathed heavily, focusing on the owner of the arms that were holding me up.

"Thanks," I breathed. I stood up straighter, trying to put the pain out of my mind.

"Don't thank me yet," Xavier said. "We gotta go." He dropped his hold on my arms and grabbed my hand, pulling me into a run.

The Takers were storming out of the building. Within a minute or two, Ariana found us. We ran away from the building in a random direction. Adrenaline took care of the pain. A couple other kids were running as well, but in the opposite direction. Seemed we weren't the only ones the Takers were targeting.

I looked back, hair flying over my shoulder. We hadn't lost the Takers. Xavier sent a spiral of fire propelling at them, which they scrambled to dodge. It wasn't enough to stop them entirely. We raced into the woods that bordered the school campus. They were still coming.

"They're catching up!" Ariana breathed heavily as we ran. The Takers' boots crunched on the ground behind us, closer and closer. I forced myself to pick up pace, but it wasn't going to be enough.

"Xavier, you have to...set fire," I said.

"What?" He gave me an incredulous look. "That'll *kill* us."

"The alternative is dying anyway. Just light the trees behind us," I panted. "It's the only...way we'll…outrun them."

Xavier took a breath and shot Ariana and me a wry smile. "You guys should run," he said. "I'll catch up." That was a good idea. Not all of us could withstand the intense heat of a forest fire. Ariana and I gave a quick agreement. "Here goes nothing."

I couldn't help but look over my shoulder as we ran. Xavier blanketed the trees behind us with a wave of flames. Then another. And another, until the back line of trees was ablaze. Soon, we were trying to outrun the flames instead of the Takers.

I forced my feet to keep moving forward as my lungs starved in the smoke-filled forest. Thin beams of sun peeked through a gap in the trees. We had to keep going. *Almost there.*

The forest's smoky entrapment finally ended what seemed like an eternity later. My knees buckled under me, hitting the cool grass. I doubled over, coughing and fighting for oxygen. Ariana heaved loudly to my side. Xavier stood against a tree, bent over slightly, trying to catch his breath too by the sounds of it. The heat hadn't taken much of a toll on him, but his coughs were as intense as ours. The smoke must have filled his lungs just the same.

"We can't...stop," I wheezed. We all knew it was true. The Takers could be onto us any second.

I stumbled onto my feet, still coughing and struggling for air. I took one wobbly step forward, beyond dizzy. Still, I took another step.

"I can't," Ariana said. Her eyes were wide with terror. She gasped for air.

"Yes," Xavier said firmly, "you can."

"Just...have to calm down," I said, the coughing almost faded.

She nodded, tears blinking out of her eyes. She managed to take in a deep breath. Granted, she coughed it right back out, but it was the start she needed. Not long after that, she was able to stand.

We trudged along at as fast a pace as we could, the energy to run sucked right out of us. I opened my eyes wider and breathed a sigh of relief as my eyes landed on a closed-in parking lot, as good of a cover as we could have hoped for.

"Guys," I nodded towards the lot. "Down here." We scanned for any nearby Takers that would see us. None had made it to the other side of the forest yet. We could get into the lot unseen.

We crept inside, quietly weaving in between the blue Solar-Cars. The pickup truck we found seemed like nothing short of a miracle. We didn't usually see many vehicles bigger than a basic mini-car in this area. We made our way around the truck to hide behind it. Ariana and I sat against the back wheel, and Xavier leaned against the front.

There, we took a breather. My whole body hurt, and I was bleeding here and there from the glass stuck in my skin. Some shards had been ripped out as we ran. Those spots bled the most. There were also the burns from stray flames that had leapt onto my skin and eaten holes in my clothes.

But none of that could compete with the smoke inhalation. It felt like smoke was swimming in my lungs, up and up, pushing out the oxygen I needed. I tried to hold in the coughing fits that tickled with more and more force at my throat. They were inevitable. Ariana was in no better shape, and Xavier would have gotten the worst of the smoke since he'd been at centre of the fire. I had no right to complain.

The peace of our hiding spot allowed us to begin breathing normally and ease some of the glass shards out of our skin.

"We'll check in the lot," a lady's voice said only minutes later. "You guys keep looking around the perimeter. Maybe they died in their stupid little fire." She sounded hopeful.

The door clicked open, its sound resonating throughout the lot. I tensed all over, and the hair stood up on the back of my neck. We were sitting ducks. They were going to catch us.

I'm gonna try something, I thought to my friends. *And it's probably really stupid, so I'm sorry.* I ignored their mental protests. *You won't miss the cue.*

I crept from car to car, out of the Takers' sight. I needed to be close if I had a chance at reaching all of them. I looked over and saw the lady and two men searching in between cars.

Get ready, I told my friends.

And then, I screamed in the Taker's minds as loud as I could. They doubled over, clutching their heads. It was working! But with the loud volume I had to transmit, I couldn't focus on much else. Hopefully my friends had taken their cue to run out of the lot. I had to believe they had. I couldn't keep this up much longer, and I still needed to get out.

I started towards the exit, but I had to run right past the Takers. I dashed past the men, their faces scrunched up in pain. I sprinted past the woman, but her hand snaked around my wrist, jerking me backwards. I stared at her, horrified, my focus broken. She straightened up, as did the others, and I tried everything to twist out of her grasp. It was no use.

The Taker lady had a vicious smile on her face as the men came up behind her. I couldn't beat them, even without their weapons. It had been a stupid idea.

"Where are your friends?" she asked, her voice honeyed. "They left without you, huh?"

I was silent, fighting to keep any emotion from crossing my face.

"Nobody would blame you if you ratted them out," she coaxed.

I gave her no response.

Her grip tightened around my wrist until I couldn't help but cry out from the sudden pain. She laughed. My face heated with anger, and I almost expected the smoke from earlier to fume out of my ears.

She curled her polished fingers around my face, squeezing. Her next words came in the form of a hiss. "Tell me where they've gone, or we can do this the hard way." She removed the hand from my face and pulled out a sleek, buzzing rod.

I spat on her cheek.

The Taker's rod slammed into my side, and I dropped to the ground convulsing. I couldn't see through the black spots in my vision, but I heard one of the men cry out. His bubbling skin sizzled.

Footsteps ran towards me. It had to be my friends. My convulsions started to fade, but I wasn't strong enough to read anyone's mind and figure out what was happening. The next thing I heard was the click of a gun. My friends' footsteps ceased.

"Just stop right there," a man said.

I turned my head to the side. I could see well enough now, and there was a Taker man waving his gun between my friends. The lady's feet were planted in front of me. Almost by instinct, unsure what it would accomplish, I grabbed her ankle, gripping tightly as anger pulsed through me. She began to crumble away before my eyes.

I let out a small yelp and released her. In a matter of seconds, she'd become a pile of ash and armour.

Confused and scared, I didn't have time to waste if we had a chance of getting out. I would freak out later. With shaky fingers, I grabbed the gun buried in the ash. I lifted it up and aimed at the last man. I squeezed the trigger. *Ke-choom!* The gun dropped to the floor, silent due to the intense ringing in my ears.

The Taker stared at his bleeding abdomen. His gun clattered to the floor. He clutched his stomach and fell against the wall, where he stayed. I had gained most of my strength back and stood. I strode over to him, my anger returning.

"We could have helped you." I looked him up and down. "But you murdered the only person who could have healed you. And who knows, maybe they'll find you, and you'll get help in time. But whatever happens, you deserve it."

I turned on my heels, trying to keep my head held high as I stalked out of the lot. My friends followed, silent. When we were outside, and the Takers out of sight, the force of what I'd just done smashed into me like a giant wave.

So, I ran. My sneakers pounded against the concrete, and my friends called out to me. I kept running. I didn't care how much pain I was in. I ran in through a mulch-filled path.

I finally stopped on a rocky ledge.

Sinking down, I pulled my knees to my chest. Sobs racked my body, fast and panicked. The tears flew from my eyes and stained my shirt more and more every second. I'd killed two people. I hadn't had to kill the man. It was cold-blooded.

I'd thought avenging Damion and my parents would help me, but I was wrong. They wouldn't want me to become *this*.

And my friends… They shouldn't have had to watch me do that.

Everything was a blur of eyelashes and tears, but suddenly I could feel an arm around me. I knew who it was without having to look up. I leaned into Xavier's embrace, burying my face in the fabric of his shirt.

"Hey." He rubbed a hand up and down my arm. "It's gonna be alright."

"How can you say that?" Even if I hadn't shot the man, a lady had turned to ash under my fingers. What part of that was alright? I didn't even know how it happened. What if I accidentally did that to one of my friends?

"I just know," he said. Would they be safer without me? "I need you to trust me on this one."

What if trusting got him or Ariana hurt? Or worse? I couldn't live with myself if that happened. They were all I had left. Would they be safer without me?

"What...what I did, Xavier," I said quietly, the fear in my voice obvious.

"We wouldn't be alive if you hadn't."

"That man." I forced the words out through my tears. "He...I didn't have to."

"He could still be alive," Xavier said. "Ari is bandaging him up with strips of his shirt. I think you hit low enough on his stomach that it won't kill him."

I sniffed. I tried to wipe the tears from my face, but they just kept coming anyway. "You think so?" I asked.

"Yeah," he answered. "Yeah, I do."

But I hadn't thought about that when I shot the man. I would have killed him. "And...and that woman," I said, shaking my head. "I don't even know what happened... What if..."

"Whatever that was, it saved us," Xavier said. He looked at me, earnestly. "That's all that matters."

I had protected them. And, it wasn't like I'd ever hurt anybody I cared about before. Maybe he had a point. "I just..." I drifted off, unsure of what to say. I looked down. "I don't know. I'm scared."

"I never hurt you when my ability was first starting and all out of control, did I?" he asked.

"Well, no," I said, wiping at my eyes again. "I guess not." He'd never burned us, though my couch had taken a small hit.

"There you go then." He gave me a small smile, meant to comfort. It did a little. "Don't worry."

"I'm sorry," I said, looking back up at him. Sorry for running off. Sorry for trying to take care of things myself. Sorry that I was a murderer.

"You're already forgiven," he said, still with that small smile.

Why was he being so nice to me? I didn't deserve it.

Then, he stood up abruptly. "Crap—Ari's there all alone. We have to get back." He offered me his hand.

I took it and jumped up beside him. "Thank you."

We half-jogged, half-tripped our way back to the parking lot. Though we kept an eye out for other Takers, they were nowhere to be seen. My breathing was still a little ragged, probably from the electrocution wand. Every step seemed to bring fresh pain. I said nothing though. I deserved worse.

We were there in only a few minutes. I thanked the universe that the man was alive. His hazel eyes widened when he saw me. He shifted nervously.

"I took his weapons. They're just over there." Ariana pointed to a corner a few feet away. There was a pistol, those strange glowing handcuffs, and an electrocution rod. "His backup will probably start suspecting something's up soon. We need to get going."

I nodded. *How is she just going on like nothing happened?* Maybe she just really didn't know what to say. I didn't know what to say either. All of this was so different, so much worse, than anything I'd seen in war history simulations.

"I don't know how far we can walk without them spotting us," Xavier said.

"Is there anywhere close we can hide?" I asked, though I didn't like the idea of staying anywhere nearby. I wanted to get far, far away, where they couldn't find us.

Xavier walked over to the weapon pile and grabbed the gun and the wand. He went to the nearest car window, then hesitated. "We have to get as far as possible," he said. "No way we'll make it more than a block walking." He took a deep breath and smashed the car window.

As the alarm blared, he unlocked the door and looked over at us. "Well, come on."

He left the gun on the ground. It might have offered us a little protection, but we weren't willing to risk somebody seeing it. Besides that, I was already struggling to keep the bile from rising up my throat after shooting somebody. I couldn't stand the thought of carrying around the weapon I'd done it with.

Ariana and I ran to the car. The government would compensate the owners so they could get to work, but I still hated this—stealing. But what choice did we have? I hated the thought of my friends dying more, and if those people caught us, Ariana and Xavier would. Stealing this car was the only way we could survive. And I'd already done far worse today.

"How do you even steal one of these?" I asked. Ariana grabbed the front seat, and I sat in the middle of the back. "Don't you have to be within a distance of the keys?"

Xavier jammed the rod in to the charging outlet and pressed down the button for all the automatic driving options. The car soundlessly came to life, and the alarm stopped.

"Manual override?" the monotone voice of the car system asked.

"Yes," Xavier said. If anyone knew about stealing cars, it would be him. His mother had worked in E-Car repair.

Backing out of the driveway was a slow and careful process. We didn't want to set off any more alarms. Once out of the parking lot, we sped off down the road. Xavier was impressively not horrible at driving. Even most adults couldn't drive manually; everything was automated.

When we made it to the highway, Ariana let out a breath that I first thought was relief.

"What's wrong?" Xavier asked her. "We made it."

She sniffled. "A few weeks ago, I was worried about, like, failing math class. How can something not be wrong?" Her words were so true they hurt.

A few weeks ago, I'd been playing games on the VirtReel with my mom, dad, and brother. I was working on art projects with my friends. I was thinking about what career path I would take. Now, I was just hoping we would have somewhere safe to sleep.

"I guess." The sniffling stopped. "We just...gotta try and make things right again."

"We'll figure it out," Xavier said.

We decided to go as far as possible. These Takers obviously weren't giving up on finding us, and no doubt they'd be on our trail soon. Going to the next city just wouldn't be enough. We drove for hours. I was barely able to stay awake. I didn't know how Xavier was managing to drive for so long.

We only stopped when it got dark, not wanting the battery to get too low. Without constant solar energy, that would happen quickly. Only people with work permits had car batteries with a long life. Instead of imposing a curfew, the government said they reduced battery life to help make things safer at night. At least we would have the benefit of empty roads.

Xavier parked to the side of a back road, in the hopes that nobody would notice us.

"I'll stay watch," I offered. "You guys should sleep."

I couldn't. Closing my eyes started a slideshow of all the bad things that had happened over the last couple weeks. Now the scene in the parking lot had been added. The crumbling of a woman to ash in my hands. The gun going off, the bullet retreating into a man's abdomen on my command.

"I can do it," Xavier said.

Ariana was already snoring softly in the passenger's seat.

"No," I shook my head. "You've been driving all night. It's fine."

"Alright," he said. "But wake me up if you're tired."

"Sure." I didn't plan on waking him up.

There was an **On-The-Go** store just ahead of where we'd parked. I hadn't noticed it at first, due to the dark, but over the first two hours of my watch, I couldn't stop staring at it. When was the last time I'd eaten? Breakfast that morning? We would need food. I glanced at my sleeping friends. I'd be able to see the car from the store. They could always call out to me if they woke up. My stomach growled.

Did I have any cred-sticks in my pockets? I could buy some food without drawing attention to us, and we could be gone by morning.

"Dammit," I muttered, coming up empty on the cred-sticks. What were we going to do for food? I was already hungry, and we would only get hungrier.

Sharp fear coursed through me. I'd never even had to think about going hungry before. Sure, I'd heard of people not getting as much food as they needed in poor areas, but what if we actually grew hungry enough to kill us? The image of the three of us slowly starving to death in some dark alley made my decision for me.

I scooted over to the door and pushed it open. I slipped out of the car, closing the door as quietly as I could manage. Using the darkness as my cover, I walked over to the store and peered inside the window. There was one person inside.

I put on my best not-suspicious face and eased the door open. I made my way to the checkout and smiled.

"Hi," I said.

The guy at the cash register looked about twenty at most. He couldn't be the brightest either because only the academically inept got stuck as cashiers. This had to work, or I had no idea what we were going to eat. "Um, I was wondering if there's a bathroom here I could use?"

He barely looked up. "There's the employees' bathroom." He gestured to the back with his thumb and begrudgingly got himself out from behind the counter. "I'll show you where it is."

"Great," I said. "Thanks."

When he had his back turned, I plucked a few protein bars off the shelves. I tucked them under my shirt, secure against my back in the waistband of my pants.

"Well, uh, here we are." He pointed to the employee bathroom. "I'll just be at the counter."

"Okay." I gave him as convincing a smile as I could muster. "Thanks again."

I hung out near the bathroom for a few minutes, flushed the toilet for believability, flashed a grateful smile at the cashier on the way out, and went back to the car. I got in and put the bars on the seat next to me.

Xavier stirred awake, then turned back to me, trying to open his eyes. "Where'd you go?" His words were sleepy and clumped together.

"Got protein bars," I said. "Want one?"

"Yeah." Xavier yawned. I couldn't help but mimic it. He sat up straighter. I handed him a bar and unwrapped my own. "Not complaining, but how'd you get these?" His voice was more alert now, if still drowsy.

"I didn't have any creds," I said. I looked at the store, and Xavier followed my gaze. "I had to take them. We needed something to keep us going... Just until we figure something else out."

"Thanks," he said, chewing on the bar.

"We should leave as soon as it's light so he doesn't see the car parked here," I said.

"Yeah."

I crumpled up the wrapper and tossed it to the car floor. I yawned again, leaning back against the seat. It became harder to open my eyes again each time I blinked.

"Why don't you sleep for a bit?" Xavier suggested.

"No," I protested. "You drove."

"You got tasered," he said. "Sleep."

But I was already drifting off.

~

When I woke up, we were on the road again. Xavier and Ariana were talking, and other cars whirred beside ours on the highway.

"Hey," Ariana said when she noticed I was awake. "We're almost to Greenville."

"That's where we were thinking of stopping," Xavier said.

"We figured it's far enough, and somebody is gonna notice sooner or later we're too young to drive. Last thing we want is to get pulled over."

"Sure," I said. "Sounds alright." From what I knew about Greenville, it was a lot like Brampton, only worse. The jobs were of even lower value, and there were only a couple schools because nobody could really afford to have kids.

"We just need to find somewhere we can, like, stay and stuff," Ariana said. "Maybe we could find a way to get an apartment or something. It's that or keep hiding out in this thing."

"Maybe we can talk to a landlord? See if they'll let us stay in an empty apartment?" I asked.

"That's a good idea," Ariana said. "Even if they just let us stay for, like, a little bit for free, and then we'll find a way to start getting creds."

"What can we tell them though?" Xavier asked. "We can't say what really happened."

They can't know we're fifteen. They wouldn't give us somewhere to stay. They'd call Child Placement, and the Takers would find us.

"It has to be something that makes us sound old enough to rent," I said, taking another few seconds to think. "We could say we worked in Services, and our jobs got shut down."

"That could work," Ariana said. Xavier nodded.

"Yeah," he said. "We can just say the landlord kicked us out because we couldn't pay."

Whoever we found probably wouldn't let us stay, no matter what story we spun, but we had to try it. We couldn't sleep in the streets, like people too far gone with D.R.D. We'd probably be found by police, who might turn us over to the Takers.

There were plenty of apartment buildings in Greenville. We picked the one that looked most run-down, in the hopes that they'd be less likely to turn us away. It took almost fifteen minutes of roaming the halls before we found the superintendent's office. I knocked on the door, and we waited only a few seconds before it opened.

An older man's face greeted us. He looked to be in his sixties and had a large, round nose. "Hello," he said, looking a little suspicious, probably because of how beaten up we looked. "Can I help you?"

"Yeah, um, we just really need a place to stay. Our work shut down, and we were sharing an apartment. We couldn't pay in time, so the landlord kicked us out." I spoke very sweetly, smiling at him. "We're looking for jobs, and we'll pay you back after we get them. But we just need a place to sleep for a few days until we can get some money. Is there any way that you could just let us stay in an empty room until then?"

The government didn't pay as much attention to housing in the Service areas. People moved around a lot more, whether it was from moving for a job or being kicked out for not paying the rent. As long as the landlords were meeting their quotas and there were no reports of trouble in the buildings, it was unlikely the government would bother screening who lived there.

"Where did you work?" he asked, looking at us carefully. "You look a bit rich to work around here."

Crap. I hadn't even thought about our designs. My friends looked like they were also trying to hide their panic. We didn't look flawed enough to work in Services. But then, Ariana seemed perfectly designed, but she had personality "flaws" that had made her parents treat her poorly.

"They got the looks part of our designs right," I said, dropping my expression. "But they messed up on the thinking and learning stuff." I tried to think of more, in case he would ask. *Please believe this.* My heart started beating faster. "We can't even go home. Our dads were so mad. They say we're embarrassing."

Before he even spoke, his compassionate expression told me that we could stay. "There is one empty room, not much in it," he said. "But you'll start paying in a couple weeks or you're out, understand?"

"Thanks, we understand." Ariana made herself sound choked up. It probably wasn't hard. We didn't talk about when our parents had been taken, but there was a certain heaviness in the air that followed us. "Thank you. So much. We'll be totally quiet, no issues at all."

"You're welcome," the man said. He placed a keycard in my palm. "Room number thirty-three."

"We'll pay as soon as we get some creds," Xavier said. "Thanks again."

"Good luck, kids."

We went straight to the room, having seen it on our way to the superintendent's. I swiped the card to get us in and heard the door lock behind us with a beep. There was a counter a few feet in front of us, which lead into the narrow, galley kitchen. Ariana dumped the two leftover meal bars on the counter.

The place wasn't bad. There was no furniture, and it was a little dusty. It was also a major improvement from the stolen car we'd ditched a few blocks down. Xavier looked around at our new space. Ariana ran straight for the small bathroom towards the back of the apartment.

Once Ariana was done in the bathroom, and we'd gotten a look at the place, we all stayed in the living room together.

"I'll keep watch and stuff," Ariana said, later that night.

"You sure?" I said. "I don't mind."

"Yeah," she said. "You did last night."

"How about we do half-shifts?" Xavier asked. "Switch out every few hours?"

"Sure," Ariana said. "Who'll I wake up?"

"Xavier's had the least sleep," I said. "So it should be me."

"Sure," Xavier said. "But we should rotate the shifts every night."

"Sounds good," I said.

I went over and made sure the door had locked behind us. The light was red, but I shook the door a bit to make sure it wouldn't open. It stayed shut, and I relaxed a little.

Ariana took position sitting in the corner of the room, facing the door, while Xavier and I tried to make ourselves comfortable on the cold floor. My arms were far too boney, but they would have to do as a pillow.

"Night," I whispered into the dark.

"Night," my friends replied.

I turned onto my back and stared at the ceiling, watching every shadow carefully to make sure nothing moved. Was it even safe to sleep? The Takers could come at any moment, and I might not wake up fast enough.

What if the door's not locked? I'd double-checked it, but what if it wasn't? *They could just walk right in.*

Stop it. You're being stupid. The door was locked. *But what if something broke, and it unlocked?* It was irrational—I'd checked it less than a couple minutes ago—but still. I turned over onto my side and shut my eyes, determined to put the thought out of my head.

What if I don't check that it's locked, and they get in and take Ariana and Xavier while I'm sleeping? They would be gone, and it would be my fault because I didn't want to double-check.

I lasted maybe twenty minutes before I broke down and got up.

"What're you doing?" Ariana asked, keeping her voice low.

"Nothing," I said, seeing that the lock was red. I went back to my spot on the floor. "Never mind."

Checking had provided some relief, but the same doubts were still creeping into my mind. I had to get up a few more times, checking the windows too, before finally falling asleep.

~

Ms. Cage, Damion, Ariana, Xavier, and I were sitting at the white table in my backyard. There was a beautiful sunset projected behind us, different shades of pink and orange mixing together to form a serene evening. There were steamed vegetables, chicken, and fruit in abundance on the table. We were celebrating the New Year. My mother was reading the traditional story of Mozaan's creation, which was read every New Year. A hologram projected from her holo-watch displayed pictures of the events and the words she read.

"And," she said, her expression warm and happy as it always seemed to be, "our first Prime Minister, Adia Mozaan, devised the solution to save humanity. The best of the human race was chosen to be saved on the last piece of healthy Earth, and it was named Mozaan after her."

I looked around at everyone else, smiling at their happy expressions.

"The government set out to ensure that such destruction never happened again and carefully watched over everybody to make sure we stayed safe."

I bit into a strawberry, my mouth filling with sweetness.

The taste of the fruit turned rotten, and the sunset vanished. The sky darkened. Bulky figures burst through our backyard with large black guns drawn. The food was decaying, and the rancid smell filled my nose. The sky was getting darker and darker, but nobody at the table noticed.

"They helped direct us into safe, productive behaviour," my mother continued, that same smile still on her face.

A beam of light came from one of the guns, striking Ms. Cage in the head. I tried to move, but I couldn't.

"Guys, run!" I was screaming, tears flying from my eyes as I struggled to move. "Get out of here!" But nobody could hear me. They shot my father and Damion, who slumped in their chairs across the table. "No!"

My mom was still reading. "Allocating jobs so everybody would contribute to a better society."

"Mom!" I screamed at her, desperate for her to see me. "You have to run!"

The intruders shot Ariana and Xavier. Ariana fell open-eyed against my shoulder. The blood from her head poured down my neck. I tried to cup her wound to stop the bleeding as I sobbed hysterically.

"They saved us from ourselves," my mom said, still with that awful happiness. A beam hit her, and she went limp in her chair.

Chapter 5: Fire Alarmed Theft

When I woke up, I had tears running down my cheeks. I struggled to control my breathing. I looked quickly to make sure my friends were still there.

Ariana was still leaning against the faded blue wall. Her head was dropped down, and snores shook her body.

"So much for shifts," I mumbled, sitting up. I looked for Xavier next, but he wasn't where he'd been.

I jumped up. "Xavier?" I called, moving into the hall.

I tried to keep the panic out of my voice. The kitchen was empty, and the bedroom door was wide open. Xavier was nowhere in sight.

"Yeah," he answered, his voice low and tired. I turned to see him standing over the bathroom sink, splashing water onto his face. His shirt was damp with sweat, as was his hair. There were dark circles under his eyes.

"Are you okay?" I asked, stepping towards the entrance of the bathroom. I blinked at the light, but my eyes quickly adjusted.

"Yeah, fine," he said, wiping off some of the water on his face with his hands. He didn't look fine. "Just a nightmare. That's all." I didn't bring mine up since his looked like it had to have been worse.

"Do you want to talk about it?" I asked.

"Thanks," he said. "But, no. I don't think I can."

I moved out of his way as he started to leave the bathroom. "Okay." What else was there to say? We both remained standing in the hall.

My entire body ached—from the burn just under my ribs, to the cuts that seemed to be everywhere, to my tight, over-worked calf muscles. Turning my head sent a stab of pain through my neck, which was stiff from sleeping on the floor. I gently massaged it.

The lingering pain was strange. Damion had always been there to heal things. I'd felt initial injuries, of course, but I could scarcely remember a time when I had to heal on my own.

"Ari kept a *great* watch," Xavier said, shaking his head.

"We're lucky nothing happened." It was a good thing I'd checked the locks, or we could have been a lot worse than injured. My eyes flicked over all of our cuts from the glass. "Wanna help me look for a Med-Kit?"

"Sure." He nodded to the bathroom. "We should check the bathroom first."

"Yeah." As I moved forward, pain stabbed through my calves with each step. I wasn't used to so much running, and the cuts didn't help. My walk wasn't quite a limp, but it wasn't balanced either. I was lucky the bathroom was only a couple steps away.

It was nearly bare, with white flooring and the same blue walls as the rest of the apartment. A small black sink and toi-let were pushed against one wall, and a narrow, glass shower was on the opposite side, in the corner. A small, light-grey piece of cupboard surrounded the base of the sink, but there was no other storage to be seen.

We knelt beside the small cupboard, pulling the two doors open. Silver piping swirled down the middle of the space and into the floor. On one side, a few black towels had been stuffed in—which was good because I didn't feel like air-drying if we got to shower.

"Perfect." I reached into the other side of the cupboard and pulled out a small red box. I dusted it off, revealing the bandage symbol that was on all the medical kits and hospital signs. I clicked open the box, which was about as long as two of my hands pressed side by side.

A half-unwound roll of white gauze made a messy blanket over most of the Med-Kit's contents. Xavier picked the roll up from the box. Stray gauze hung down from it. It was almost as tall as his pinkie and twice as thick. He began to roll it back up, and I grabbed for the next item I saw.

"Someone had priorities." I let out a short laugh and tossed Xavier the MintPower mouthwash.

"Fine." He put it on the ground beside himself. "Don't have any."

"Hey." I put my hands up in mock surrender. "Not saying I don't appreciate it."

I picked up a small booklet. "Ooh. First aid and CPR guild." I slid it across the floor to him. "Ari'll be all over that."

"Hey." He looked at the first page of the booklet. "There's stuff on burns and cuts too."

"Cool," I said.

Xavier picked up a white-and-red tube that looked like toothpaste. "Jackpot." He waved the tube in the air. Pain relief cream.

"Good," I said, letting out a breath of relief. He put it on the floor with the other things.

We ended up with a good array of supplies and quite a bit of burn gel.

"Do you have any idea how to use half this stuff?" I asked, as we began to neatly pack the contents back into the Med-Kit.

"No clue." He shook his head. "But I'm gonna go out on a limb and say *maybe* we shouldn't use trial and error." I picked up a couple small, paper wrapped rolls and read the front of the label.

"What even is ammonia inhalant?" A brief smile appeared on my face as I shook my head. I put more items away in the Med-Kit.

"A respiratory stimulant," Xavier said.

"How'd you know that?" I asked. "Chem project?"

Xavier had always had a niche for chemistry, especially when he got to blow things up. "I read the back of the label." He tossed one of the doses into my palms, and I put it in the Med-Kit.

"Label of what?" Ariana asked, appearing in the doorway. She yawned loudly. "Why'd you guys let me sleep like that?" She rubbed a hand over her neck.

"We found a Med-Kit," I said, gesturing to the box. "All sorts of presents in here for you."

"Like what?" she asked, sitting cross-legged beside us. There was hardly any room to move in the small bathroom.

"Lots of ointments," Xavier said. He slid the box over to her.

"And a booklet about treating stuff," I said. "Thought you'd like that."

"Yeah," Ariana said, smiling. "This'll be, like, perfect since we're all cut up and stuff."

It didn't take long to disinfect all the little cuts and gauze the larger ones. We even figured out how to treat my burn from the electrocution wand, then bandaged it up.

All the medicine in the world couldn't fix our hunger though. We needed food. If we were going to find a way to earn credits to buy food, we needed new clothes and soap. Which also cost credits.

"We could try and get a food-stick," Ariana said. The government handed out those sticks to poor people who registered, and they could use them in place of a cred-stick to get a certain value of food products. But that wouldn't work for us.

"We can't," I said, dismayed. We really were on our own. "Government would see us register."

"Right," she said, frowning. She sighed. "I'm starving already, and those meal bars are gonna have to last awhile."

"And I don't think asking is gonna work for food," Xavier said. People didn't even talk to their neighbours, so it wasn't likely they would just be willing to share their food, especially since most people here wouldn't have much.

"Maybe we can try and get jobs fast?" I suggested. "How long could we go without eating?" Not long, probably, and most jobs paid bi-weekly.

"We couldn't get hired looking like this," Xavier said, gesturing to all of our ripped-up and bloodied school clothes. "If we tried, they'd probably call the police thinking we're cranked."

"There has to be some way we can get the clothes and food we need," Ariana said, her tone optimistic. "I mean, we only need a little bit, just until we find some kind of jobs."

"What if…" I really didn't want to finish the thought. We'd done so much stealing already, and the people here were so bad off. But were any of them at risk of starving to death? They could at least get government aid, as small as it was. And we wouldn't take enough to really hurt them. "We could try and find a way to get a couple creds from one of the apartments."

"I dunno," Ariana said, looking unhappy with the idea. "This isn't a rich area or anything."

"We'd only need a little," Xavier said, considering it. "Just enough to print some cheap outfits and soap… Maybe a bit of food."

"And we could maybe do a couple apartments," I said. "So we wouldn't be taking too much from anybody."

"Well, if we only take a little bit…" Ariana said, reluctantly. She frowned and seemed to be looking for another idea. "I guess we don't really have another choice."

"How would we do it though?" I asked. Doors automatically locked when closed, so it wasn't as if we could just wait for people to go to work.

"I could set off the fire alarm," Xavier said after a moment. "Don't the doors unlock in case the firefighters need to get in?"

"Yeah, they do," Ariana said, nodding. "And that would get everybody out of the building too."

Our postures were slumped, and our expressions were miserable. We had to try this. There was no other option, but that didn't make it suck any less. We took a minute to stew in our decision.

Xavier left the apartment, and we waited for the alarm to blare. Red light and wailing noise washed over the building, and within seconds, the quick movement of feet could be heard in the hall.

We waited for the shuffling to cease, and I peeked my head out the door. The hall was clear. Xavier must have already ducked into another room. I motioned for Ariana to follow me out, and then we split up, both going to a different room. I checked repeatedly over my shoulder; somebody could come back any second. I creaked open the white wooden door of my chosen apartment and stepped inside.

The apartment had the same layout as ours. The walls were coated in vibrant blue paint, and the people who lived here had furniture to fill the space.

The bedroom was simple, with the same blue walls and a white double bed in the centre. A black dresser with gold trim was standing against the wall, taller than me. I pulled open the top drawer, revealing bundles of grey socks. I moved them around to check for credits. My dad always kept his valuables in the top drawer of his dresser. There were usually more valuables than socks in it. In this one, there were only socks. I pushed the drawer closed, then opened one after the other. Nothing of value.

There was an air vent just to the left of the dresser. I stepped in front of it but couldn't feel any air. I put my hand up parallel to it. Nothing was coming out of it. I dug my fingers under the rim to pull off the metal vent. It took a couple seconds, but it eventually came off. I tossed it onto the bed before peering inside.

Prepaid credit chips. They were scattered along the bottom of the hidden compartment, varying from 20 credits to 300. I stuffed a couple low-value ones in my pockets. If my friends and I each grabbed a couple, it should be enough to get us some clothes, and maybe some soap.

I quickly scanned the cupboards, checking to see if there was a stock of meal bars. There were, but the supply was minimal. I decided to leave it. Ariana or Xavier would probably find some.

There was a faint scuffling in the hall. The residents were coming back. I picked through the thoughts of people entering. They were still by the front doors. I had to take my chance getting out now, or I might not get out at all.

I crept to the door and rested my hand on the silver handle, my heart beating quickly. What if I got caught?

I listened for any thoughts coming to the door, which was hard when so many people were cramped in the hall. From what I heard, there were people really close, but nobody was coming inside yet. Before I could overthink things, I turned the knob. I slid out of the apartment, breathing a quiet sigh of relief when nobody saw me.

The crowd was thick in our section of the hall, and I merged in. Despite my odd appearance, nobody glanced twice at me. Not a lot of people paid attention to the world around them, outside of their VirtReels and holo-watches. Everyone was probably in a rush to get back to their false realities, away from the people in the hall whose names they didn't know, despite living in the same building.

I can't believe we had to evacuate, and there wasn't even a big fire, a man thought, as he used his chubby elbows to push past others.

I found Ariana and Xavier in the crowd once I was close to our apartment. We reached our own rooms without anyone noticing us, though I got a few more bruises from being elbowed by those rushing back to their homes.

Inside, Ariana collapsed against the door with a dramatic sigh. "Let's, like, never do that again." She stood up again and peered through the small rectangular slit window in the door. "Do you think anyone saw us?"

I tugged her away from the window. "They're gonna see you if you keep staring like a creep," I said. "Come on, let's put the stuff on the counter."

Xavier had already dumped some meal bars on the white countertops. I fished into my pockets, curling my hands around the cool chips. They clacked loudly as I placed them on the counter. Ariana and Xavier did the same. Ariana had even found mini soaps for each of us, which meant we could shower today. I hadn't counted the credits, but it looked like we might have enough to get by until we found some work. *If* we found some work.

"I hope the people from the apartments don't notice," Ariana said, looking down at what she'd gotten. She flicked her purple eyes back up to me. "Do you think I took too much?"

"It's fine," Xavier said, his tone reassuring. "They can get help if they need it. And nobody will risk calling the cops if they notice. The police will just think they're cranked."

The sad truth was people in low-class areas struggled to afford much and received little respect for their jobs. The resulting need to escape meant that tons of people in these areas suffered from D.R.D. The police were more likely to assume people had gone crazy than to believe a couple of low-value items had been stolen.

"Yeah," she said, nodding. "You're probably right."

I put the credits into a neater pile, counting them. There were about five hundred total, which wasn't a lot considering a single cheap shirt would probably cost us almost a hundred. Then I looked at the mini-soaps.

"So," I said, "who gets to have a shower first?"

I didn't care all that much. I'd get a shower eventually, and it hadn't been long since my last. It may have felt like forever ago that we'd been at Xavier's aunt's, but it hadn't even been two days. I left it up to Ariana and Xavier to see who could go first.

"You ready?" Xavier asked her. He held up his hands to play Earth, Fire, Water, which would decide who got the first shower. "You know you're going down."

"Yeah, whatever." She rolled her eyes. "Let's hurry up, so I can have my shower faster." They each put a fist on top of their palm.

"Earth, fire, water!" they both shouted.

"Ha!" Xavier tapped his three fingers over her curled fist. *Why would she pick Earth? Did she really think he* wouldn't *pick fire?* "I win."

"Three outta five?" she asked.

"Nope," he said. He scampered to the bathroom and locked the door.

"You suck," she called. Though he couldn't see, she stuck her tongue out. The sound of water raining down from the tap was Xavier's reply.

Ariana and I walked back to the living room. We sat beside each other, against the wall at the back of the room, the door in sight. We were silent for a while, listening to the water.

"Do you remember when I showed up at your house?" Ariana asked. Her voice was faint, almost drowned out by the sound of the shower.

"Yeah," I said. "It's not something I'd forget."

My door had buzzed over and over within the span of a few seconds. I'd run over to see who it was and found Ariana standing there. Dark lines had dripped down from her eyes, like she was melting. Water had filled her eyes. Her hair had been frazzled, and there'd been no shoes on her feet. What had caught my attention most was the bright-pink mark on her cheek, roughly the size of a hand.

"Come in." I'd ushered her into my house, closing the door behind her. I had brought her over to the couch, rubbing her back.

"I can't go back." She had stammered while, more water poured from her eyes.

"You'll never have to," I had told her. Ariana's parents had always been horrible to her, but they'd never, to my knowledge, hit her before then.

"I'm a freak," she'd sobbed, making it hard to understand what she was saying.

"No, you aren't." I'd left no room for debate. "I don't care what they told you."

"Can normal people do this?" She'd looked at her hands. A blue light had flickered in them for a split second before disappearing. She'd seemed startled by herself.

"When did that happen?" Up until then, only Damion and I had manifested our abilities.

"Today." She had sniffed again, wiping her sleeve across her nose. "She tried to...to hit me, again. It stopped her." Ariana had been crying more heavily by then.

"Your parents just let me live with all of you," Ariana said now. "They did so much for me, for all of us."

"They loved you." I looked down at my knees. I didn't want to talk about them.

"What if," she said, "it was my fault?"

I looked up at her. Her eyes shimmered with tears. "It wasn't your fault, Ari."

She shook her head, wiping at her eyes. "Your parents called the cops," she said. "I put your family in danger when I came to your house."

My parents had finally had grounds, and they'd called the police on hers. They'd been arrested and had said all kinds of things about Ariana. They'd told the police she was dangerous, wrong. The police hadn't seemed to think anything of it.

"How else would the Takers have heard about us?" She started to stumble over her words again.

"That was a year ago." I tried to be reassuring, but I wasn't in the best place either. I didn't want to talk about what had happened. "They would've come earlier if it was something your parents had said."

"I just... What if it was?" she asked, quietly. "What if they're gone because of me?"

I looked away. "It wasn't your fault." The water stopped running in the bathroom. "You should go have your shower."

Despite my poor comforting skills, Ariana seemed a bit more at ease. She nodded and stood. "Yeah," she said. "Okay."

Xavier opened the bathroom door, steam stepping out with him. He and Ariana switched places.

"God," she said when she reached the small bathroom. She turned around to face him. "How hot did you have the water?"

"Hottest it goes." Since Xavier was made of fire, he couldn't be burned. It was the opposite actually. Heat energized him, made it easier to use his powers. "Have fun."

She huffed, closing the door behind her.

He sat down beside me. His hair was still damp, with pieces falling across his forehead, but everything else was dry. He'd washed his clothes, but they were dry too.

"Good idea," I said, gesturing to the light-blue shirt that rested against his cleaned skin.

"Thanks," he said. "But we should probably ditch the school uniforms soon."

He was right. We needed to appear old enough to have this apartment. It was amazing the superintendent hadn't noticed.

"Yeah," I said. "We need to find a printer, get some clothes."

"Did you see how many creds we have total?" he asked.

"Only about five hundred." I sighed. "It might get each of us a shirt, but we can't get pants too." The pants we all wore were plain, light-grey dress pants. They would be fine to wear without arousing suspicion. The shirts, however, would be recognized instantly with the school crest set below the collar.

Xavier ran a hand through his hair. "We're gonna need money to keep living here."

"Yeah," I said. "How do you think we can work? We're not exactly in the CareerPath program any more." The government assigned people their careers, so how could we find work?

"Most of the Service jobs aren't part of the CareerPath," he said. "We'll have to hope we can find something."

The people here, the ones who worked in the Services, usually had to find their own jobs since they weren't deemed essential by the government in any field. While it might have sounded like more freedom, none of the jobs were good, and none paid nearly enough.

"Right." I slumped against the wall. I could never follow my dreams of being a biologist like my father. Would the rest of my life be full of crappy work hours and little sense of purpose?

"It won't be so bad," Xavier said. He gave me a small, reassuring smile. "With all of us working, we should be okay."

"Yeah," I said. I pressed my lips firmly together and tried to smile back. "I know."

Maybe we would be okay, but I wasn't sure we would ever be good.

Chapter 6: Print

After we had all had our showers, we sat on the floor of the living room. We ate the meal bars we'd stolen, and Ariana took her turn to look through the Med-Kit.

"We can go to a store and print the shirts once we're done," I said. "Change, then check for job listings."

People in low-class areas couldn't afford to have personal printers. It would just be another bill at the end of the month. So they went to community printing places, where they paid per print.

"How does it work anyway?" Ariana asked. "Do we just, like, give the money to someone and they print it for us?" I'd never been to a community printer, but that didn't sound right.

"No," Xavier said. He played with the wrapper from his meal bar, singeing the ends with his fingertips. "You print it yourself, but there's a scanner for cred-sticks and cards, so they can charge you."

Xavier had lived in our neighbourhood, but his mom had worked extremely hard to keep them there. He hadn't had a printer at home when we were younger because they couldn't afford the extra bill.

"Oh," Ariana said. She balled up the wrapper from her meal bar, thinking for a moment. "That's kinda cool. Like, going out to buy things... Do people hang out and go printing?"

"I dunno." He gave her an odd look.

I crumpled up the wrapper from my meal bar too. "Seems weird," I said. I shifted my body slightly, and pain exploded under my ribs. "Ah." I twisted my face up from the sudden pain. I'd almost forgotten about all the injuries.

"You okay?" Xavier asked, leaning forward.

"Yeah." I gave a tight smile.

Had my family been in pain? I had chosen to believe that it had been quick, that they hadn't felt anything, because considering the alternative made my stomach churn.

"We should get that burn fixed up," Ariana said. She packed the stuff back into the Med-Kit. "And all the bigger cuts. We can't walk around like this." She took the kit in her hands and rose to her feet.

We threw our wrappers down the chute and went to the small bathroom. We put the lid down on the toilet, and I sat down. I lifted my shirt just above the burn, wincing as the fabric skimmed it. Xavier's eyes widened when he saw the injury, which looked raw and oily.

"Ouch," he mouthed.

"Yikes," Ariana said. "Okay. Here we go." She dug through the Med-Kit, pulling out various ointment packets, the roll of gauze, and medical tape.

"Are you sure you know what you're doing?" I tilted my head, looking over the packets.

"Instructions," Ariana said. She pulled out the manual from the Med-Kit and waved it at me. "See?"

"Alright." I took a deep breath, which only sent more pain shooting through me.

Ariana turned to the page on electrical burns and read the instructions aloud. She took one of the dampened towels and soaked the end with icy water. The water was a relief on the burn, sending cool waves through my body. The ointment, which stung sharply, was less of a relief. The gauze stung at first too, but Ariana secured it tightly enough around my stomach that it wouldn't shift against the burn.

"Thanks." I let my shirt fall, covering the bandage.

Next, we cleaned up the bigger cuts made by the glass. Xavier and I both had two, but Ariana had escaped almost all of the glass with her force field. It didn't take long to tie some gauze around the cuts once they were cleaned. After that, we had no more reasons to delay finding a community printer.

As we left our apartment, I found myself constantly looking over my shoulder. It felt as if someone could jump out and shoot at us any minute. My friends seemed similarly anxious. We padded quietly through the halls and didn't say a word.

At the corner leading to the elevator, we slowed, peering around cautiously. I couldn't see anybody outside the silver elevator.

"Let's go," Xavier said. We picked up our pace and reached the elevator in a few seconds. It sensed our weight in front of it and dinged, rising up from the floors below. The doors slid open, and we stepped into the steel box.

I stared forward in anticipation as we arrived at the main floor. Would there be guns waiting for us on the other side? My heart pumped a bit faster. What if they had found us again?

The doors slid open, revealing an empty lobby. My heart settled again as we walked out of the elevator.

When we made it out of the building, still air met my face. The sun was starting to lower in the sky, which was now a soft blue. The pavement leading away from the apartment had faded from black to grey and was full of cracks. On the other side of the street was a plaza full of rundown buildings. They were basic, black, printed buildings, some with broken windows and signs. The store at the right end was small and square, with a sign that had some of the lights busted. It read CommuPrint.

"I think that's what we're looking for." I pointed to the store's sign.

"Yeah." Xavier nodded.

I scanned the road in front of us. No E-Cars to be seen. "Let's go then," I said.

We doubled-checked for E-Cars before darting across the street. My calves still burned, and I couldn't help being glad the run was short. I pushed against the glass door and walked into the shop.

The walls—like the outside—were solid black, as were the floors. All that was in the room were four tall printers, backed against the far wall. They were about as tall as I was, thick and silver. We walked to one in the middle and tapped the screen.

"Select a category." The monotone voice rang throughout the nearly empty room. I tapped the picture of a T-shirt. "Clothing. These are the trending clothing prints. For additional options, change the organization type."

I changed it to give us the most inexpensive clothing options. Once all was said and done, we had just enough credits to get each of us a shirt and a package of underwear.

Back in the apartment, I took the bedroom, Ariana took the bathroom, and Xavier stayed in the living room. I laid my things on top of the white nightstand. It was in poor condition, with one of its three drawers refusing to close all the way.

I changed as quickly as I could without hurting my stomach further. I smoothed down the shirt I'd picked. It was a plain black T-shirt that fit snugly around my body. I didn't usually wear black, and if I did, there was always a colourful logo to brighten it. Damion had claimed he always wore black because he hadn't wanted to waste his time matching things. My parents had hated it, which was probably part of the reason he'd done it.

I tucked the pack of underwear and my torn-up uniform shirt into the top drawer of the dresser, then opened the door.

"You good?" I called to Xavier.

"Yeah," he said. I walked out to the living room to meet him. He was wearing a navy-blue cotton T-shirt that had a small dip into a V-neck. The blue suited him, calling attention to his warm, brown eyes.

"There's a nightstand in the bedroom," I said, nodding over to the room. "If you wanna put your stuff away. Top drawer's mine."

"Alright, thanks." He gathered his things into his arms and went to put his stuff away.

Ariana still wasn't done in the bathroom. I knocked on the door. "Ariana, it's not like you have a lot of clothes to choose from."

"Sorry," Ariana said. She opened the door. "What d'you think?"

"Very nice," I said. She was wearing a pale-green shirt with a wide neckline. It was plain, which Ariana had complained about, but it complemented both her violet eyes and dark skin.

"Ready to go?" Xavier asked.

We had to go back down to the lobby to use the Screen, so we made another trip in the elevator. There was a seating area, with wide cushioned chairs, towards one corner of the lobby. The Screen was mounted on the wall between two of the chairs. Ariana tapped the Screen, and it lit up in blue. She typed in the keywords, and the results window popped up.

There was nothing. Nowhere within walking distance was hiring one person, let alone three.

"What're we gonna do now?" Xavier asked.

He clicked off the Screen. We sat in the big chairs, slumped back. Hunger prodded at my stomach.

"Maybe..." Ariana said, leaning forward, chin resting on her palms. "Let's try again. Maybe we missed something."

"We checked everything." I rested my head against the back of the chair. "No one's hiring." We needed jobs. That superintendent wouldn't let us stay for free forever, and we would need more food soon.

"Well, we have to do something," she said. She pushed her dark hair out from behind her ear. "We can't just, like, wait here to starve."

"We can't use the fire alarm again," Xavier said. "People'll know something's up."

"You're right," I said. I sat straighter. "There has to be a job." *What can we do? We can't get jobs any farther away without a car.*

"Maybe surveys..." Ariana drifted off. Surveys required someone to have a personal Screen, not to mention they were usually government-run.

"We could try what we did with the superintendent," I said, frowning. *Begging worked once, maybe it can work again...* "See if we can convince someone to hire the three of us."

"I don't think someone would pay three workers they don't need out of pity," Xavier said, shaking his head. "Everyone here needs all the creds they can save."

"We could..." I didn't want to do what I was thinking. These powers had gotten us into trouble, but it seemed they would be the only way to help us survive now. "I could read somebody's mind, maybe find something that we could use to, sort of, make them hire us."

I just wanted us to be safe and have what we needed to survive, but what else was I willing to do to make sure that happened? We had already done things I'd never imagined I would have to do. When would it end? When could we go back to trying to be good people?

"I don't think we should." Ariana frowned. "It just feels... dirty."

All of the things we had done recently did. But maybe if we did this one last thing, it could all stop. If we had a job and somewhere safe to live, if we could support ourselves, then we could go back to living without going against our morals.

"It's dirty to snatch people from their homes at night," Xavier said. His jaw tightened. "But here we are. Maybe it takes playing dirty to survive."

"Well, it's up to Renee." Ariana looked at me. "Whatever you pick, it's your power."

"Let's do it," I said. Her face fell a little. I pressed my lips together. "I mean, I don't like that we have to, but we *have* to."

"I guess," Ariana said. She sighed. "Where should we go?"

"Somewhere that needs more than one employee," I said. "More than one person could get complicated."

"There's a FitHub across the street," Xavier said. "They've got pools too."

"They'll need lots of workers then," Ariana said.

I nodded. "It could work." I looked out the large window. "We should go now. Sooner we get some credits, the better."

We got up from the chairs, a slow and ache-filled process. We left the lobby, ran across the road for the second time, and walked into the FitHub. A man behind the counter greeted us.

"Hi," he said. He sounded exhausted. There were dark bags under his eyes, and his cheeks were sunken in. "Have you been to FitHub before?"

"We'd like to speak to the manager," I said.

"Sure," he said, monotonously. He tapped his finger on the holographic counter. He leaned his head down, speaking towards a small microphone. "Some kids asking for you."

"Thanks," Ariana said, giving him a small smile.

"It'll just be a minute." He turned back to tapping at holograms. We were left in awkward silence. I looked around the gym, fiddling with my fingers.

Behind the counter were vibrant yellow walls and a plain grey floor. Rows of black exercise machines lined the space. It was a more modest gym than back home, mostly filled with treadmills and ellipticals. In the more high-end gyms, there were machines that essentially moved people's bodies in the workouts for them. My dad hadn't liked them; he'd said that people should be able to push *themselves* in a workout. I was never a fan either. It had felt odd being pulled around like a puppet.

A man stepped out from the elevator on the right. He had dark skin and black hair to his shoulders. He wore a salmon-coloured suit and tie with shiny black dress shoes. The other man, without looking back up from his game, jabbed his finger in our direction.

The man in the suit turned to us. "Ah, hello." He gave us a tight smile. "How can I help you?"

"Could we talk in your office?" I asked. We couldn't do this in front of his employee.

"Uh." His eyebrows dipped down in confusion. "Sure."

"Great," Ariana said. Her smile was fake. All of our smiles were fake. I wasn't sure they'd ever be real again. "Thanks."

He led us into the elevator, and a stony silence blanketed us. The silver box rose until it reached the second floor. A light flashed, and a *ding* cut through the silence.

"Just this way." The man motioned to the right. He led the way and then opened a door, holding it for us. We walked into the small office, sat down at the end of the table closest to the door, and waited quietly for the man to take his seat on the other side. He did, his eyebrows still furrowed. "Well? What would you like to discuss?"

"We're looking for jobs," Xavier said.

I tried to dig into the man's thoughts for anything useful.

"I'm not hiring," he said curtly. *Don't these kids know how to read? Who asks for a job without reading the listings?*

"We know," Ariana said. She made herself sound disappointed. "But, we were just hoping you might...change your mind. We really need them."

I was probably gonna post soon, but it's not like I want a bunch of inexperienced kids working for me.

I looked at my friends and shook my head. I didn't think just asking nicely would do it, but it had been worth the try.

"Sorry, but like I told you, I'm not hiring right now," he said. "Honestly, you kids should just look somewhere else."

Where are these kids' parents? Why didn't I think about that before? If these kids are runaways...

Not many people got jobs before their CareerPath was chosen. There were never any Service jobs open for kids to fill because of how many adults stuck in Services were forced to have multiple in order to live off what they earned.

"Is there anything you'd never want anybody to find out?" Xavier asked. "Something that could ruin your life?"

The man's eyebrows had gone even lower, which I hadn't thought possible. "Who the hell are you?" He stood up from his chair, making a loud squeak as it scraped against the floor. "Get out!" He pointed to the door. His thoughts gave away to what I needed.

"You're going to give us jobs here," I said, hardening my gaze. "Or I'll tell the authorities that you've been hacking your electricity bill."

He had been hacking into the system that monitored his electrical usage to lower his bill. From what I understood, it was common in the poorer areas of Mozaan. Doing that, he'd actually managed not to be too bad off. It might not hurt him too much to pay the three of us, which was a relief. I didn't think I could have gone through with it if he had been struggling.

"How did you—" His bright-blue eyes were wide now, and he stepped back. "Who are you?"

"You can pay us the minimum," Xavier said. He looked the man straight in the eyes. "But we work here starting tomorrow. Alright?"

"Not like I have a choice." He looked between the three of us. "Why here? How did you know I hacked?"

"I'm sorry," Ariana said, "but we aren't gonna tell you that."

"What time does our shift start tomorrow?" I asked.

The man sat back down, trying to appear calm. He wasn't. If the government found out about his hacking, they would arrest him and let somebody else run the business. Of course, we couldn't really go to the government. It was an empty threat, but as long as he didn't know that, we would be fine. At least, as fine as we could be.

Chapter 7: Purpose

"Here," the man in the salmon suit said as he handed us our uniforms the next day. "Get changed and then we can discuss the, er, the job."

We went to the bathrooms, holding crisply folded uniforms in our arms. As Ariana and I walked into the plain, white women's bathroom, I picked the first stall and closed the pigeon-grey stall door behind me. The cool plastic latch clicked softly as it locked.

I changed into the uniform, bunched my old clothes up in my arms—in a messy way that neither my mother nor Ariana would approve of—then made my way over to the counter that stretched across the length of the bathroom. It was the same white as the walls, with three silver sinks spaced out along it.

I folded the clothes and set them on the counter below the mirror. The uniform shirt, a dry-fit tee, clung to my skin. It was the colour of juiced beets, with white rimming the neck and sleeves. The pants were looser fitting and solid black. At least it was better than the school uniform. My hair was still a mess though. It was frizzed at the top, and many of the loose curls had tangled together.

I made a part in my hair with my nails and tried to comb through the locks with my fingers, but I was quickly forced to stop and rip apart pieces that had tangled together.

Ariana came out of her stall as I worked, clothes already folded as neatly as humanly possible. I refolded my own pile of clothes, matching all the edges and smoothing out the wrinkles. My mom would have found the result unusually acceptable. Back at home, my dad, Damion, and I had all been banished from folding laundry.

Ariana placed her outfit on top of mine, and I grabbed them to bring with me to the desk I was working at. We didn't want to risk anybody taking them.

"Ready?" Ariana asked, smoothing over her hair in the mirror. Her mouth had twitched into a small frown, which she tried to bring up into a smile. "First day of a new life."

The air deflated out of me, and a sigh escaping my lips. "I don't want a new life."

An earthquake had collapsed on our lives. We were the only survivors, and the rubble was suffocating, like sandbags hung from my body that dragging me down. I lifted my lips into a small, fake smile again. "But nobody ever really gets what they want, do they?"

She reached out and pulled me into a hug. "One day," she said. When she let me go, her face was serious. "We will. Life's gonna pay us back for all the crap it gave us, and we're gonna be happy."

How could life ever pay my parents back? My brother? They were gone, and there was no way the universe could ever make that up to me. I shook my head. "The world isn't gonna change for us, Ari," I said, my tone heavy and without hope.

"Then we change the world." She sounded like she was really trying to look for the best. Didn't she realize it was pointless? We were going to be stuck hiding and working Service jobs for the rest of our lives, however long we managed to survive.

"How are we supposed to do anything with our lives? Change the world?" I gestured around the small bathroom. My voice rose, wavering somewhat. "This is us. Forced to blackmail some guy just to get enough money not to starve to death."

"I don't know!" she said, almost shouting. Her hands flew down to her sides. "Maybe I just want to believe it'll get better, okay? Maybe I wanna think that after everything bad that's happened—"

There was a knock on the door. "You guys almost ready?" Xavier asked.

"Yeah," I called back. I walked over to the door and yanked it open. Xavier stood just in front of me. "Let's go."

Xavier was stuck taking care of the pool and cleanup. Ariana got the lifeguard position after assuring the boss—Nigel—that she had taken medical training courses in school. I took the place of the man at the counter. A few hours later, I understood why he'd been so lifeless. I was either being yelled at by customers or left all alone. I tried not think too much while I stood there by myself. If I thought too much, the sandbags would become too heavy for me to function.

With the three of us working, we had enough for our basic needs—rent, food, soap, and other necessities. After a while, there was a little extra. Not much, but it was something. We saved. We went to work, ate bad food, and slept on the hard floor of our apartment. Then, we went to work, ate somewhat decent food, and slept on air mattresses.

It all felt the same. Empty. Every night, I was still afraid to go to sleep. I still had to double-check the locks on the windows and door. I still woke up some nights from horrible nightmares that weren't as bad as Xavier's, which woke him up in sweaty shivers most nights.

What was I supposed to do now? A month of our new lives, and there was no sign of Ariana's "greater purpose." Or any purpose. We were just meant to stew in our misery.

The sandbags were getting heavier and heavier.

Ariana kept trying to talk about what had happened. Some days, she seemed to be alright, like she had hope that we were going to make things better. Despite her efforts, I could still hear her crying most nights.

She wanted me to talk and try to heal. I wasn't stupid. I knew that I had issues... But therapy wasn't a safe option, and I didn't want to dump my issues on either of my friends when they had enough to deal with.

I also didn't want to heal from it. I didn't want to be okay. How could I be? No matter how much talking I did, my family would still be dead. What right did I have to ever be okay after that?

Xavier worked as late as he could. Most nights he only came home to try and get some sleep, which was almost always interrupted by nightmares. A lot of the times when I woke up in the night, he wasn't there. I would find him in the bathroom, the same as our first night. Sometimes he talked to me about the nightmares, but try as I might, I wasn't all that good at comforting him. The dark circles under his eyes seemed permanent now.

On a Tuesday, no different than any other, Ariana and I returned to our new home after work, and I looked back to make sure the door had locked. I placed our keycard on the counter and went over to the windows. They were locked too. Good.

"They lock automatically," Ariana said, not for the first time. "You really don't need to check all the time."

I shrugged, mumbling something like "whatever."

"I'm gonna shower," I said, walking past her to get to the bathroom. The shower was the only place I felt comfortably alone, less pressured to function and make conversation. I tried to do all of my crying in there so the others wouldn't hear. The water washed away the evidence.

I selected the heat and pressure levels I wanted—mildly scalding and high pressure—and closed the door behind me, pushing the button that locked it. I stripped down and stepped into the shower, letting the hot water soak my hair and roll over my skin.

I washed my hair and body with the cheap unscented soap we had, nothing like the body wash I'd had before. It had smelled like cocoa and made my skin feel fresh and moisturized. But it was way too expensive. We didn't even have separate body wash and shampoo now, so my hair always felt dried out.

I lathered my legs with a new coat of soap to shave, then took the blue plastic razor from the ledge. As I shaved, the flash of black on my wrist jumped out at me, and I angled my it to see the whole tattoo. It taunted me now. Why had I survived? Tears welled up in my eyes. I hadn't asked for this, to have to wake up every day knowing my family was dead.

It wasn't fair.

"How am I supposed to make my happiness out of this, Dad?" I whispered, hot tears pouring out of my eyes. I didn't want to be the only one left with this stupid tattoo.

I looked down at the razor in my hand. I could just get rid of the tattoo. Stop being the last surviving member of my family. Stop waking up every day knowing they were dead. Just...stop.

And maybe there was some kind of afterlife where I would see them. Or maybe not. Either way, at least the pain could finally stop.

I lifted the razor to the offending wrist, my hand shaking. What was I living for anyway? I started pressing the metal to my skin.

Why do you check the locks every night?

The answer was simple. *Ariana and Xavier.* I wasn't worried for myself, but I couldn't do this to them. I couldn't add to their pain.

I put the razor back on the ledge and sat down with my knees pulled to my chest, crying until the water turned off.

You have to pull yourself together. I sniffed and rubbed my hands over my eyes. *You don't want Ariana to hear, and she'll know something's going on if you don't come out of the bathroom.*

I got out of the shower and wrapped a towel around myself. I washed my face in the sink and wiped it off with the corner of my towel. I stood there awhile, breathing in and out. Once I felt a bit more in control, I went to the bedroom and got changed into my pyjamas.

The apartment door opened, and Xavier's voice called out. "Hey." He was home a lot earlier than usual.

I came out of the bedroom to greet him. "Hey," I said. "You're early."

"I'm not staying late any more." There was conviction in his voice. Ariana stepped out from the galley kitchen. "We're gonna start doing something," Xavier added.

"Like what?" I asked, frowning. Even Ariana seemed confused.

"We're gonna train," he said. "Get fit. Ready for a fight if *they* come again."

"How?" Ariana asked, tilting her head.

"We'll start small," he said. "Exercise here, look up workouts."

"I'm in." Ariana nodded. "I think it'll be good to feel like we're working towards something."

"Okay," I said. I wasn't excited about it, but I wasn't opposed either. It might not protect us if they did come, but it couldn't hurt.

~

Turned out, training gave me a way to stop thinking. Physical pain and exertion was so much easier to handle than mental. When I wasn't busy working, eating, or sleeping, I was training. Going faster, getting stronger—pushing myself beyond my limits. Maybe it wouldn't help us a ton, but just like with the locks, it became a need of mine to get stronger. Bad day? Train. Need to escape my thoughts? Train. Nearing the edge of an emotional breakdown? Train.

Any time I considered skipping a day or going easier, I thought, *What if they came and I could've stopped them if I were just a bit stronger?* I pushed myself harder than I'd thought possible, trained every day. I wouldn't let a lack of training be the reason we died if they came for us.

Then came that "greater purpose" Ariana had been hoping for. It walked right into FitHub and started doing weights. There was a tall woman who couldn't have been more than eighty pounds. She was sickly pale, with the strained eyes of a virtual-addict and the sunken cheeks of someone close to starving. She also picked up a fifty-pound weight in each hand like they were nothing.

I watched her carefully, making sure she didn't catch me looking. She was tentative picking up heavier weights, unsure of herself. But as the weights got heavier and heavier, she still showed no sign of struggle.

She didn't know about the Takers. She didn't know she should be hiding her ability.

Leave it alone. Down-low, remember?

"Hi," I said with my best customer service smile, walking over to her anyway. "Is this your first time at FitHub?"

She put the weights down and turned to me. "Uh, yeah." There was a slight narrowing of her eyes. "Why?"

Good question. What could I tell her? Address. I needed her address. "I was just looking at my screen," I said, glancing over to it. "And it hasn't got your address registered yet."

She tilted her head to the side, her dirty-blond hair shifting on her shoulders. "Sorry," she said, her eyes narrowing further. "Why do you need that?"

"It's this thing to make sure people aren't using more than one FitHub per membership." I tried to sound bored. "Standard. It'll just take a sec."

"Alright," she said.

We walked over to the counter, and I pulled up the Notes section on my screen. "Okay," I said, gesturing for her to tell me the address. "Go ahead."

"Thirty-Two Mystic Court," she said.

"Great," I said, smiling at her as I typed it in. "Thanks."

It would be dangerous, but I had just found our purpose.

Chapter 8: Tripping

You wanna warn her?" Xavier asked. The three of us were sitting on my air mattress in the living room. Ariana's lay across from it, and Xavier's was in the bedroom. We'd stopped bothering to take shifts guarding at night soon after we started working at FitHub. Ariana just fell asleep, and Xavier and I were up enough throughout the night as it was.

"Yes," I said.

I pressed my lips together. Maybe it was a bad idea. I shouldn't have been asking them to risk everything. What if this got them killed?

"I'm in," Xavier said.

"Me too." Ariana nodded.

"Really?" I furrowed my eyebrows. "Just like that?"

"Well, yeah." Ariana rolled her eyes. "Did you think we'd say no?"

"It's what we've been waiting for," Xavier said. He looked at Ariana, then his dark eyes bore into mine. They flamed with determination. "This is how we get back at the Takers."

I nodded. "Alright." I took a breath. "I guess we're doing this." Dangerous or not, there was no point in protecting ourselves if our lives were just wasting away anyway.

We went down to the lobby and gathered around the Screen. I tapped it to life and typed in the woman's address. A map came up, showing a blue dot where we were and a red flag at the address. It was a few streets over, behind the FitHub plaza.

"That's not even too far," Ariana said. She reached over, tapping to get walking directions. "Twenty minutes."

"That's good," Xavier said, nodding. "If she flips out or something, we can get back here fast."

I peered at the map, trying to memorize it. I was better at memorizing things, thanks to my genetic enhancements. "You guys ready?" I asked as I erased our search. I powered down the Screen and straightened up.

"Yeah," Ariana said. She tightened her long ponytail and nodded. "Let's do this."

Xavier straightened up too. "Let's go," he said. A brief, small smile lit his features.

I let a similar smile drift onto my face as we walked out of the apartment building. We bolted across the street to FitHub as usual, but this time, we continued behind the plaza. Mystic Court wasn't far, and with our five months' worth of training, the walk felt like nothing. Less than fifteen minutes later, we were facing the plastic door of Thirty-Two Mystic Court.

"So, who's gonna ring?" Ariana asked, her voice hushed. The entire street was quiet, with only the low humming from the ground disrupting the silence.

"My idea." I brought my shoulders back in an effort to appear confident, though my heart was beating harder. I tapped my finger on the button above the door handle, which flashed red. It beeped faintly. I stepped back on the porch.

We waited for a minute or so, and there was still no answer. Had we come all this way for nothing?

"Probably gaming," Xavier muttered.

He moved up to the button, brushing lightly against my shoulder as he walked past. He tapped the button four times, in rapid succession. As he stepped back beside me, movement could finally be heard in the house. Footsteps stomped towards us, and an eventual grumbling sounded on the other side of the door.

The door swung open, revealing the sickly-looking woman from the gym. "Look, whatever you're selling—" She stopped when she saw the three of us. "Who're you?"

"We're here to tell you something important," Ariana said. She smiled. "Could we step in for just a sec?"

"What?" The woman scrunched her eyebrows. "No. Get away from my house." She started to close the door, but Xavier put his foot in the way.

"Sorry." He gave her a tight smile. "But we just need a couple minutes."

Her face changed into alarm. She opened her mouth to speak—or yell—but then saw me. "Hang on." She pointed at me. "You're that girl from the gym. You took my address!"

"Just calm down," I said, putting my hands out just in front of me and motioning downward. "We need to talk about that recent *strength* you've had."

Her hazel eyes grew wide. She stepped back and let go of the door. Xavier moved his foot away.

"How...how do you know about that?" she asked. "Do you know what's happened to me?"

"We're like you," Ariana said, her voice soft. "We wanna help."

"Prove it," she said, eyeing us suspiciously.

"Inside," I said, matching her gaze. "It's dangerous out here."

She hesitated before easing the door open the rest of the way. She moved to the side, motioning for us to come in.

The foyer was nearly bare, save for a couple beat-up pairs of shoes. The walls were black, like the outside of the house, and the floors were a solid teal.

"How do I know this is even real?" she asked suddenly. She latched the door and shook the handle to make sure it was locked. "What if I'm tripping out on VR?"

"It's real," I said. "You'll have to take my word for it."

"And you're all strong?" she asked, turning back to us. "Like me?"

Xavier shook his head. "Not exactly," he said. Fire danced along his fingertips, and she watched with awe. He closed his hand and put out the flames. "But close enough."

"And you two?" She turned to Ariana and me. "You can do stuff too?"

"Yeah," I said. Ariana flickered a small force field out from one hand.

The woman stared for a minute. She shook her head and put a hand to her forehead. "This is cranked. This is game stuff."

"It started last week?" I asked her, after hearing it in her thoughts.

"Uh, yeah." Her eyebrows furrowed again. "How did you—"

"You tell anyone?" Xavier asked, looking her straight in the eyes.

"No." She shook her head. "Why? Why are you here?"

"There are these people," I said. "We think they're part of the government."

"They kill people like us," Xavier said.

"They what?" she asked, her eyes so wide I thought they might snap back like an elastic. "I don't understand…"

Ariana put a hand on her shoulder. "It's okay," she said. "That's why we're here. To warn you."

"What's gonna happen?" the woman asked. "Are they gonna come for me?"

"Did anyone see you?" I looked her in the eyes. "It's important."

"No." she said quickly. "Nobody."

"You should be safe for now," Xavier said. "But you can't let *anyone* find out about this."

"And that means no lifting heavy stuff," I said. "No going to the gym. Don't test the waters."

"I—Okay," the woman said. I read her thoughts to ensure she understood the severity of what we were saying. She wasn't going to tell a soul. "But what do I do now? Now that I know about all this?"

"Pretend you don't." Xavier turned away from her. He unlatched the door.

"Good luck," Ariana said, her lips curving into a smile.

"Thanks," the woman said as we left. "You too."

It had gotten dark. There were no street lights here, and the FitHub plaza in front of us was full of black, looming buildings. As we grew closer to the plaza, the dark spaces in between the buildings became more distinct. We would have to go through one of them to get back home. My chest tightened as we approached. The silence was horrible, broken only by the sound of our breathing.

"Is there, like, any way we could not go into the scary alley?" Ariana whispered, as if breaking the silence would alert something to our presence.

"It's fine." I kept my voice low. "It's not even a hundred yards." I eyed the space we stood in front of.

"So?" she asked. "What good things have you ever heard of happening to teenagers going down dark alleys? You've been in simulations, right?"

"You've been in too many," Xavier said, his voice at a normal level. "Come on."

He started to walk forward. I followed, stuffing down the nervous feeling in my chest. He was right. We were worrying for no reason.

As Xavier and I entered walked into the alley, our footsteps echoed against the building walls, but there was a lack of footsteps behind us. I turned to Ariana, standing back where the alley began.

"Come on, Ari," I said. Xavier and I paused. "Faster you walk, faster we'll be outta here."

The sound of her taking a deep breath reached my ears, and she ran toward us. I was debating whether we should just run through the whole alley, but I didn't want to sound childish suggesting it.

We kept walking in silence for a few seconds. The feeling in my chest loosened. It was stupid to think anything would happen. It wasn't as if there were animals out here, and there was no way the Takers would have waited in such a public place to attack us.

A rock scraped on the concrete ahead of us.

I took a sharp breath.

"Oh god," Ariana said. She stepped closer to me. "What was that?"

"It—" I was about to tell her something about it being just the wind, but I was cut short by rubber slapping onto the concrete.

"Someone there?" Xavier called out into the dark. A vague outline of a human figure was coming toward us. Slow footsteps padded closer.

"We don't want any trouble," Ariana said.

The figure came closer. His face was thin, but a beard hung down a few inches past his chin. His clothes were black, baggy, and wrinkled...

"Students!" Upon seeing us, he clapped his hands together. He came closer, his rubber shoes quickly tapping against the ground. "Here to join my resistance."

I glanced at my friends.

"What?" Ariana asked.

"Against the Kyritone Empire," the man said. He tilted his head.

D.R.D., I thought to my friends. They nodded.

"So you'll aid our cause?" he asked.

"Sorry," I said. "We can't join." We were so close to being out of the alley.

"What? Why not?" the man asked, his voice rising. "If you aren't with us, you must be an enemy spy." The man pointed a semi-sharp rock at us.

"Just put the rock down," Ariana said, trying to sound calm. "We aren't enemy anythings."

"I'll kill you!" The man got closer, waving the rock between us. His voice was almost a shout now.

He's too loud, I thought to my friends. *He's gonna call attention.*

"You stole our lives!"

I knocked the rock from his hand in a swift motion, but his ramblings grew louder.

"What're we gonna do with him?" Ariana asked, her voice back to a whisper.

The man grunted and lunged toward me. I jumped at the sudden movement and managed to twist his arms behind his back. I held him there, his attempts to struggle unimpressive.

"I dunno," I said, heart pumping faster. He was yelling swears now. Somebody was going to notice.

Xavier brought his elbow down over the yelling man's head so fast I hardly saw the movement. The man slumped instantly in my arms.

"Guess that's one way to solve it." I set the him down on the concrete.

"Won't people freak if they see him?" Ariana asked.

I shrugged. "Not like they'll know it was us. They'll probably think he just passed out. Look at him."

"Besides," Xavier said as we started walking again, "he'll be up in a few minutes." We exited the tight space, reaching the front of the plaza.

I stretched my arms out. "Glad that's over."

We made it back to the apartment without any further problems. I locked the door behind us, and we all went to our normal spots on my mattress.

"I can't believe we just did that," I said, shaking my head. I smiled broadly. Our training was working.

"Yeah." Xavier nodded. His lips twitched up into a smaller smile. "Makes me wonder if maybe *we're* the ones tripping."

"Maybe," I said. I felt lighter after warning that woman, like the sandbags had been lifted. For the first time in months, there was a point to our lives. We'd helped somebody.

"What do we do now?" Ariana asked after a few minutes of silence.

"What d'you mean?" I asked, lowering my eyebrows slightly.

She tucked some of her dark hair behind her ear. "Well, it felt really good, finding her and warning her." She took the time to pass her eyes over both of us, and her tone seemed almost pleading. "And I don't want that to just, like, go away. It finally felt like we were doing something, and I don't wanna just go back to eat, work, train, and sleep, y'know?"

"You wanna keep warning people?" I asked. I definitely wanted to. I wanted to hold onto that light feeling and to prevent people from feeling as heavy as I did most of the time.

"Yeah," she said, nodding. She fiddled with the ends of her hair. "I think we have to. There's so many other people that the Takers could hurt. If we can even help a few of them, I think we need to do it."

"I'm in," Xavier said decisively. "If the Takers can make our lives crap, the least we can do is make theirs harder." There was a fierce determination on his face. The two of them looked at me.

"In," I said in a "duh" tone. If I could, I would have destroyed Prime Minister Cameron's government for what they did to us. For the moment, stopping her minions from perpetrating Outlier genocide would have to do.

Chapter 9: Little Did We Know

Y ou know how we're warning people?" Ariana asked a couple weeks later.

We had successfully managed to warn a few people, and scary as it still was, it might have been helping me a little. I'd had a couple days where I actually felt like doing things, where I didn't want to just stare at the wall for hours. I was trying my best not to let the guilt about surviving eat away at me. It was hard.

"Yeah," I said. We were sitting at our little plastic table, eating meal bars for dinner...again. I still missed meat. There was no way the three of us could afford it, but I couldn't help longing for my dad's roasted turkey—a ridiculous thing to complain about when my family could never eat anything again. How could I be missing anything except for them?

"What's up?" Xavier asked Ariana.

"Well, I was thinking." She bit her lip and shifted in her chair. "What if we made a group with the Outliers we find? Y'know, talk about what happened, our powers..."

"That's a good idea," Xavier said, sitting straighter in his chair. He had that fire in his eyes. "If we get enough and train them, we could go after the Takers. They'll want them gone as much as we do."

"We can't," I said, shaking my head. My breathing sped up a little. "What we do is already risky enough. Now we're gonna have big, suspicious group meetings *full* of other Outliers? We'd just be rounding ourselves up so the Takers could catch us all at once."

A group meeting regularly also meant extra attachments that I didn't want. I worried enough about Ariana and Xavier, and I'd already lost my family. I didn't need to be getting attached to new people who could be taken at any time.

"Yeah, it's risky," Xavier said, still all pumped up, "but this is our chance! We can make them pay for what they did to us."

"What are we gonna do?" I asked, raising my eyebrows at him. "Charge in with a few other kids hoping to take down an entire government? We can't get revenge if we're dead."

Xavier's "shoot first" attitude was going to get him hurt.

"Renee's right about that," Ariana said. "We can't try to attack anybody. But I still think we should form a support group or something. It wouldn't be too suspicious. Like, people do have friends they see."

"*If* we did make a group," I said, "we still couldn't meet regularly or too often. And it couldn't be a support group because nothing has happened to them yet. *If* we made a group, it should just be to enlist more people to warn others." It was important to warn as many as possible, and if we made a group this way, Ariana and Xavier would get what they wanted, with much less risk.

"I guess that could work," Xavier nodded, even if he seemed a little reluctant not to go after the Takers.

"So you'll do it?" Ariana asked me, excited.

"If," I said, putting my hands out in front of me. "If we do it the way I said. Irregular, no group therapy."

"Fine," she said, rolling her eyes.

And the warning group was born.

~

"Found one a few blocks down," I said as I walked through the door, almost a year later. The electronic lock gave a soft beep as I shut the door, and as I always did, I looked back to make sure it was red.

My friends were already home, chatting and filling up on some meal bars. I pulled out my earpods and set them on the kitchen counter. Unfortunately, they weren't connected to anything. It just looked less suspicious if I had music when I went for my "run" every night. That way, I didn't appear as if I were walking around the neighbourhood aimlessly when I was really listening for the thoughts of other Outliers.

"Newport again?" Xavier asked, hidden by a wall from where I stood in the kitchen.

"Yeah," I said, opening the cupboards. My eyes drifted across the bright meal bar packages, dried fruit, and boxes of oatmeal staring back at me. "They seem to have a lot."

I reached up on my tiptoes and curled my fingers around a meal bar wrapped in maroon. It was cherry-and-fig flavoured, with the usual insect protein. When I closed the cupboard, the plastic doors squeaked shut. I pulled at the wrapper of my meal bar as I walked toward my friends.

I grabbed the white back of my chair and pulled the cool plastic seat backwards. I sat down, still struggling with the wrapper.

"What ability this time?" Ariana asked. "My bet's on night vision."

Though most people were too freaked to join, our warning group had grown to almost twenty. People who could see in the dark seemed the most common, but we hadn't seen one in almost a month. We still hadn't run into anybody with the same ability as me.

"No," I said. "She's like that little boy we saw a couple months ago. Breathes underwater." When I finally got the wrapper open and bit into the meal bar, the taste of cherry and figs exploded in my mouth. Cherry was my favourite flavour of everything, and I had been looking forward to that meal bar all day. I leaned back in my chair, chewing.

"Wanna go soon?" Xavier asked. "It's dark enough."

I bit into my meal bar again as he crumpled up his wrapper and set it on the table. He looked out the window. The sun was already down, and the sky had turned a deep navy dotted with white stars. I nodded.

"Yeah," I said, after swallowing the last of my meal bar. I crushed the wrapper in my hand and set it down on the table. "If we wait too much longer, she might be asleep."

Ariana had finished her meal bar a while ago, and her wrapper lay neatly folded in front of her. We composted our wrappers and headed out. The sidewalk was empty, but streetlights provided circles of yellow light every couple feet.

"I don't like all these people from Newport," I said, my voice lower than usual. We didn't want to draw any attention to ourselves. "They're all so stuck up."

Newport, better known as "Cop Street," was a rich pocket in Greenville. Some government people, including the Greenville Police Force, were forced to live in this area for their "highly paid" work. That didn't mean they lived like poor people though. Newport was a street full of large, beautiful houses that looked completely out of place, and almost all of the government employees in Greenville lived there. So we were extra careful on that street and made sure the people we warned weren't even *thinking* of turning us in.

"I know," Xavier said, shaking his head and rolling his eyes. "It's like they think everyone else is sub-human."

The government seemed to think that people like us, with abilities, were sub-human too. It was ironic that some of them had abilities of their own. Did they ever make exceptions for their own people? Or would even their most loyal members be carted away? It was like the historic days of prejudice and anti-diversity that Ati used to scare us with.

"Still though." Ariana gave a half-shrug. "Never know. I doubt every single one of them is like that." I wasn't so sure, but Ariana always tried to think the best of people.

Fifteen minutes later, we reached the street of big pearly-white houses. Each had bright-green lawns with neat trims, vibrant flower gardens, and walkways made of actual stone. We used to have a small lawn and a garden. The soil had been squishy and moist in my hands when my father and I planted new seeds. It was one of the few luxuries I still missed with an ache. What I wouldn't have given to be gardening with my dad right then.

The house we wanted was the third one down on the left side of the street. It looked like all of the others.

"This one," I said, nodding to it. My voice was down to a whisper now that we'd reached Newport.

Ariana pressed her finger to the doorbell, and a faint dinging sound could be heard from where we stood on the grey stone porch. She took a step back so that she was beside Xavier and me again, and we waited.

A girl opened the wide teal door after a minute or so. She tapped her foot on her glass floor, scanning us up and down. She looked about eighteen and wore short pyjamas, with a tight, low-cut shirt and shorts not much longer than boxers. I shouldn't have judged. We hadn't exactly had a comm-chat beforehand to let her know we were coming. She wasn't wearing any makeup, but it wasn't like she needed it. She must have had expensive designing. Her face was without a blemish, and all of her features were perfectly proportioned. Her silvery-blue eyes shone under the porch light.

"Who are you?" she asked, raising an eyebrow.

"Not important," I said, shrugging. "We know about your underwater breathing."

She inhaled sharply. "Don't know what you're talking about." She tried her best to cover up her shock and sound annoyed, but there was no masking the surprise on her face. "You're cranked."

"We need to explain some things," Ariana said, her lips turning up into a gentle smile. "But you'll have to let us inside."

The girl stared at us and gave a short laugh. "Yeah right. So you can rob me? No thanks." She started to close the door, but Xavier made fire dance across his fingers, stopping her in her tracks. She stared at him but kept her grip on the door.

"You gonna let us in or what?" he asked, stopping the fire.

Her gaze left his hand and met his eyes. She opened the door slowly. "You've got five minutes," she said, her lips pursed. "And don't touch anything."

I rolled my eyes and stepped past her into the house. The foyer was nearly as big as our apartment. It held a small bench against the wall, a shoe rack that was overflowing, and a large Screen on the wall toward the back. The walls themselves were the soft grey colour of a wolf's fur, and the floors had thick layers of white frosted glass. A small black chandelier lit the room, dim against the darkness that peered in from the large window in the door.

The girl closed the door behind us and crossed her arms. We explained everything to her about the Takers and the government.

She seemed to take it better than most people. Her entire demeanour changed. She nodded, thanked us, and smiled occasionally. I checked her thoughts anyway. While she had some quite ignorant opinions of under-designed and design-flawed people, she did believe what we were telling her. That meant we could ask her about joining the group.

"If you want to help," Ariana said to her, "there's a group of us warning people. You could join."

"I think I could do that." The girl nodded. "Where do you guys meet?"

"We don't have a set place," I said. It was too dangerous to meet at the same place all the time. "Every once in a while I'll send a message to everyone saying when and where to meet, and we just sorta share updates and ideas."

"Okay," she said. "Yeah, I'd like to try and help. But these Takers won't catch us, will they?"

"We can't know for sure," I said, honestly. "They haven't yet, and we're very careful."

"I'll do it." She smiled at me. "Just let me know."

"Great," Xavier said. "We will."

We left her house a few after we got there. Ariana was especially excited about having another group member. All we could do now was go back to our small apartment and get ready for bed.

We had done some serious training before I went on a run to look for new Outliers. Between the training, the running, and the walk, I was exhausted by the time we got back. I could hardly keep my eyes open as we went up the elevator.

As always, I looked back at the lock once we were inside and checked to make sure it was red. Then I went over to the windows and did the same. They were good.

"Night," I said to Ariana as I flopped down on my mattress. I turned over so that the wall was to my back and tugged my plain black blanket over my shoulder, balling the end in my fist.

"Night," she said, lying down on her own bed.

I closed my eyes, drinking in deep breaths of air. I'd made it through another day. I was glad to be going to sleep. I would need it because tomorrow would be exactly the same as today, too long and mentally exhausting.

Chapter 10: Would You Please Jump Off That Ledge, My Friend?

*B*ang. *Bang. Bang.* Knocks pounded on our apartment door, far too loud for it to have been the old superintendent. Each bang sent a tremour through the plastic door. It couldn't have been one of our neighbours either. Nobody talked to each other when passing in the halls, let alone came over to others' apartments.

We all fell silent. I crept closer to the door, staying low. The door shook from the impact of the fists that continued to pound it. I opened my mind to hear the thoughts on the other side. What I heard was pretty much what I had expected, but it still sent a wave of shock through me. I scrambled back to my friends, nodding to confirm what we had all feared.

The Takers had found us.

It had to have been the new girl we'd asked to join our group. She must have freaked out after we left.

Without a word, we all made our way to the window. I nodded to Ariana, and she formed a large blue force field in front of herself. She shoved the force field forward, colliding it with the glass. There was a sharp sound as the glass exploded into tiny shards that flew out the window.

Next came the scary part. I stared down at the concrete below the building. Our apartment was two floors up. If we didn't land with absolute perfection, we were road pancakes.

I took a deep breath. We had known we would have to jump if it came to this. It was a scenario that had played many times over in my head and one that we had done our best to prepare for. We'd known the risks of warning strangers about the Takers. I shouldn't have decided to warn that first woman. I shouldn't have gone along with the idea of continuing to warn people or starting a group. Now we could all die.

Ariana and Xavier could die, and it would be my fault.

"That's really far," Ariana said. She leaned closer to the window and looked down with me.

Fists pounded the door even harder, shaking it so much that I feared it would break off the hinges any second.

"What if we don't make it?" she added.

"Not much of a choice," Xavier said, his tone resolved.

Without another look down, he crawled through the window frame and jumped. My breath caught as I watched him plummeting down. Farther and farther. It didn't look like he was going to make it unscathed.

Then, at the last second, he rolled into the perfect landing. He got to his feet and turned back around to look up at us. My breath came rushing out. He was alright. He gestured urgently for us to jump too.

"I'm scared." Ariana looked at me, then back at the window. "I...I don't think I can." She had to.

"It'll be alright," I said, trying to give her as much comfort as I could manage given the circumstances. The pounding on the door had stopped. My heartbeat quickened. They wouldn't just give up. They must have gotten a keycard. "Whatever happens, it's better than if they catch us. Jump."

"We'll be okay," she said to herself. Her breath hiccupped. Tears leaked from her eyes, leaving black mascara trails along her cheeks. She sniffed and crawled into the window frame. She glanced back at me and stiffened her lip. She looked down again and pushed herself out of the window.

The electronic lock clicked, and the small circle on the silver handle lit up green. At least it had bought us a little time. Someone flung open the door, smashing the handle into the wall behind it. People in black-and-white suits filled the doorway.

There was no time to hesitate. I took in another large breath. Getting a good grip on the bottom of the frame, I crawled into the window. I pushed myself out. Glass cut into my palms as the Takers bounded across the small room.

Wind rushed through my clothes and blew my hair up around me. The concrete grew closer and closer. I only had a few seconds to prepare myself for the landing. I tried to relax my body, press my legs together, and bend my knees. As my feet touched the ground, I tucked my body inward, bringing my knees closer to my chest. I rolled as I landed and sprung to my feet. My friends were ready, and we didn't wait another second after I was up off the ground.

My sneakers slapped against the pavement, and the air rushed against my face. We sprinted as fast as we could to our emergency meetup place. My friends were just ahead of me.

Maybe we had gotten lucky.

As my friends turned the corner to exit the apartment building's parking lot, someone jerked me to the side. They grabbed me so tightly that I could barely move, try as I might. A large hand, covered in a black leather glove, slapped against my mouth, muffling my screams.

Chapter 11: MIA

An intense ache coursed through my body, clouding my thoughts. My arms were suspended above my head, and some kind of burning shackle held both my wrists and feet in place. The pain was worse in those spots. I must have been in a vehicle of some kind because, every so often, there was a bump that jostled my whole body. I groggily blinked my eyes open, my vision blurry.

A woman stood in front of me, but mostly I just saw black blotches. Eventually, my vision started to clear, and I could see her better. She was tall, with light skin that contrasted the black Takers' uniform. She was carefully designed, with bright-red hair and lips whitened in the latest fashion. She stood waiting in front of me. My eyes eventually focused on her flaming hazel ones.

Oh, plat. I was with the Takers. I started to struggle frantically against the restraints that held me, but my movements were slow and painful. Had Ariana and Xavier managed to escape? Hopefully they hadn't come back to look for me.

"Good," the Taker said. The corner of her whitened lips turned up. "You're awake."

I gave up on struggling; my body hurt too much to keep moving. I took a few seconds to orient myself before I replied in a raspy voice. "No thanks...to you."

I saw the slap coming, but there was nowhere I could go to dodge the woman's hand. The impact snapped my head to the side, leaving my cheek burning and stinging.

"Do not speak unless spoken to," the woman said. Her nose was crinkled, as if I were something bad she was smelling.

"You're speaking to me now," I said, giving her a look full of ice and clenching my jaw. I had wondered how I would feel if this moment came. Depressed? Angry? Terrified? Relieved? It seemed that anger had won for the moment.

The Taker whipped out an electrocution wand from her belt and jammed it into my stomach. This pain was different—intense, sharp, and burning. She held it there for a few seconds while pieces of my shirt burned off, revealing my skin to the device.

I couldn't help but cry out in pain. I couldn't help the water that filled my eyes. I couldn't stop the terrible, body-racking convulsions that ripped across me as she stood there, satisfied. I slammed my wrists hard against the cuffs as I thrashed.

When she finally removed the wand, I couldn't seem to get enough air.

The Taker waited a minute or so, allowing me to catch my breath, somewhat, before speaking. This time, she got straight to the point. "I want you to tell me where those little freaks you warned are hiding."

"I want—" I started. She would never know what I wanted because she reared her fist back and smashed it into the side of my face before I could finish. Blood dripped from my lip onto my shirt.

I spat a wad of it into the woman's eye. I didn't care if I was making this more painful for myself. It was worth it.

She wiped her eye. A sound, like a growl, came from the back of her throat. "I know you think you're being smart, little girl," she hissed, leaning close enough that I could smell her flowery perfume. "But you are nothing. You hear me? *Nothing.* I could kill you right now if I wanted to." It seemed to be personal for her.

"If that's true," I panted, "why am I alive?"

I struggled to read her mind, but the pain was too much for me to focus. My being alive didn't seem like it was up to her. There was probably some sort of protocol. Otherwise, why wouldn't they just kill me right away?

"We have your friends," she said, avoiding the question. The hair bristled on the back of my neck, and it became hard to swallow. Was she lying about my friends?

"I'll kill them in front of you, with this knife." She pulled out a blade and trailed it along my cheek, making a deep gash.

I flinched as the knife cut into me and blood trickled from the wound, but I refused to cry out this time. I stared back at the woman with an expression made of stone. I couldn't know for certain that she wouldn't kill Xavier and Ariana. I had to stall.

"Then what?" I asked.

"What do you mean?" She furrowed her thin brows. She obviously wasn't used to questions like that. Most people were probably shaking with fear.

Terror coursed through me at the thought of her hurting my friends, but I couldn't let her know that.

"And. Then. What?" I said, dragging out my words. It was all I could do not to give in. "If you kill them...you've got nothing to make me talk." What if she called my bluff? What if she killed them and left me alive to suffer?

"No," she said, a tight smile on her lips. "But I can certainly torture them until I have you begging on your knees."

I hadn't thought of that. I tried not to show my fear as I searched for anything that could save my friends from that fate.

"Wait, so you mean..." I said, making my expression falter. I let my voice sound scared for the first time, shaky. "So, you're saying... You'll just hurt them to make me watch? I'm the reason you'd hurt them?"

"Exactly." She smirked. She thought she'd found my breaking point. She leaned forward and whispered. "Gotcha."

It was my turn to smirk. She blinked and took a tiny step backward. I was powerless and in pain, and my friends were being threatened. She must wonder what I had to be smug about.

"You're stupid and arrogant," I said, erasing my fearful tone and expression. I was nearly snarling. My lip twitched up in anger. How dare she threaten the only people I had left after already destroying everyone else I cared about? I looked her dead in the eyes. "You won't torture them if I don't have to watch. You just said so."

"Wha—" she started, then her eyes grew wide. She must have realized my plan. It might kill me, but maybe it was time. We were all going to die anyway once the Takers took us wherever we were driving. At least this way, I could save my friends some pain.

I dipped my head down and then, with all of my force, whipped it backward into the hard wall behind me, finding my way into darkness.

~

When I regained consciousness—again—I was on a cold floor. I shifted slightly, sliding my arm out from its uncomfortable position under me. We must have still been in a vehicle because the occasional bump jostled my now aching body. And the cuffs were still attached to my wrists, pumping me full of pain.

I could hear other people breathing. I tensed, which only put me in more pain. A soft, pain-filled sound escaped my lips.

I blinked, and my heart plummeted when I saw the dark figures of my friends. They hadn't escaped. But at least they weren't being tortured. My plan had worked.

I struggled against the blazing pain and into a sitting position on my knees. I took a moment to catch my breath. Across from me, Xavier shifted, and he looked like he might be about to say something. I managed to create a faint telepathic message.

No. They can't know I'm awake.

Chapter 12: Going Down Swingin'

I could sense my friends' curiosity, but I couldn't form another coherent sentence if I tried. My head felt like it was imploding. All my thoughts were out of focus. Blurry. Breathing took up all of my attention.

"Why can't they?" Ariana whispered.

I groaned. They must not have been able to see how extensive my injuries were, or they would have given me some time. Even with my ankles free of the cuffs, my thoughts were swirling around, difficult to catch.

"Renee?"

Please, I thought to her.

The pain inside my head intensified to a level I didn't think was possible. It was like my brain was being pulled apart. I bit my lip to stop from screaming. Huge mistake. The cut on my lip reopened, and blood filled my mouth. I pulled my knees up to my chest, rested my head on them, and shut my eyes. The burns on my stomach sparked with hot pain as my stomach crunched forward. I grimaced but refused to make a sound.

"I'm sorry," Ariana said. She sounded scared.

"What's wrong?" Xavier asked in a hushed tone. I heard him shift. "Ari?"

"She needs time," Ariana said. Her voice was quivering, but she managed to keep it low. "I think...I think she's hurt really bad."

I fought to get a grip on the pain. It wasn't getting better, but I was figuring out how to handle it.

I closed my eyes and took a deep breath. *It's my head. Worse than I thought,* I thought. Hammers pounded behind my eyes, and claws stabbed into my skull. I pushed on. *Wanted... where others... Were...hurt you...make me talk.* I wasn't even sure they'd only interrogated me to find out about the Outliers we'd warned were.

The Taker woman had seemed angry with me personally. Did she know about what happened in the parking lot a couple years ago? *Found a way out.*

After a long silence, Xavier was the first to speak. "You can use your abilities with the cuffs on?"

No. Speaking...simple... And...every word...hurts.

"Well, then stop it!" he whisper-yelled. His jaw was probably clenched in anger. "You're going to make your head *worse.*"

I huffed out a breath of defeat. My shoulders slumped. I hated that we couldn't do anything. Xavier had been right though. My head had gotten ten times worse. I squeezed my eyes shut and balled my fists.

We sat in silence that only broke when the vehicle finally stopped. I tensed all over and opened my eyes wide. I could hear my friends trying to get into better defensive positions. A sigh escaped Ariana's lips as if she'd been about to speak.

The back doors burst open, letting in a nauseating burst of light.

"Get out," commanded a deep voice.

I blinked rapidly, trying to adjust to the blinding light. I could hear more of them outside.

"No," Xavier answered, still managing to be stubborn. I loved that about him.

"Now," the voice said, his tone demanding.

"We aren't moving." Xavier spoke as if he might laugh.

He knew we would back him up, even if it was a pointless protest. We wouldn't accomplish anything. But we would go down fighting. We would go down together.

The Takers had destroyed my life, my family. I was going to make this as difficult as possible for them.

The man—who I could somewhat see now—motioned to the other Takers. A few of them ducked into the vehicle and came toward us. I backed up against the wall. Xavier kicked one of the Taker's legs out from under him. The man landed with an *oof* but got up quickly. He didn't look too happy.

He wrapped a thick arm around Xavier's neck and yanked my friend up to his feet. Xavier struggled, to no avail. The sight of him clawing at the man's arm, unable to breathe, made my heart clench.

I need to help him. But I couldn't even manage to sit up straight. I shouldn't have used up all of that energy to communicate with my friends. It had been stupid.

Within seconds, I was also hoisted to my feet by a pair of rough hands. Ariana was next. I went limp. I refused to assist them in dragging me out. I was too hurt to fight, but I could be a dead weight. Ariana made me proud with all the kicking and swearing she did.

None of it could help us escape. Even if we had, where would we have run?

A Taker held each of us as another van pulled up. Two more Takers hopped out. They went around to the back and ripped open the doors of the other vehicle.

"Out!" one of them barked. "Immediately."

The people inside obeyed. The first was a man with bright orange hair and a face so thin and pale it made him look ill. His blue eyes were wide with fear. He shook where he stood. A Taker grabbed hold of his arm and dragged him along to meet us. The other stayed, waiting.

"Hurry it up!" a Taker woman yelled.

A girl about our age, with short blond hair and a petite frame, walked slowly out of the vehicle. The Taker took a tight grip on her arm, though the girl's drained, pain-filled face showed she wasn't going anywhere.

"You too." The Taker called into the vehicle.

A rotten feeling settled in my stomach, and a lump formed in my throat. A little girl came next. She couldn't have been more than seven years old. She had light-brown hair that came to her shoulders. Her orange eyes were wide as saucers and shining with tears. A small whimper escaped the child's lips as the Taker woman latched her fingers latched the girl's bicep. The woman walked over to us with both the Outliers in hand.

Once the merry little band was together, we began our walk to the building. The threat of a gun kept me moving forward. Sand puffed up around my black sneakers as I dragged my feet. All of my attention was on putting one foot in front of the other. I needed to just rest for a minute and close my eyes. I doubted the Takers looked highly upon napping breaks.

Then I remembered I didn't care what they wanted. They were going to kill me no matter what. I might as well make myself comfortable.

I came to a sudden stop. The Taker that came to an abrupt stop too. She'd probably thought if anybody was going to put up a fight, it wasn't going to be the most severely injured person there. I dropped into a cross-legged sitting position before she could react.

I casually leaned back, with my cuffed hands resting on my stomach, and stared up at the sky. The clouds were fluffy and white, a simulation, but I didn't care. A few bright specks dotted the navy-blue blanket above me.

I loved stars. Nothing on Mozaan could touch them or put them out. They were far away, but they weren't hidden. Free to shine their brightest and burn their fiercest. You could wish on them, and they could guide you. I wished on the brightest star that I could join them when I died.

Ariana giggled. Xavier made an amused sound, and out of the corner of my eye, I saw his impressed expression. I smiled, though it stung to stretch my cracked lips.

We were facing death, and there was nothing to do about it. We had nothing to lose except our pride. Nobody with fancy handcuffs and guns was going to take that away too.

"Get up now," the woman ordered me. "Or I'll put a bullet through your pretty little head." She was blocking my view of the cloud shaped like a bunny.

"Yeah, whatever," I said, my voice barely above a rasp. "But can you move to the left a bit, please?"

"What?" she asked, her tone both shocked and irritated. I assumed that I'd struck her completely off guard.

"Move. Left," I said, trying not to pant my words. Talking was hard. "Your...fat head is in the way of the cloud. Oh look what you've done now!" I huffed in anger, hiding the pain from my face. "See? You...didn't move. Now it's something else."

"I'll shoot." She pointed her gun in between my eyes as she hovered right over me, leaving only a sliver of the sky visible.

"What even is that?" My voice was growing fainter. I was running out of breath. I ignored the cold barrel against my forehead and tried to see past the woman's face. "A dragon?"

"Get up." She scrunched her black eyebrows down and furled her lip upwards

"You won't shoot." I was almost worried she wouldn't hear me. I could barely hear me.

"What makes you so sure?" she asked. She pressed the gun harder into my forehead.

I made an attempt at a shrug, but it probably looked more like I was twitching. "One, I'd already be dead. Two, I'm guessing there's a reason you're taking us into a building... Less mess?" I tripped and stumbled over the words, but I managed to get them out.

She scowled.

I kept going, even though my throat was dry and my head was screaming in pain. "Three, you think I'm pretty." I forced a wink.

That, apparently, was the last straw. My friends cried out, and I was once again in darkness.

~

Coloured blotches filled my vision. For the third, fourth—I'd lost count—time, I woke with a throbbing head. I blinked slowly. Where was I?

The first thing I focused on were the thick glowing restraints clamped onto my ankles. They were attached to one end of a silver table I was on. My hands were secured above my head on the other end. There was a small monitor in the ceiling above where I lay. I could just make out my reflection. White stickers were attached to different spots on my head, with wires that connected to a vibrant screen on a nearby table. The screen showed wave patterns and what had to be scans of my brain.

Someone's heels clacked loudly on the marble floor. I jerked my head to the side to see who had come in. My neck cracked with a sickening sound, and a sharp pain raced down my spine. A woman stood a few feet away from me. She had layered blue hair and wore a bleached-white lab coat. She came closer and sat down on a wooden stool next to the table I was strapped down on.

She plucked a needle from the jar on the metal counter. I'd never experienced a needle before. All my immunizations were done by design, and I'd never needed blood work or an IV.

I tensed and tried to pull away from the woman. What was she going to inject me with? Was this it? A lethal injection? They used them on Mozaan for death sentences, but I'd never imagined the Takers might use them.

But when I thought about it, it made sense. They were government, and we were considered criminals, even if we'd done nothing wrong. I struggled frantically against my restraints as the woman came closer. Adrenaline fought off the horrible pain coursing through my body.

I was going die. I'd known when they took us that we would be killed, but the terror was only now setting in. In a few seconds, I wouldn't exist. *Let me become a star,* I wished again.

The woman grabbed my arm. As the debilitating pain came crashing back throughout my body, I stopped thrashing. She slid the silver tip of the needle into my arm. I refused to die crying. She pulled up on the plunger of the needle. It filled with crimson.

Blood. She was taking my blood.

"What are you doing?" I asked, my voice just above a whisper.

"My job," the woman answered.

I closed my eyes and breathed a sigh of relief. I had never considered that they would do tests on me. But it actually wouldn't have made sense for them to give us lethal injections. There were so many abilities that option wouldn't work on—like unbreakable skin— it would be a waste of time. The same would have gone for shooting us. And talk about messy.

I peeled open one eyelid, much to my discomfort. The woman brought a thin, rectangular rod in front of me. So what it would be then? Asphyxiation? Acid? Would they just starve us to death?

Where would they put all the bodies?

A blue light went over my eye and shone into it. I needed to blink, but the Taker held my eye wide open. The machine beeped quietly. I'd used retina scanners almost every day in my old life. That was how most schools were secured.

"This feels very violating," I said. The momentary relief of being alive gave me a second wind. "Just thought I'd let you know."

She ignored me. They weren't a customer surveying type of organization. I turned my head to watch as the woman went over to the computer with the brain patterns on it. The movement hurt so badly, like something stabbed my head. I hoped all the blood from when I smashed my head would stain their stupid table.

"Hmm," she said, more to herself than me. She pursed her uncoloured lips. "That's unusual."

"Oh, dammit." I tried my best to sound devastated. It was pretty easy considering I was in excruciating pain and could be killed at any moment. "Do I have a tumour? Am I gonna die? Tell me straight, doc."

"Shut up, you insolent child." She reread the scan details. She raised her wrist just under her mouth to the holo-watch strapped around it. She spoke aloud, but not to me. "Brain scans more active than the boy's. More activity in other regions too."

"What?" I narrowed my eyes in confusion. What boy? Were they doing this to Xavier too? Was he even still alive?

He had to be. If he had died, I would know it. I'd feel deep in my bones that the world wasn't the same.

"Tell me," she said as she turned to face me. Her expression was made of stone. "What are your defects?"

"You've..." I closed my eyes, trying to overcome a wave of dizziness brought on by the pain. Everything hurt so much. How much longer could I stay awake? "Got my brain right there."

"Tell me." This woman was the kind I could never imagine smiling. Like she must have been stern and detached since birth.

"I can eat a whole meal in a matter of minutes. Does that count?" I clenched my teeth and focused on breathing for a second before continuing. "Or, like, never-ending sarcasm? Yeah... that must be it."

She pressed a button. The wires on my head sent electric shocks pulsing through my body. I cried out as my body convulsed against the hot restraints. When it stopped, I did my best not to cry like an idiot. This was too much.

"Tell me," she repeated. Her expression didn't waver.

"Okay." I breathed. Not the electricity again. I couldn't do it. "I hear thoughts."

"That's not it." She shook her head. Her finger hovered over the button. "Tell me what else."

"Um," I said, panting to catch my breath. "I send messages. In people's heads." My breathing was laboured and sporadic, no matter how hard I tried to make it normal. My eyes didn't want to stay open.

"That's not it!" she said, her tone irritated and frustrated. She slammed her hand an inch away from my face. "Tell me *everything.*"

I flinched. What was she talking about? That was it. "That's it."

She pressed the button again. I couldn't escape the electricity, no matter how hard I struggled against the restraints.

"Stop!" I screamed. Hot tears leaked from my eyes.

The shocks ceased. My arched back thudded down onto the table. The cold metal was a relief on my burning skin. I closed my eyes and struggled to control my ragged breathing.

"What did you do?" Her voice sounded far away.

Nothing. It didn't matter if I had. Did she think I was capable of speech at the moment? If she was a scientist, she was exceptionally bad at her job.

"How?" She was talking to herself. Was that fear? She was so far away now it was hard to tell.

The stool screeched back as she stood. I didn't have the will-power to open my eyes again. Her heels clacked on the floor. They got farther and farther. The door beeped faintly behind her. Or maybe I imagined it.

The world seemed distant, just out of reach. My mind was a random collage of pictures and words that I couldn't make sense of. The throbbing in my head was a lullaby, soothing me into a half-sleep.

Blurry scenes wandered through my brain. Poking fun at Damion's bangs. Learning to skate with my dad on a little pond. Painting with mom. Having a picnic with Ariana and Xavier.

"Her injuries are fairly extensive," a new faraway voice said. Was she real or part of the dream? "But we have enough infor-mation. Even in this state, it's too dangerous to keep her around any longer."

Part 2

ASHES,
WE ARE ASHES
DUST FROM THE FLAMES.
SCARS DANCE ON OUR SKIN
WE DARE NOT FEEL ASHAMED.

THE WAR RUINED MUCH.
THIS WE KNOW TRUE.
HOWEVER MY DEAR,
ONE THING IS CLEAR:

IF NOT FOR THIS WAR,
WE WOULD NOT BE HERE.

Chapter 13: Brother

*B*oom-boom. *Boom-boom. Boom-boom.* My heart pounded in my chest. *In and out. In and out.* I was breathing. I was alive.

Someone held my hand. Theirs was warm, calloused, and familiar in a way that seemed impossible. I forced my eyes open. My breath caught in my throat.

What I saw *was* impossible. Tears formed in my eyes.

"Damion." My voice was almost a whimper.

Was I hallucinating? Was I dead? I would take this over being a star any day.

I sat up fast enough to make myself dizzy. I wrapped my arms around my brother, squeezing him so tight it was a wonder he could breathe. I didn't care how he was here.

He was here.

My brother returned the hug, holding me snugly in his arms. Tears flooded out of my eyes, dripping onto the leather jacket he still wore.

"Hey, hey," he said. He rubbed my back. "It's okay. You're okay."

"You were *dead.*" I sniffed and tightened my hold on him.

"Almost," he said, nodding. "I'll explain everything later." He pulled away and wiped my happy tears with his thumb. "You've grown up so much." His eyes were glassy.

"I know."

Damion looked older too. He was taller, leaner. His features were sharper, his face less babyish. His dark hair was longer, if only a little. It poked out from under his ears, in a way I would probably tease him for later, and fell in a longer-than-ever side-bang over one of his eyes.

The small twin scars that curved just under his right eye had been joined by a couple others scattered across his face. One, short but a bit thicker, cut through the bridge of his nose.

For the most part, his clothes had remained the same—black cargo pants, black T-shirt, and black leather jacket. Even the white lanyard with our house's keycard and the small turtle keychain I'd bought him years ago still hung from his neck. Only his shoes had changed. They were mud-brown combat boots now.

I had turned that Taker woman to dust, I thought to myself. *And I'd shot that man. The blood had gushed from his stomach. He'd been terrified.*

I had definitely grown up. But not necessarily in a good way. I tried to put the images out of my mind.

"I'm sorry," he said. "I wasn't there."

"You're back." I laughed. I gestured to him with both my hands. "You're here."

"You're stuck with me for good this time." A small smile twitched at the corner of his mouth. "I promise."

I pulled myself back more, sitting cross-legged to give him room to sit. "I just don't understand," I said, after he'd shifted into the centre of the bed and sat in front of me. I shook my head. "How?"

"Not everyone died in the Fall," Damion said. "Some of us have been surviving here, on Earth."

I blinked. "The Fall? Earth? What?" I asked. "I was at that Taker place. Their HQ..." I glanced around the room. It definitely wasn't the lab I'd been in. It was smaller and had white walls. And I was on a cot, not that metal table.

"Right," Damion said. "Ariana and Xavier said the Takers knocked you out before. You were in really bad shape when we found you."

"Ari and Xavier?" I flicked my eyes around the room once more, as if I might see them, before looking back at Damion. "They're okay?"

"Yeah." Damion smiled. *Maybe the universe is paying me back.* "Don't worry, they're just looking at different jobs they could do around here."

"Back to here," I said. "What is this place? What did you mean the Fall?"

He nodded and sat up a little straighter. "So, in the HQ, there is this sort of...hole. You remember how Mozaan's just above earth?"

"Yeah," I said, nodding too.

"Well, that hole, it basically spits out right above Earth," Damion said. He paused a moment. "And the Takers threw us down."

What? He couldn't be saying what it sounded like. It was crazy.

"That's where we are. This is Earth."

"It…" This was crazy enough that I thought I might be dreaming. "But Earth decayed... That's why we had Mozaan."

"That's what everyone thinks, up there at least." Damion pointed up. The corners of his lips turned up into a smile.

"Some of it *is* still dead and grey, like where we landed, but we found this place. There's tons of life around here."

I took a moment. *Outliers are being thrown down to Earth? And surviving? How is that even possible? The government, my teachers, everyone always said that Earth's irreparable.* I still couldn't fully take in that Damion was there, sitting with me.

"I just can't believe it," I said, with a breath of laughter. "Earth, and you, and…"

Another question, one of millions, popped into my head. "Are Mom and Dad here? Can I see them?" A glimmer of hope sparked inside me. I sat up straighter and started to bring my legs over the edge of the cot.

"No," Damion said, his expression dropping for the first time since I'd woken up. "I'm sorry. It's just us. They… They didn't make it." He explained that hardly anybody had survived the Fall when he'd first gotten to the Base. Since then, he and the other survivors had put some spare mattresses and soft things, like moss, under the area where people fell. He said it had helped quite a bit, but a lot of people still didn't make it.

"You didn't have any of us?" I asked, my shoulders slumping. I'd had Ariana and Xavier, and I was barely able to cope. How had he done it, with strangers on a strange planet? "God, Damion, I'm so sorry."

"Don't be. It's not your fault," he said, shaking his head. His expression lifted again and his smile returned. "I'm just glad you're here. We've got so much to catch up on."

"Is there any way we can catch up over some food?" They had to eat food of some kind if they were surviving. "I feel like I haven't eaten in days."

"You haven't," he said. "You've been out a couple days."

I raised my eyebrows in surprise. "Really?" That explained the gnawing sensation in my stomach. "That long?"

"Yeah." He got up and gestured toward the door with his head. "Come on, let's get you something to eat."

As we left the small room and walked down a hall toward the dining area, Damion kept filling me in about Earth, answering my questions and asking ones of his own.

When we arrived at a bar-type counter in the dining area, Damion explained to the cook, Jarred, that I was new and asked him to make me a plate. There was a certain authority, but also friendliness, to Damion's voice. He'd vaguely said he was really high up in the Base but hadn't delved into much detail about it yet.

A few minutes later, Jarred handed me a steaming plate of food. I hadn't realized just how starving I was until I started eating. The plate full of vegetables, wild rice, berries, and turkey was the best thing I'd ever tasted. Or at least the best thing I'd tasted for the past couple of years. I'd almost forgotten what meat tasted like. I scarfed down the food, bite after bite. Despite Damion's warnings that too much might make me sick, I barely took time to breathe.

"How did you get so hurt?" Damion asked. He frowned briefly. "The others didn't look so bad."

I raised my eyes up up from my nearly empty plate. "They wanted to know about other Outliers we were warning." A look of understanding passed over his face, saying he was sorry without words. "Then they did tests on my ability."

"Ari and Xavier told me you were warning people," Damion said, nodding.

"Yeah." I stabbed a carrot onto my fork. "For a long time actually. We even had this group thing going, but the last chick we warned probably turned us in."

"You must've helped a lot of people." The pride on his face filled me with guilt.

"Well," I cast my eyes down to the wooden table. "I don't think the Taker really *needed* to know about the ones we warned." If they had, why hadn't they tried interrogating Ariana or Xavier?

Damion tilted his head to the side. "What's wrong?" he asked, his expression growing concerned.

"I...I think they wanted payback." I traced my fingers over the knots in the wood. "When we were first on the run, they almost got us, and I..."

I couldn't say it. What would he think of me? He was supposed to be reuniting with his sister, not a murderer.

Damion noticed my hesitation. "It's okay," he said, putting a hand over mine. "You can tell me."

"I killed one of them," I said. My voice was small and low. "I don't know how, but I did. And then, there was a man, and I didn't have to shoot him. But I *did*, Damion. I would've let him die, and I just..." My eyes were starting to water. I took a deep breath and looked up, blinking. I would not cry with all these people nearby.

"We've all done things." He squeezed my hand and gave me a small smile. "You just gotta learn to be better than the Takers."

I nodded and picked at a loose thread on my pants. "I'm sorry. I shouldn't be dumping all this on you." He had come back from the dead for me, and here I was putting my guilt on him. I wiped at my eyes, though no tears had spilled over.

"Hey," he said, smiling again. "We've got two whole years of emotion dumping to make up for."

I sniffed. A smile worked its way onto my face. "Thanks." It was time to change the subject. "Did they do experiments on you too?"

He seemed to notice the somewhat forced subject change but didn't press. "No, it's weird. I think that only happened to you." Damion gave a half-shrug. "Maybe it's because you evaded them for so long, or maybe it's your training. Maybe even that you were able to take out one of them. But they didn't test Ari or Xavier. No one else has reported anything like that."

"Really?" I straightened my posture a bit.

"Well, there is this one guy," Damion said. "My friend Elliot. He said they ran some tests on him. He can hear thoughts, like you can. Said they seemed pretty interested in that."

They had been interested in that with me, for sure.

"Why would the Takers care what kinds of abilities we have anyway?" I raised an eyebrow. "They just kill us."

"My theory," Damion said, his voice a bit lower now, "is that they want to find a way to use the mind reading to their advantage. That way, they can pick us out, detect traitors and stuff."

"But they hate people with abilities," I said, shaking my head. "They wouldn't want to have their own."

"Renee, if it's the government like we think, then they just hate us 'cause they're afraid of us. We're different. Stronger. They can't control it. Historically speaking, people tend not to like those who are different from them, especially if they find them threatening." His words made a lot of sense. "They could never *really* get rid of all of us anyway 'cause new people keep getting abilities. They'd have to get rid of the whole human race to make sure there's no more of us."

"So they just do it to make themselves feel better?" I asked. "Until they find a way to either be more powerful or stop people from getting abilities? That's nice."

Just as he opened his mouth to respond, a familiar voice called out. "Renee!" Ariana said, her tone high and excited. "You're awake!" She ran over, and I stood up to hug her.

"As are you." I nodded, glad to see her.

Xavier and a blond girl followed behind Ariana. They also came over to our table. Xavier had a wide smile on his face too, and I wrapped my arms around him next. The faint, pleasant scent of charcoal filled my nose. I realized several seconds later that I had probably been hugging him too long and pulled back. "Hey."

"Hey," he said. "Glad you're up."

"How do you feel?" Ariana asked, scanning me up and down for any sign that I was unwell.

"I'm fine, Ari," I said, as the three of them sat down at our table. She knew Damion had healed me. "You don't need to worry."

The blond girl looked familiar. She had a short pixie cut framing her heart-shaped face, green eyes, a small nose with a sharp angle to it, and fair skin. Where had I seen her?

"Damion explained everything?" Xavier asked.

I smiled, glancing at my brother again. He was here, right across from me. "Yeah." I gave a small chuckle. "Well, I get the gist anyway. Still have a million questions."

Oh. I'd seen the girl when we were being dragged toward the building on Mozaan. With the redheaded man and the little girl. She must have fallen with us.

"How'd the job tours go?" Damion asked.

"Good," Xavier said, sounding enthusiastic. "It was cool to see all the different stuff people do."

Damion had mentioned briefly that everybody had a job, but he hadn't gone into much detail.

"How's that all work?" I asked.

"This guy showed us all the different jobs and stuff, said we'll get a few days of free food and everything until we get one." The blond girl told me. "I'm Thalia by the way." She reached her hand across the table, and I leaned forward to shake it.

"Renee." I said, sitting back against the chair.

"We basically tell them what we're good at and then, like, if there's a certain kind of job we'd want to do most." Ariana said. "Then they put us in a job, depending on what group needs more workers."

"What kind of stuff are you thinking about?" I asked.

Ariana's eyes were bright, and she was twisting the ends of her hair. "I wanna try and be one of the doctors," Ariana said. "They do the more long-term stuff, so that way Damion can focus on the really bad injuries."

On Mozaan, Damion hadn't had to do too much healing, but injury on Earth had to be more common. It was a good idea to have the doctors; all that healing would be a bit exhausting for him.

"I'm sorry, Ari. I don't really think we need any more yet," Damion said. Her expression dropped. He offered her a smile. "But I think you'd be great for going out on the rescue missions. You'd get to be saving people every day, and we could use another pair of hands."

"You mean, like, bringing people back after the Fall?" she asked, tucking some of her hair behind her ear.

"Yeah," he said, nodding. "I think it'd be right up your alley."

"I think I might like doing that," she said, sitting up straighter and bouncing a little in her seat. "Thanks." Was she blushing?

I agreed with Damion. Ariana would do great at welcoming new Outliers to Earth. It was a shame she couldn't be a doctor—she'd wanted to since we were little—but this seemed like it would be the next best thing. I looked over to Xavier and Thalia next. "What about you guys?"

"There's a guard option. I might do that," Xavier said, tilting his head a little as he considered it. "Said they need some more people, and I've got the training."

That was interesting. I was definitely going to look into guarding. I wanted to do anything I could to safeguard what I had on Earth.

Xavier must have known this, too. "You might like being a guard, and hey, you've got my reference," he said. "You kick butt at defence. And offence," he added, a smile tugging at the corner of his lips.

"I think I will," I said, laughing. "Sounds about right. What about you, Thalia?"

"Not sure yet," she said. "I think I kinda like the idea of guarding too actually. I'm not sure what else I'd like. I mean farming? Blech." She made a face, then chuckled.

"What were all the other jobs?" I didn't want to have to go on a whole job tour. The idea of guarding was already firmly planted in my mind.

"Well, there's the guarding, farming, ranger-ing? Is that a word?" Ariana asked. I made an "I don't know" gesture with my palms facing up, and she continued. "Then there's gardening, cooking, hunting. Um, there's different jobs where you make different things, there's foraging, and water-collecting... That's all I can really remember."

"You got all the major stuff," Damion said, with a nod. He turned to me. "The other stuff is mainly cleanup and small jobs. If you want, you can just do the guard test, and you can go when Xavier and Thalia do." He still knew me so well. "Basically, after the first few days of touring the Base and adjusting, working is how everyone earns their rations. So people won't just not work and take food."

"Makes sense," I said.

Better keep moving, I heard a man's voice in my head. *Looks like those power-people are nearby...*

I blinked, confused. I hadn't meant to read anybody's mind. But the way that man had been thinking—did that mean he *wasn't* a power-person? Was there somebody else on Earth? Somebody who didn't like Outliers?

I looked around the room, unsure of what I expected to see. There couldn't be a Taker *here*, could there?

"What are you looking at?" Ariana asked. No, surely I must have imagined it. I was just being paranoid. We were safe from them.

"Nothing." I turned back around and rejoined the conversation, brushing away what had to have been my mind playing tricks on me.

We all sat talking for a half hour or so, speaking in eager whispers as we rushed to catch up on everything we'd missed. Damion was excited to take me on a tour of the Base, so after we'd cleared our plates, we headed out of the dining area to look around. The others had already been on their tours, so they hung back.

We went to the training area first because it was closest, just up a short hallway, and I saw racks of metal weapons and wooden dummies set up in the corners. People were shuffling about and grabbing the things they needed. A couple were even practising knife-throwing on the dummies.

"How do you guys get all the metal?" I asked, as I walked over to the first rack and picked up a small knife. I turned it over in my hands, looking at the metal and how it was jammed into the wood handle. They'd obviously been made by the other Outliers.

"There's a couple kids that can turn organic stuff to metal," Damion said with a soft chuckle. I couldn't count all the times over the past couple years that I'd wished to hear him laugh again. "They help *a lot* around here."

"Cool," I half-smiled and put the knife back in its place on the rack. "It's amazing what you guys have done down here. I mean, the fact that there even is a *here* is just..." I shook my head, unable to find the words.

"You're gonna love outside," he said. "It's so different than it was on Mozaan. And you can study the different animals to your heart's content. Some of the plants are even different here."

"Can we go now?" I couldn't wait to get outside. There were two metal doors on the other side of the room just calling to me. To breathe fresh *Earth* air.

"Sure," he said. "But let's go to the main gate. That way, we'll pass by the sleeping quarters, and I can point them out to you."

"Alright." I turned to him with a grin on my face. "Sounds like a plan."

We walked out of the training area and into a different, longer corridor.

"Are they big?" I asked. "How many people live here anyway?"

"Biggest areas in the Base," Damion said. "There's about two thousand people in the Base. Most sleep in the quarters, so I guess that's pretty big."

Two thousand? How are people on Mozaan not noticing this?

"Some people don't use the quarters?" I asked. We'd reached a spot where the hallway branched off to the left.

"That's the girls' quarters." Damion pointed out the space to me before we continued walking. "Yeah, some people build their own little huts outside the actual Base. We've got a fence enclosing everything, so they still feel safe enough. It's mostly families that do that, but anybody can."

"That's cool," I said. "Did a lot of families survive together?" It wasn't fair that my parents hadn't made it. Damion must have been so devastated. He'd been thrown down to a strange planet with no family or friends.

"No," he said, with a tone of dismay. "Not really. It's mostly teenagers and younger adults that survive the Fall. Siblings and cousins aren't too uncommon, but we don't get many full families."

We'd reached a large set of metal doors that I assumed lead outside.

"Is this it?" A feeling of giddiness spread through me. I was about to be outside on Earth. With wild plants and animals and soil underneath my feet.

"Yep," he said, smiling as he looked at me. "You ready?"

I took a deep breath and nodded. He pushed the large doors open, letting natural light wash over us. The sky was a sort of greyish colour, with dark blue powdering it. The bright, nearly white sun was half down, leaving streaks of orange underneath it. Overlapping the sky were thick trees, most of their leaves green, but an odd tree stood out from the rest with its strange colour, like purple. In front of the forest, only a short gravel path away from me, was the gate for a short wooden fence, made mostly of thick, round tree branches. It was so overwhelmingly beautiful and strange that I almost wanted to cry again.

"Whoa." I turned my head toward some high-pitched laughter. There were some children playing in a small, enclosed area to my side.

"That's the daycare," Damion said. "To keep an eye on the couple of little kids we have while their guardians are working."

Beyond the daycare stood a few long wooden tables, each with various goods on them. Lots of other Outliers came up to look at the items.

"What is that?" I turned to Damion and then nodded over to the tables.

"That's the Stands. It's where everybody trades stuff they've made, came with, or found for stuff other people have." What an odd idea, especially because it looked so social. There was nothing like that on Mozaan. But Damion talked about it like it was nothing special, which I guess it wasn't for him any more. All of these strange things were normal to him now.

"Ariana would like that," I said. She'd been so intrigued by the community printers on Mozaan. "Did you show her?"

"Yeah." Damion laughed. "I think she's already done a trade."

"Everything's so different here," I said. "But I guess it is like another planet. Sort of."

Over on my right, there was an area of people who seemed to be making and fixing things. Farther, there were horizontal farms. Nobody was there, so the job must have been done for the evening. Beyond the farms, there were some large, metal barrels with smaller containers in a neat stack to the side, which Damion said were for food and water storage.

After I'd looked around at everything visible from where we stood, Damion took me around to the back, where it was just some open space and people guarding at the fences. Beside the left gate, he pointed out a of couple rusty black trucks that looked older than anything I had ever seen and had separately attached solar panels.

"We use those for rescue missions," Damion said. "They didn't work at first, but my buddy Wayne has an ability for fixing stuff that comes in pretty handy. Still have to repair them now and then, but they get the job done."

"Where did you guys get all this stuff anyway?" I asked. "The Base and the trucks... You didn't make it?"

"No," he said with a laugh. "Honestly, it was probably just a stroke of luck. I think it must have been a military bunker or something from before Mozaan. Maybe some people got left behind when Mozaan was made and tried to survive in it. Might not have saved them, but wherever it came from, it sure has saved us."

After we passed the trucks, we came around to see some of the little huts that Damion had mentioned. There were a bunch of them, with no uniformity at all.

"Do you have one?" I asked my brother. As leader of the place, I assumed he would. "A hut?"

"No," he said, shaking his head. *Weird. Doesn't he want the privacy?* "It's better if I sleep in the quarters. That way, I can keep an eye on things better. I'm closer if there's an emergency."

"Oh, that makes sense," I said, nodding.

"Besides," he said, a smile quirking up on one side of his face, humor in his tone. "I doubt I could make one if I tried."

I smiled with him, trying to remember every moment carefully.

We walked back around to the path that led to the main gate. "Beyond the gates," he said, "there's forest, a couple clearings, rivers, and a lake. There's the Powerhouse, down there." Damion pointed in a general direction past the main gate. "It's a sort of rocky area that a lot of people go to so they can practise the more dangerous abilities. Mainly beginners who can't control it as well and might wreck stuff if they practised here."

"Cool," I said with enthusiasm. It was really a community full of Outliers, fully encouraged to use their abilities. There was no hiding here. I was starting to wonder if maybe this was all just something I'd dreamed up. Would I wake up tomorrow in our apartment, eat a crappy protein bar, and go work at FitHub? Or worse, go back on the metal table?

When we went back inside, we passed somebody in the hall. "Hey," he said, waving to Damion. He looked at me and smiled. "Welcome to the Base."

I blinked. In Brampton, no one said "hey" to people in the hallway unless they really knew them, and people definitely didn't acknowledge strangers.

"Hey," Damion said.

We kept walking.

I felt bad for not thanking the stranger, but he'd startled me with his friendliness.

"Sorry," I said to Damion. I glanced back down the corridor. "It's just weird. Are you guys friends?"

"Not really." Damion shook his head. "I mean, everybody knows each other for the most part around here, but I don't hang out with the guy or anything." On Mozaan, it was like people didn't even see each other. This casual friendliness would be a bit hard to get used to.

Damion briefly showed me around the few places we'd missed inside, and hours later, extremely late at night, we forced ourselves to separate and go to the sleeping quarters.

The girls' space was one large room. I couldn't see too much in the dark, but it was full of tons of cots, side by side.

Ariana was already inside, her snores guiding me to where she was asleep near the back. I was lucky enough that there was an open bed beside her, in a corner no less. I took off my shoes and socks, placed them on the small shelf over my cot, and laid down in my clothes. I wasn't sure if I would get something new to wear tomorrow, like Ariana and Xavier seemed to have gotten, but I definitely wasn't asking now. I'd just have to deal with it tonight. It wasn't like that was new.

I couldn't sleep.

I looked over at Ariana to make sure she was still there. For the past two years, the only two people I had left to care about had been sleeping in the same lockable apartment as me, so close I could hear them breathing. Ariana was still close, as her snores proved, but with all these people around and the open space, anything could happen if I fell asleep.

And I couldn't see or hear Damion and Xavier. Who was to say they were safe? Who was to say they were still here? Who would stop something from happening to them if I was far away and sleeping?

My breathing started to quicken. Logically, I knew they were still here. I knew in my head that they were safe, that nothing would happen to them. But logic couldn't stop the doubts from creeping into my mind. It couldn't keep the fear from quickening my breathing and my heartbeat.

Damion? I mentally called out to him, needing to reassure myself.

Yeah? he asked.

Night, I love you, I responded, relieved to hear his thoughts.

Love you too, he thought.

I reached out to Xavier in the same way, not caring if I woke him. I needed to know he was okay. He was awake anyway. Much like my fear, his nightmares hadn't gone anywhere just because we'd left Mozaan. We talked for a while, about how strange Earth was, about his nightmares, and about my worry of not having any locks to double-check. I felt at least a little bit better by the time we finally decided to try and salvage some sleep.

Even then, I still woke up in the night. I had to call out to Damion and Xavier, and I kept looking over at Ariana's bed to make sure she was still there. It didn't help that I was feeling queasy from the Earth food. Or that I'd heard that strange guy's thoughts about power-people. I was happy when morning final-ly came, but immensely tired all the same.

~

"So, just line your vision up with the target and try to make a *J* motion with your hands, okay?"

I already knew how to throw a knife, but I nodded anyway, not wanting to be rude. The guy instructing me was only doing his job.

Without hesitation, I threw the blade. It sank into the surface of the board, landing right where the heart was on the per-son-shaped target.

"Whoa, where'd you learn to throw like that, newbie?" the guard asked. He was supposed to be seeing if I was fit to guard. I was confident I could secure a spot.

"Summer camp," I said, in a joking tone.

"Must have been one hell of a summer camp," he said, an impressed look playing on his face.

"We trained with this kind of stuff before they got us," I explained. *Not that it helped us when they came.* But it was good it hadn't. Now I was on Earth, far from the Takers, and more importantly, I had Damion back.

"Oh, okay." He was quiet for a few seconds. "So, just do a couple throws with the knife. Or you can try the bows if you want, but I think there's a pretty good chance you're in."

I already knew I was. Mind reading came in handy at times. "Sure," I said, repositioning myself to throw. "I'll just use the knife a few more times."

"Yeah, go ahead." He smiled. He did that a lot, partly because he was a nice guy, partly because he was impressed, and partly because he thought I was pretty, from what I overhead in his thoughts. "It's mainly the hunters that use the bows anyway."

I walked over and plucked the knife from the target board. I threw it a few more times, calling out what I aimed for, and I hit each spot without fail. A couple people had been stealing glances in my direction as they trained. The guard overseeing me still had on that impressed expression.

"Well." He gave a short laugh. "I think it's safe to say you made the cut. We just need to find you a partner now, and they can show you the ropes. That's if you wanna do guarding. Were you going to check anything else out?"

"Nope," I said. "I think I like this. When do you think I can start?"

"Couple days, max," he told me.

I smiled at him. "Great."

I was glad I would be able to contribute to the Base and help protect it. I could actually have a place in this society and do some meaningful work.

Chapter 14: Gangs, Voices, and Bears, Oh My!

I've partnered you with my friend Elliot," Damion said three days later. Since Damion pretty much ran things around the Base, he got to choose who I was partnered with. He had been the one who convinced everybody they should have people guarding. Apparently the Base had been pretty unorganized by the time he got there, and he'd helped straighten it out.

Damion had told me there were quite a few sick and injured people when he arrived, and that was what really started it. He'd healed them, and all of a sudden people respected him, started asking him what to do. He guessed they thought if he could make all those people better, he could make the Base better. They hadn't been wrong by the sounds of it. Now, a few of the adults on the Base acted as his advisers, and things seemed to be running pretty smoothly.

"He should be here in a minute." Damion motioned towards the door. For my first day of guard duty, I had dressed in the sleek black guard clothes—tight-fitting pants, my own pair of sneakers, and a protection jacket, which came just past my hips and strongly resembled a motocross jacket from the simulations I'd seen. I'd also slung a nylon, webbed weapon belt around my waist and tucked knives into a few of the pockets. It hung loosely, so one of the blades tapped rhythmically against my thigh when I walked. I didn't mind though. It was an odd comfort to know it was there, protecting me.

"Oh." Damion nodded over to the entrance of the training area we were in. "There he is."

I followed his gaze to the boy walking towards us. He looked close to my age, but he was much taller than me. His dirty blond hair was wavy and spiked up in the front. His mouth had a deep Cupid's bow and curved into a carefree smile that showed off his teeth. His eyes were a startling electric green—obviously designed to stand out. I was willing to bet he'd been rich on Mozaan, or at least well off.

"Hey," Damion said as the boy—Elliot—stopped in front of us.

"Hey," Elliot said. He turned to face me. "Hi."

"Hey." I held out my hand for him to shake. "I'm Renee."

He gave me a smile and shook my hand. "Elliot Halstead."

"Alright," Damion said. He turned around, talking as he walked backwards to leave. "Sorry I can't stick around. Truck's waiting on me to go." He had to go out with his ranger group and check for anybody that had fallen from Mozaan to the Fallsite, as they called it. Apparently there were usually a couple people every day, though only some survived.

"Yeah, no worries, man," Elliot said, giving him a half wave. Damion had explained the gist of the job, but I hoped Elliot would answer any questions I had.

"See you later!" I said with a smile on my face, waving to him as he began to turn around.

Happiness filled me since I would, in fact, see him later. I would get to see him again, and again, and again, like when we'd lived in our house on Mozaan. Only now I knew to fully appreciate it. There was still no Mom and Dad, but I had Damion back. It was enough to make me think that maybe, just sometimes, the universe could be a little kind.

"See you later!" he called back as he headed out the door.

Love you, I thought to him as he disappeared from sight.

Love you too, he thought back.

We hadn't said it enough before. We hadn't realized we might not get the chance one day. I wasn't making that mistake again.

"Ready to go?" I asked, turning to Elliot.

"Sure," he said, smiling. "We're at left gate; come on." He nodded in the general direction.

The gate wasn't far, and in a few minutes, we were already standing behind it. There wasn't much to do but stare at the land beyond the uneven fence. It was mostly forest, vibrant and full of animal life. In the couple of minutes I'd spent out there, I'd already seen more bigger, real-life animals than I'd seen my whole life on Mozaan. It was funny how we'd always been taught that Earth was this uninhabitable wasteland, devoid of life, yet there was more natural beauty just in this part than the whole of Mozaan.

"So," I said, still taking in the scenery. "What exactly are we looking for? Damion mentioned gangs?" It was hard to imagine many threats. The whole place seemed like one peaceful dream.

"Yeah," Elliot said. "You wanna keep an eye out for any rough-looking people. Or big animals, like bears."

"People live outside the Base then?" I scanned the land in front of us, as if somebody would pop up at any moment.

"Some," he said. He turned to look past the fence too. "People we've had to kick out, mostly. Sometimes they form gangs, and some hide out in the forest. But they usually only try and attack the hunters for the most part because they can find them in pairs, away from the Base."

I think this is far enough from both camps. I heard that same man's voice again. *Just better hope there's food around here. The taste of that deer meat almost makes me wish I hadn't run.* Why would he run? From the Base? Or from some other camp. He'd mentioned two. My heart started to pound.

No, I told myself. *He's probably someone who got kicked out of the Base. A criminal or something.* But my mind wouldn't let it go. Like this man represented something awful here on Earth. Something worse than animals or gangs. Something like the Takers...

"Don't worry." Elliot looked at me, seemingly taking my distress to be about the gangs. He shook his head. "They're pretty unorganized, and they haven't succeeded yet." I tried to make myself seem more at ease. I couldn't screw this all up by being paranoid and hallucinating things. Things were going to be perfect here, and I just had to learn to let them be.

"Why do they attack?" I tried to put the crazy thoughts out of my mind and focus on my conversation with Elliot. It seemed stupid for a small group to attack so many people. It would be like us trying to win an attack on the Takers—impossible.

"Well," Elliot said, a hint of humour to his tone. "We don't just leave random, nice people to fend for themselves. We get rid of the really bad criminals, and they usually aren't too happy with that. Most of the time, they want revenge."

"You think anything'll happen today?" I fiddled with part of the fence, moving a sliver of the wood back and forth.

"Prob'ly not."

I'd expected as much, and it was a good thing. It meant that the Base was stable, safe. And I concluded the man whose thoughts I kept hearing was just that, a criminal. But the knot in my stomach didn't release, no matter how many times I told myself the man meant nothing.

"We'll have to check everybody that comes in or out of this gate, which we do every day, but I doubt much else will happen." Elliot said the words as it as if they would relieve me, so I gave him a small smile, then turned back to the forest.

Two squirrels raced each other up and around a tall, thick tree. One of the squirrels was fat and a light shade of brown. The other was thin and glossy black, with a stub for a tail. They twisted in between the branches until they were hidden by the odd tree's unnatural purple leaves.

What caused the strange colours? Maybe chemicals, pollution, or bad genetic engineering? Radioactivity from the nuclear weapons countries used to fire at each other in the time before Mozaan? I had learned about all the things that had plagued the Earth and created the need for Mozaan in history class. Now I couldn't be sure if it was all true since I was also taught Earth was uninhabitable.

Maybe we're like the trees. Anomalies evolved from the chemicals and designing, and who knows what else, on Mozaan.

"Do you guys use your powers a lot out here?" I asked Elliot. It was strange, living somewhere we didn't have to hide our abilities. No more locking doors and double-checking that the curtains were closed just to practise. Here, we would be free to push our limits, to reach our potential.

"Yeah, most of us," he said with a nod. "There are a couple people who refuse, but they usually aren't doing work outside the Base anyway. We don't train powers or anything because there's so many different types, but people practise on their own. I never asked, what do you do?"

"Oh, uh…" I was so used to our abilities being secret. Even when we first got our powers, before we'd ever seen the Takers, we'd never shared them with anybody but each other and my parents. My parents had worried that somebody would try and hurt us, dissect us, or turn us into a freak show. They'd made us promise not to let anybody else see what we could do, and though we'd probably taken more risks than we should have, we hadn't shown a soul. Still, in a place where we were free, I hesitated.

"I read minds," I told him eventually. Damion said Elliot could too, which was exciting. I had never met somebody with my ability.

"Really?" Elliot asked. He tilted his head and rested his arm on the fence. "I've never met anyone else who can do that."

"Me neither," I admitted. "Hey, I wonder if I can read what *you're* thinking." I'd never been around another mind reader, but hopefully he wouldn't be able to read my mind as easily as I read others'. Ironic as it was, there were just some things I would rather not have anybody else know.

"I dunno," he said with an easy smile. "Try it."

Just like that? He's not worried at all?

"Alright," I said, concentrating. I got inside his mind without any trouble and heard the stream of his thoughts like anybody else's. "It's working."

"I know." *It's like that feeling when somebody is watching you*, he thought. Nobody else had ever been able to tell that I'd entered their mind.

Suddenly, like a door being slammed in my face, I was booted out. I blinked, startled. There was a small pain in my temple, lasting only a second.

"Cool," he said. "Wanted to see if that would work."

"How'd you do that?" I asked.

"Just sorta put up a wall, I guess." He shrugged. "It kinda feels like closing a door and holding it closed while someone tries to break in."

"Hmm." I tilted my head. "Interesting."

I would need to be able to do that if he ever tried to read my mind. My thoughts were the only things that were truly private, truly mine. I wasn't about to lose that.

"Here, you try," he said with a smile.

His tone was friendly, and though I knew he meant no harm, that didn't make me any more okay with it. I didn't have time to protest before I could feel that I wasn't alone in my mind. I panicked, shoving him out with all my force.

"Ah," I groaned as another flicker of pain appeared in my temple.

"Sorry." He rested two fingers on his temple, too.

"S'alright." He ran a hand through his hair. "Feels weird, doesn't it?"

"Yeah," I said, shaking my head. "Let's not do it again."

"Agreed." He nodded. "It sorta hurt."

"Yeah," I said. There was a pause. "So, do you use your ability a lot?"

"Yeah, most of the time," he said. "I like everything to just be open."

"You read everyone's minds?" I asked.

"Why not?" he asked, pushing back some of his hair. "I always figured if you don't have anything to hide, why worry about it, right?"

"I dunno," I said. "I know I like my privacy, so I give my friends theirs."

"That's cool," He leaned back casually on the fence, supported by his elbows. "I'm just used to not having to wonder, y'know? My moms always encouraged it when I was growing up, and now it'd be weird not to know what people are thinking."

I nodded. "Yeah, I guess I understand that."

We fell silent, so I glanced around. On the gateposts, I noticed some small, and crudely done, sketches were nailed to it. I asked Elliot about them, and he said those were the people they had banished. We had to check and make sure each person that came in wasn't one of them.

Throughout the day, a pair of people would come in every so often, but most came closer to the end of our shift. We checked each of them over. At least one person in each pair had a solar-watch strapped to their wrist. Unlike the holo-watches, these were basic and old, only telling the time.

"Do we get watches?" I asked as another pair of hunters walked into the base.

Elliot showed me his wrist. Sure enough, it held a sleek blue-and-black watch. "We need them to tell shifts," he said. "But we don't have enough for every single person. It's usually one per pair of partners."

"Oh, alright," I said, somewhat disappointed.

"Speaking of which..." Elliot looked at his watch. "We've got three minutes or so left."

"Really?" I asked. "How long have we been out here?" I could get so lost in thought staring out into the forest. It didn't feel like too much time had passed.

"Six hours," he said.

"Oh, wow." I hadn't thought it had been nearly that long. "So, when we're not on shift, can we just wander around the Base?"

He laughed. "Yeah, pretty much. I mean, you can't be distracting to the other workers, but you can get food, check out the trading shops, and train some more if you want."

"So, our shift starts at the same time tomorrow, right?" I asked just as the watch beeped, signalling the end of our shift.

"Yep," he said, popping the *P* as we headed inside. We kept walking until we reached the hall that broke off into the separate sleeping quarters. After a quick goodbye, I headed into the girls' area.

I sat down on the bed I'd chosen the night before and quickly changed into the simple outfit I'd been given to wear. I still kept the one I'd arrived in—a brownish-green pair of cargo shorts that came down to my mid-thigh and a plain black T-shirt—folded on my shelf. But it wasn't practical because there were more than a few holes. The outfit I had on was a plain cotton shirt with a shallow V-neck and a pair of knee-length shorts with a drawstring that I had to tie tight to make the shorts stay on.

I folded up the tight black clothes and armour I'd been wearing and placed them carefully on the shelf beside my other outfit.

I left the sleeping quarters in search of my brother, who'd said he would be in the dining area after the shifts. Besides, I was starving. I didn't waste time in the dining area and went up to the counter to get my food.

"No problem," the guy behind the counter said. He smiled at me. "You're new, right? Damion's sister?"

Damion's sister. Back in school, people had always asked if I was his sister. He'd definitely been well liked and known. I'd always had a good amount of friends, but I lacked his kind of charisma. That was fine though; I wouldn't have liked all that attention.

"Yeah," I said. The guy turned around to gather my food. "It's my first day working." He handed me a plate steaming mashed potatoes, carrot rounds, and a small amount of turkey. "Thanks."

"You're welcome," he said.

I scanned the area for my brother. It only took a few seconds to find his et-black hair. He sat at a table with a couple of other guys. They looked at me with curiosity when I pulled up a chair and sat down beside my brother.

"Oh hey," Damion said, turning to face me. "How was your first day?"

"It was good," I said. "Not much excitement though."

"So, Damion," one of the guys said. He had toffee-coloured skin and light-brown hair reaching to his neck. His eyes were a bright, crystal shade of blue. "You feel like introducing us to your lady-friend?"

Damion rolled his eyes, partly annoyed and partly amused. "Sorry," he said to me. "That's Gray, and he's an idiot." He turned around to face his friend. "This is my sister, Renee. You know, the one I told you about, what, five minutes ago?"

"Oh, right." Gray laughed, and I raised an eyebrow at my brother.

He opened his mouth to defend his friend, then closed it again. "Yeah, I got nothing."

Gray punched him in the arm. I gave a small tuff of laughter. Then Damion's other friend spoke. "I'm Wayne, by the way," he said, reaching out his hand. I took it, giving his hand a brief shake. His hair was dark red and in a mountain of curls. He had a pale, oval-shaped face with a soft jawline.

Ariana and Xavier joined us soon after that, pulling up chairs and introducing themselves to Gray and Wayne. It turned out that Xavier had the same guard shift as I did. Ariana had been trying out a job on the rescue team.

"I really liked it," she said when I asked her. Her face was glowing with excitement, her grin stretching from ear to ear. "Because we know that, like, every person we bring back will survive—thanks to Damion—and I really feel like we're helping people."

"That's great, Ari," Xavier told her, and my brother and I hummed in agreement. I smiled and gave her a thumbs up. She rolled her eyes.

"Yeah, awesome," Wayne said, standing up slowly. He seemed bored. "But I think I'm gonna get going. You coming, Gray?"

"Nah, I think I'll stay here, enjoy the view." He winked at me.

My brother pointed to the door, annoyed. "Gray, go."

"Fine," Gray said, sighing. He stood up. Wayne nudged him toward the door, and he begrudgingly complied. He turned back and mouthed "comm-chat," motioning to his wrist.

When they were out of sight, I furrowed my eyebrows together. "Do they even *have* holo-watches here?" I asked Damion.

"Nope," he said, shaking his head.

I laughed, then took a moment just to look at Damion. He was real, he was here, and I couldn't have been more grateful.

I glanced down to the black tattoo on his wrist, identical to my own. I wasn't the only one that had it any more. I wasn't the last member of our family left, and I was going to make sure it stayed that way.

Chapter 15: The Air of Mystery

I yawned as I looked out at the trees. Again. A week later, the most dangerous thing we'd seen was a five-legged rabbit. I knew I shouldn't want something to attack us. That would be stupid. But I had trained in combat every day for over a year and a half. I couldn't help but feel antsy. Maybe I needed to do some training in my spare time.

Elliot and I talked to pass time. We were growing to be friends, despite the fact that he was much more easy going than I was.

"So, do you ever hear any weird thoughts out here?" I asked, hoping he would have an concrete explanation for the voice I'd been hearing.

"Yeah," he chuckled. "This one lady, all I could hear when I read her mind was scary-passionate thoughts on basket-weaving."

I laughed along, but disappointment washed over me. He didn't know what I was talking about.

"Wow," I shifted my weight onto one foot. "That's... interesting."

"Yeah," he said. "Sometimes I really wonder about people."

"Bet you've heard all the gangs and stuff before they attack you though," I said, still hoping he might have heard something like I had. "You probably hear what they're up to all the time."

"Well, I only really listen for them when I'm guarding," Elliot shrugged one shoulder. "But it has helped a few times."

So he wasn't hearing anything by accident. I didn't understand why it was only me hearing these thoughts.

"Oh." I told myself I was probably just anxious that was making it harder to control my ability. "That's cool."

~

"Nobody knows what to make of it," Xavier said as we walked to the dining area after our guard shifts. "The foragers said that it was sucked completely dry."

"How can an entire river evaporate?" I asked, utterly dumbfounded. "Are there any explosives or anything here?"

"Not sure," he said. "But I doubt even the gangs would be stupid enough to destroy a main water supply."

"Maybe somebody with an ability similar to yours did it," I suggested.

Oh great, just what we need. I heard Xavier think. *Somebody with the ability to dehydrate us all.*

I stumbled from unintentionally hearing his thoughts. That had only ever happened when I was first developing my abilities, when they were getting stronger and I couldn't control them. But since coming to Earth, I'd heard that weird man's thoughts and now Xavier's.

"What's wrong?" Xavier touched my shoulder, his brows furrowed in concern. If I'd read Xavier's thoughts by without meaning to... Could that man's have been real too? I thought about mentioning it to Xavier, but I knew how cranked it would sound to say I'd been hearing a voice in my head. I finally had Damion back and things at the Base were supposed to be good. Why couldn't my mind just leave me alone?

"It's nothing." I shook my head. "I must have read your mind by accident."

"Is my head *that* bad?" he asked in a joking tone. I forced myself to smile like everything was alright, but I started to fear I was losing it.

"Yeah." I pretended to shudder. "I think I might have to sue you for emotional distress."

I wonder if they have lawyers here, he thought. *Doubtful.*

I laughed, and it was for real. Xavier seemed to have a way of always lifting my mood. I told myself, again, that the man must have been a criminal running in the woods and that the fear and stress of being tortured and trying to adjust to a whole new life here that was getting to me. But I couldn't shake the idea that this man was more than that. That he represented something truly dangerous like the Takers. I closed my eyes, took a deep breath, and tried to dismiss the thoughts. I was safe. Damion was here. My life had finally gotten on track since that awful night when the Takers came on Mozaan.

"So, you can read people's minds by accident?" He tilted his head, and his dark eyebrows dipped downward.

I frowned. "Not usually, and that's the problem." I pressed my lips together. "But... Maybe you just think *really* loudly compared to other people."

"Maybe."

I wasn't sure I'd fully convinced either of us that was it.

When we walked in to the dining area, we spotted Ariana. For a few minutes after we sat down with her, we didn't talk since we too busy shoving our food in our faces like animals. It was always a long wait between breakfast and lunch.

Ariana ate slower, at a normal pace. Good for her for having table etiquette. I followed her example and slowed down—a little.

Ariana was the first to speak. "Did you guys hear about that river?" she asked, leaning forward.

Xavier had just popped some chicken in his mouth. He finished chewing before he answered. "Yeah, I was just telling Renee about it."

Thalia came into the dining area. She looked around uncertainly, hesitating before coming to our table. "It cool if I sit?" she asked, her thin lips pressed together.

"Sure." I smiled at her. "Pull up a chair."

Thalia found an unused chair at the table beside us and set it down behind Ariana and me.

"Oh, here," Ariana said. We moved our chairs over to give her room. The legs scraped against the metal floor.

"Thanks," Thalia said with a grateful smile. She sat down and placed her plate on the table.

"You hear about the river?" I asked.

"No," she said. She tilted her head and frowned a little. "What about it?"

"It's gone." I scooped some mashed potatoes into my mouth. I resisted sighing in contentment. I loved potatoes with a passion. Down here, we usually had at least one kind with a meal because they were easy to grow and, therefore, abundant.

"What?" Thalia asked. She put down her fork and leaned forward a bit. "It's just gone?"

"Yeah," Ariana said. She stabbed at something on her plate. "The foragers went out this morning, and it's just, like, evaporated."

"How?" Thalia shook her head, a wisp of her short hair bouncing from side to side. "It doesn't make sense."

"Nobody knows," I said, twitching my shoulders upward.

"Everyone's trying to guess though," Ariana said. "Some people think it might have been one of us." She jabbed a thumb in Xavier's direction.

"Hey!" Xavier feigned an indignant tone but smiled wide enough to let us know he wasn't really offended. It made me smile too.

"I wonder who it could've been though." Thalia talked behind her hand as she chewed. She swallowed before continuing. "I mean, it couldn't have just vanished."

"There are some other people with fire abilities," I said. I took another bite of mashed potatoes.

"I can't think anyone here would do that though." Ariana frowned, resting her chin on her fist. "Like, they need water too."

"Maybe that's it," Xavier joked. "Maybe somebody was just *really* thirsty."

Ariana rolled her eyes, and Thalia seemed to consider it. I gave a small tuft of laughter.

Damion's voice reached my ears as he walked in with Wayne and Gray. He saw me and flashed a smile in my direction. He said something to his friends, and they came over to sit with us.

They took chairs from the same table Thalia had. We all shifted around to make room. The table was getting crowded. I was nearly squished between Thalia and Xavier. It could have been worse though. I could have been Damion, stuck between Wayne and Gray.

"Hey," Gray said, to me in particular. He slowly ran a hand through his light-brown hair. Damion shot him a glare.

Gray turned to my brother. "What? I was saying *hi*." His voice feigned innocence. Although, the smirk on his face made it hard for him to be convincing.

"Don't," my brother said.

I pressed my lips together, trying not to laugh. Damion was just trying to be protective. It was sort of sweet.

Gray had been a shameless flirt all week. The winking and the running his hands through his hair seemed like a compulsion for him. This had not gone over well with Damion.

"You guys know about the river, right?" Wayne asked, earning a chorus of "yeahs."

We continued to marvel at how strange it was. None of us were sure what should be done about it. There was a lake nearby, so water wouldn't be a problem. Unless somebody decided to take that too.

We kept talking through the evening, long after our plates were cleared and glasses empty. Ariana was the first to leave for bed, sometime after ten. I left soon after to get some sleep before my shift the next day.

After having my gear on all day, my wool pyjamas felt like a cloud resting on my skin. It was bliss, finally being able to take off my warm cotton socks. I fell back onto my bed. The sheets were cool. I relaxed against them, letting my muscles rid themselves of their tension.

Ariana was already snoring. She always snored, another "flaw" she had always been self-conscious about. Most people minded, but I didn't. After almost three years living together, I was used to it. If anything, it was a comforting reminder that she was alright.

I still had to call out to Xavier and Damion before I went to bed each night, sometimes more than once if I woke up from nightmares or was startled awake by a little noise. They didn't seem to mind, and Xavier would usually stay up and talk with me awhile. His nightmares still woke him up too. He liked talking and staying awake because a lot of the time he was afraid to sleep. I probably would have been too, if my nightmares had been that constant and terrible.

Chapter 16: There Will Be No More

The next day, I was changing into normal clothes after my guard shift when Ariana came into the quarters looking more than a little distressed. She must have just gotten back from the rescuing.

"Hey," I said as she came over to me. "What's wrong?"

"You're not going to believe it," she said, shaking her head. "Oh my god, it's just so horrible."

"What happened?" I patted the spot on the bed next to me. "Sit down."

She sat beside me and ran her hands over her face. "They were all dead," she said, keeping her voice quiet. "All of them."

"What?" I asked, turning so I could see her better. "Nobody survived the Fall?" They'd brought at least a couple people back each day we'd been at the Base.

"They were...they were already dead," she said, her eyes still wide and horrified. She looked like she might cry. "They... the Takers must have killed them."

"Hey." I wrapped my arms around her in a side hug. "It's alright. It's gonna be alright," I repeated, even if I wasn't so sure. If they were being killed, that meant the Takers knew we were surviving. Why else would they do it?

"What're we gonna do?" she asked. "What if they come for us? Damion said he doesn't think they will, but what if they do?"

"You're sure it was the Takers?" I asked, though I didn't really doubt it. Of course the nightmare wasn't over. How had I been stupid enough to think it could be? "It's not just a coincidence?"

"They had, like, no fatal looking injuries. It couldn't have been the Fall that killed them."

The Takers just had to ruin it. Every time I was even starting to be somewhat alright again, they had to come and crash down on my world. Well, they weren't taking anybody else I cared about. I had just gotten Damion back, and my friends were okay. I was not letting them take that away from me.

"They won't come for us," I tried to assure her and myself. But then I thought about the man in the woods. Maybe they already had... "They'd probably have to send people down, and what would be the point? We're stuck on Earth anyway, far away from them. Killing us wouldn't do anything for them." As I spoke, I started to become more sure it wouldn't make sense for them to be here. But then, why did they bother killing the new Outliers? Were they afraid of there being too many of us, even trapped down here? Or was there something else, something we were missing?

"But those people," Ariana said. Her eyes were watery now. "We can't do anything. The Takers are killing them all, and there's nothing we can do to help save them."

"I know." It was awful knowing there was absolutely nothing we could do, no hope to stop the new Outliers from being killed on Mozaan. "The best we can do is try to protect all of the Outliers that are already here." I started to think that maybe I should tell Damion about the things I'd heard, just in case. He'd probably conclude, like I had, that the man in the woods meant nothing, but he still needed to know. And soon. Just in case.

"Yeah," she said, with a small sniff. "Do you think... Are there any guarding spots left?"

"I think so." I nodded. "Why? Do you want to guard?"

"Well, I can't be a doctor," she said, with a shrug. "And I just... I still want to be helping people, y'know? If I can protect them, that's pretty good."

"It is," I said, letting her out of the hug. "We can talk to Damion. I'm sure I heard him say there were some spots left."

We'd need all the help we could get if the Takers really did have plans to come after the Base.

Chapter 17: Scouting

Word spread fast in a community so small. Within a couple days, all people talked about were the dead bodies at the Fallsite. Despite all the talk, people weren't as worried as they should have been. Some were disappointed there would be no new recruits, but not many of them stopped to think about what it meant for those of us who were already there.

I did. I couldn't stop thinking about why the new Outliers were killed.

I plucked my knife from the target board and curled my fingers around the black handle. I went back to where I had been and threw again. The Takers must have been giving us some kind of message. They knew some of us had survived. I repeated my circle to the target board, took the knife out, and returned to my starting position. The knife again sliced through the air into the head that was drawn onto the target board.

If the Takers didn't care that we had survived, they wouldn't have bothered to kill the new Outliers. It was possible it was a warning to stay out of their way, but I doubted it. Something told me the Takers had to be behind the river disappearing. I believed it, from some place deep inside me, just like I believed the man in the woods meant trouble.

"Hey, you're not at dinner," Damion said as I threw the blade again. I jumped a little, and the knife missed its target. "What's up?"

"Not hungry," I said, looking back at the board. I could tell he was rolling his eyes without turning around to look.

"You're *always* hungry," he said. He walked over and took the knife from where it had embedded itself in the board. "Cut the crap. You've been distracted all week."

"It's the Takers," I admitted. "They aren't gonna leave the rest of us alone."

"No," he said. His tone and expression were serious. He handed the knife to me. "Prob'ly not."

"If they came down here, do you think we'd have a chance against them?" I asked, tucking the knife into my weapon belt. "I really believe they stole the river."

"I do too." So he *had* been thinking about the river too. "But right now, we don't even know what we're up against. And we can't stop them from killing the newbies either."

"So you think we're just screwed?" I asked.

He shook his head. "I don't think they can kill us without coming down here, and we haven't seen any sign of them. We don't know anything for sure yet. Maybe they found a way to take things without leaving Mozaan."

I thought about the man. What if the Takers *were* here though? Something had been off about that man from the moment I heard his thoughts. Again, I considered telling Damion. As leader, he should know. But before I got up the nerve to tell him about my mystery man, he spoke.

"We'll have a chance at surviving as long as they don't suck all the resources dry and leave us to die that way," Damon said.

It made sense they couldn't kill us without being down here. They wouldn't want to try and bomb us or do anything else that would cause mass destruction because, if they had taken the river, that meant they needed the resources on Earth to stay intact. So, if somehow they found a way to take things and stay on Mozaan, we should be safe for the moment.

I reminded myself that the man was likely just a criminal and dismissed the worry. I'd tell Damion if it became important. I hadn't really heard the man think anything that would lead me to believe he was a Taker, and I couldn't burden my brother with my potential insanity in the middle of a real crisis.

"We should start training more guards," I said, instead of saying what I really wanted to say. "In case they do come down here."

"Yeah, I've already got some more people in training," he said. *Always one step ahead.* "The extra foragers, basket weavers, and stuff." He paused.

Uh-oh. He had his concerned-big-brother face on. "Speaking of the guards, you really should come down and eat something. I'm holding a meeting for all the guards in a half hour."

"Alright," I said, dragging out the word. "I'm coming."

I followed him down the hall, grabbed my food, and sat down with a large plate. I ended up finishing everything. At first, I was just eating to appease Damion, but I had been I lot hungrier than I'd thought. I was actually still hungry after eating, but I said nothing. We might all get a lot hungrier soon enough.

Damion and I headed to the training area together after dinner. The rest of the guards, now including Ariana, met us soon after we got there. I went and stood beside Ariana and Xavier while Damion stood a few feet away, facing us.

"Alright," he said. "If everybody's here, I'll start."

"Is this about the Snatchers killing the newbies?" somebody asked before Damion even had the chance to start talking.

"No," he said, surprising me. I'd figured that was what this meeting was about. "This is about the river. I'm sure you've all heard?" There were murmurs of agreement. "The river doesn't impact us too badly because we get our water from the lake. But, that being said, we have no idea what was behind it, or if it could happen to something else. As of right now, we have enough food and water to support everybody, but that's been very dependent on the nearby resources. Our numbers are bigger than they used to be, and if something else nearby vanishes, we're going to need an immediate substitute."

"How does this affect us?" a guy asked. "Wouldn't this be a problem for the hunters and foragers?"

"It affects you because I'm going to send out volunteers on scouting missions," Damion said. "I need them to be guards so they can adequately defend themselves. They will go beyond where we usually get resources, try to see exactly where all this 'healed Earth' stops, and mark where we can find certain things we need."

"Would people just be going out on their own?" a woman, only a couple years older than us, asked. With gangs and cannibals nearby, going alone would be too risky.

"No, of course not," Damion assured her. "I would be sending groups of five."

"And how long will they be gone?" she asked.

"That would depend on which direction they head and how soon they reach the Grey Area. If they reach it within less than a day, then they might not even have to camp out before they come back. If they don't reach it for a while, they might be out a few days. Because they will be gone so long, I have arranged for Elliot." Damion gestured to Elliot, who gave a wave to all the guards now looking at him. "To keep in contact with the scout teams telepathically, so we will know if a group isn't responding and can keep up on their progress. Are there any more questions?"

There weren't, so Damion asked that everybody who wanted to volunteer stay behind. Naturally, Ariana, Xavier, and I all stayed. There were around twenty others, plus Elliot.

Damion kept the three of us together because we worked well as a unit, and he added two more members—Thalia and a guy named Hamisi. They walked over to join us as Damion divided up the other groups.

"We meet here tomorrow at five a.m. sharp," my brother said once the groups had all been decided. "Alright?" There was some groaning—with Ariana contributing—but everybody agreed.

We all headed to our quarters to get some sleep—except Damion, who was called away to go heal somebody.

"This could be fun," Ariana said, as we reached our rooms. "I haven't really seen much outside of the Base, except for the way to the Fallsite."

I had seen a bit, but I hadn't gone too far. It had taken a while just to adjust to all these new things at the Base, so I had mostly been exploring and getting used to the swing of things here. Besides, I wanted to spend my free time with Damion, and other than the rescue missions, he mostly stayed close to the Base in case something came up.

"Yeah," I agreed. "It'll be nice to see everything. I've been hoping to see a bigger animal, like a deer or something." It was a shame I didn't have my sketchbook. There were so many beautiful things on Earth.

"That would be so cool!" Ariana said, her expression bright. "Deer are the ones that look like little horses, right?"

"Yeah." I pulled my pyjamas off of my shelf. "I've been in simulations with them. They're sort of like small horses, but they're a lot prettier. They have these sort of horns—I think they're called antlers—that look like tree branches."

"How common are they?" she asked. "You think we could actually see one?"

"I'm not sure," I said as I changed. "I think they were pretty common before Mozaan, but I don't know about now. They aren't extinct though because we eat them sometimes."

"Oh my god," Ariana said, her eyes getting a little wider. She stopped folding her guard clothes. "Is that what that weird meat is? What if we eat them out of existence?"

"I'm sure there's enough for us to eat a couple now and then."

"I hope so." She still looked convinced we could hunt them into extinction.

I wasn't sure if I should feel bad or laugh.

Once we were changed and ready for bed, I checked on the guys and said goodnight to Ariana. I lay down, and allowed my mind to drift off into sleep.

~

I was just outside the Base, but still inside the fences, with my brother, Xavier, and Ariana. We stood on the gravel path that led to the main gate, looking around.

"Everything is so great here." I said. "We finally feel safe."

The birds were chirping, and the sun was shining. I could see all of the forest that surrounded the Base, the lush greenery giving me a rare sense of peace.

We were all talking and laughing about something.

"Do you feel that?" my brother asked. The gentle breeze had started to pick up into a harsh, stinging wind.

"Look!" Ariana pointed behind us, where all of the forest had disappeared. Things were being tossed around by the wind, and people were running into the Base for cover.

"It's happening everywhere!" Xavier yelled over the wind.

The forest around the Base was vanishing, leaving only darkness behind. More and more dissolved as the black wave rapidly approached. The fences were being ripped apart and disappearing into the void.

"Run!" I shouted to the others. "We have to take cover!"

We ran toward the Base, the darkness close behind. The trading posts and daycare had already been torn away, taking the screaming people who hadn't gotten to cover yet with them.

"We're almost there," Damion said. The darkness was coming at us from all directions. If we could just get to the inside...

"Got it!" I yelled, yanking open the doors. The Base disappeared right in front of me. I turned back to the others, terrified. They had all been swept up and were flying into the black void. "Damion!" I tried to grab his hand. Ariana and Xavier were already gone.

I almost had him.

A sudden gust of wind hit my brother, sending him flying into the dark.

"No!" I waited to be ripped away too, but I wasn't. I was left standing on a small circle of ground while death swallowed up everybody else.

~

I woke breathing heavily. I looked quickly to make sure Ariana was still beside me. She was. I wanted to check with Damion and Xavier, but it was close enough to five that I would see them soon. I forced myself to get changed into my guard clothes instead of contacting them.

After getting ready, I went and got myself an early breakfast. By the time I was finished, there was about fifteen minutes left until we were supposed to meet. I decided to go back to the quarters and make sure Ariana was awake and getting ready. She wasn't.

"Ari, come on," I said, shaking her by the shoulder. "Time to go."

"Alright," she grumbled. "I'm getting up."

Once she was ready, we headed down to the training center. Only Damion, Xavier, and Elliot were already there, so we had to wait on everybody else. I was almost glad for the wait. I wasn't super eager for my brother and friends to be outside the Base after the nightmare I'd just had.

After everybody else had arrived, the supply packs were distributed. Blankets had been turned into makeshift backpacks using a kind of vine-rope. We each got one, which contained another blanket, some food rations, two weird metal water bottles that looked similar to wine bottles, a stick of charcoal wrapped up in a leaf to avoid mess, and a couple sheets of lined paper.

"So," Damion said, after we had all split into our groups. "You all know which direction you're headed?" There was a chorus of "yeahs."

"Good. Remember, Elliot will be checking in with you. Make sure you answer. Otherwise, we'll think you're dead. Once you get far enough, start jotting down notes or doing small sketches of where things are. Always do shifts at night. And use your rations wisely. Got it?" Another chorus of "yeahs" and some nodding went around the room. "Alright then. You're good to go."

He stopped me just as I was on my way out. The others continued to stream out.

"Yeah?" I asked. He looked me straight in the eyes, his expression serious.

"Be careful, okay?" His posture was tense, and I knew this was hard for him. It was hard for me, too, knowing I would be so far away from him. Anything could happen while I was gone, and I was beyond worried that I wouldn't be there to make sure he was okay.

"I will," I said, pulling on the straps of my backpack. "I promise I can take care of myself."

"And if anything happens?" he asked.

"I'll contact you." I wrapped him in a hug, which he returned tightly. "And you better contact me too."

"I will," he said, letting me out of them hug.

"I mean it." I looked at him seriously. "If you get so much as a paper cut, I wanna hear about it."

"Alright, deal, he said. He looked towards the door and sighed. "Go catch up. I love you."

"I love you, too." I kept him in my sight as I started out the door. "I'll be back soon."

Chapter 18: You Won't Like What You Find

We'd been gone for almost the whole day, but I hadn't seen any deer yet. I had seen a pretty fat rabbit, but not much else. I wasn't too disappointed though. There were so many other cool things to check out. We'd even passed by the lake, where a couple of us spent a good ten minutes trying to catch tiny fish in our hands. We didn't have any luck. They were extremely fast.

Now, it was mostly forest. There was no sign of the Grey Area yet, so that was good. Since I had been unconscious when we landed, I'd never actually seen it, but Xavier told me the ground was like ash.

"Oh, there's some orange trees," Ariana said, nodding over to them. She'd loved oranges on Mozaan. "How come we never have oranges?"

Damion had told me all about the oranges, but it seemed nobody had mentioned it to Ariana yet.

"They get you all tripped out," Hamisi said. His voice was deep, which suited his tall, buff stature. He had dark skin and eyes and short hair. "I really don't recommend eating any."

"Oh." She frowned. "That's weird. Well, I'll mark them down anyways so Damion knows that's what's here." She had her charcoal in hand, but she just stared at the paper. "It's so hard to see now."

It had gotten pretty dark in the last hour. Hamisi's watch said it was only around seven, but we would probably end up camping out for the night soon. There was no point in stumbling around in the dark.

"Here." Xavier lit some fire in his hand so Ariana could see better.

"Thanks," she said, scribbling down some notes.

As we continued, Xavier kept the fire in his hand. It was enough light that we got in another hour or so of trekking before we had to call it a night.

We set up in one of the clearer areas of the forest, around a fire Xavier had lit for us. He'd made it a pretty good size because it was a bit chilly already, and it wouldn't be good for him if he got too cold at night. The cold had a way of draining his energy, the same way the heat gave him more. Cold also hampered his ability to use his powers.

Out in the dark, I was a bit conflicted. On one hand, it was nice having both Ariana and Xavier close to me at night again. On the other, Damion was way back at the Base, and we were in a totally open area, where something could find us at any moment. As they often did, my thoughts drifted to the man in the woods, and I panicked.

Damion? I called out to him.

Yeah? You guys doing alright?

I breathed a faint sigh of relief when he answered. *Yep. We're calling it a night, so I was just checking in.* We told each other good night, and I was left alone with my thoughts.

There was no way I could sleep. I didn't care that we were doing shifts. What if whoever was up fell asleep? Ariana probably would. And I didn't really know Thalia or Hamisi. Every noise made me turn my head to find the source. I struggled to keep my eyes open, but I couldn't let myself sleep. I couldn't let my guard down.

I was almost relieved when Thalia shook my shoulder and told me it was my shift. My mind had jumped to thinking *Taker* before I saw it was her, and I had whipped around, grabbing her arm pretty hard.

"Sorry," I said, letting go right away. "Are you okay?"

"Yeah." She rubbed her arm a little. "That's alright. I get it."

I sat watch for the the hour I was supposed to—timed thanks to Hamisi's watch—and when it Ariana's turn came, I just let her sleep. I wasn't going to fall asleep anyway, so she might as well sleep through the night.

Xavier started to struggle in his sleep, shifting back and forth with his face scrunched up. I was leaned up against a tree, not far from him. I went over and shook him awake. He jumped at first, then relaxed when he saw it was me.

"Thanks," he said, keeping his voice down. He sat up, careful not to make any noise.

No problem, I thought to him, figuring that was the best way to keep quiet.

Have you been on shift long? he asked.

You could say that. It's supposed to be Ari's turn, but I couldn't sleep.

It was close to Xavier's shift already. *Why don't I just start watch now?* he suggested. *You can try and get some sleep. You know I'll watch carefully.*

I hesitated. I didn't want to risk something happening while I slept. But I did trust Xavier.

Are you sure? I asked.

Positive. Try to get some sleep.

I wouldn't be much good for protecting anybody if I was utterly exhausted. *Okay. Thank you.*

Night, he replied.

Night.

I went quietly back to my original place on the ground, and he took my place by the tree. I managed to drift off a few minutes after he started watch but soon awoke to sunlight streaming across my eyelids. I sat up, checking right away to make sure my friends were accounted for. Ariana was sleeping a few feet away, and Xavier was sitting at the tree.

"Morning," he said.

"Morning." I stood up, stretching. Everybody else was still asleep. I went over and sat beside Xavier.

"Get any sleep?" he asked.

"Yeah." I gave him a smile. "Thanks. It's just really weird sleeping outside, y'know?"

"Yeah," he said, with a light nod. "I like having walls around me. I guess it just feels safer."

"Exactly," I said. "Here, there's movement and noises and stuff coming from everywhere."

Hamisi woke up not much later, closely followed by Thalia. We all had a small bit of food and water before deciding it was time to wake up Ariana.

She took a while to wake up but was in a good enough mood once she ate. She thanked me once she realized I had let her sleep.

No problem. I thought to her. *I wasn't that tired.*

I didn't want to tell her that I'd trusted Xavier to keep watch and not her. He'd promised not to mention it.

We got going soon after that. As we walked, I looked over at Xavier, with his blanket around his shoulders, and laughed. "Really?"

He pulled his blanket tighter. "It's cold!"

The morning air was a bit chilly, but it wasn't bad, at least not for me. It got warmer over the next couple hours, and eventually, he put the blanket back in his bag.

The forest was thinning out a bit, and I swore I could see some lights beyond the trees. "Do you guys see that?" I asked, pointing to the lights. "Up there?"

"The lights?" Thalia asked.

"Yeah," I said. We were getting closer to them, and the trees were becoming more and more spread out. "What are they?"

"We should watch out," Hamisi said. "It could be a gang."

We all quieted down as we continued on. After a minute, I could make out the torches, which were very clearly electric. I put my arm out, gesturing for the others to stop walking.

"Hamisi?" I asked, keeping my voice as low as possible. "There's no chance that a gang would have electricity, is there?"

"No." He paused. "Why?"

"Those are electric lights," I said.

We all knew what that meant.

"Takers," Ariana whispered after a moment.

Part of me was scared, but the other part was a little relieved. I had been right to worry about the man in the woods. But then guilt crashed down on me. I should have told Damion. I should have warned him and the others.

"I'm gonna go get a better look," Xavier said. He started to step forward.

I grabbed his shoulder. "You can't go over there alone. I'll come."

"Okay, that's good," he said, giving a nod. "You can listen and—"

"Does nobody think we should let Damion know about this?" Thalia asked, and I turned around.

Takers are here, I thought to Damion. *I'll have more information soon.*

Be careful. Even his thoughts held that brotherly warning tone.

"I just let him know," I said. "We're gonna have a quick look to confirm it's them and to see how many there are."

"Be careful," Ariana said. She knew we wouldn't be talked out of this. "Please."

"We will." Xavier gave her a quick smile. "Promise."

The two of us crept closer to the lights, hiding behind a couple of the sparser trees. It was the Takers alright. Electric torches surrounded their camp in a circle. There were several tents set up, and several Takers walking around. I could count about seven of them, but there were probably a few more asleep.

Plat, I thought to Xavier.

They were here. The Takers were on Earth, which meant we were all in danger. They were only a day out from the Base. They could find it at any moment, if they hadn't already.

Agreed, Xavier thought as we both stared at the camp full of enemies.

This meant they *had* taken the river. It wasn't a fluke.

You know, there aren't too many of them, Xavier thought, edging a bit closer. *We could probably take them out right now.*

We can't just charge in there. I pulled on his arm. *They have guns, and there's only five of us. Besides, what if there's more of them close by? We have to think this through.*

I could set a fire, he thought, glancing over to the camp again. *We wouldn't even have to stick around.*

Xavier. There could still be more close by. And we don't want to start any wildfires. Let's get back to the Base so we can make a real plan.

Alright. He nodded, running a hand through his hair. *It's just that they're right there, y'know?*

Trust me, I know. I glanced over at the camp. *I hate that we have to go back to the Base knowing they're not far.*

I guess we better start heading back now, he thought. *We're gonna need that plan ASAP.*

After telling the others what we saw, we hightailed it out of there. We all went as fast as we could back to the Base, managing to make it just as it was getting dark. We told Damion what we saw, and he said we would meet tomorrow in one of the office rooms to discuss it. Between everything that was going on and running the Base on top of that, he must have been under a lot of stress. Hopefully he would actually let us help, rather than trying to deal with it all on his own. No matter what he said, I was going to have a part in taking down the Takers.

Chapter 19: Man or Fiction?

Y ou said there were around ten?" Damion asked first thing the next morning. He'd called the five of us who were on the scouting mission—plus Elliot, Wayne, and Aukai, a ranger friend of Damion's.

"Give or take," I confirmed. We couldn't account for how many had still been in their tents.

"So, that's attackable, right?" Thalia asked. "I mean, just the nine of us could do that."

"Yes and no," Damion said. "Sure, we could probably take on those ten, but there's a lot we don't know yet. They could have camps all over. They could have had some people out when you guys saw them. We don't know if they know where we are. We don't even know exactly why they're here."

"Aren't they here to kill us?" Ariana asked. Her worried expression hadn't changed since we found the Taker camp.

"I don't think so, at least I don't think that's the only reason," Damion said. "It just wouldn't make sense that they would come all the way down here only to kill us. Since the teleports only go one way, everyone who came down would be stuck here. That's a big just to kill some kids." He paused for a minute. "It also doesn't make sense that they'd come in such low numbers if they were only here for us. Plus, they could have sent a whole host of deadly things down to the Fallsite to kill us, but they didn't. There has to be another reason they're here."

"It must be something to do with the river," I said. "There's no way that's a coincidence."

"I agree," Damion said. "We need to know what they're doing here. It's dangerous having them this close, so the sooner we know more, the sooner we can make a plan to do something about it."

"You thinking more scout missions?" Xavier asked.

"Yes," Damion said. "But the other guards aren't going to be told about these. I want this to stay as quiet as possible until we have a clearer idea of what we're dealing with. It'll just be the nine of us. No one has to go if you don't want to. I'll completely understand."

"I'm in," Thalia said.

"Me too," Aukai said. She was an extremely petite girl, with bright pink eyes and a pale face. Her voice was so soft and quiet that I almost didn't hear her.

"Me three," Ariana said.

The rest of us chimed in too. No one wanted to back down.

"You're all sure?" Damion asked, though I felt he was looking more at me. "I'm not going to lie. It's really risky."

"We're sure," I said with no hesitation. I was going to do everything in my power to keep the Takers away from what we had here.

"Wait," Hamisi said, lowering his thick eyebrows in confusion. "How are we going to get information from them? We aren't going to kidnap one, are we?"

"No." Damion clearly wasn't thrilled about what he said next. "We'll need a mind reader on every mission and somebody to help protect them while they listen. We'll need information from the Takers minds as well as recon of the area."

"I'd like to go." I turned to Elliot. "You don't have to, if you don't want."

"Are you sure?" Damion asked, turning to me with an expression that was trying to mask his concern. "Because I was actually thinking Elliot would go on most of them since he, uh…" There was a slight pause as my brother probably tried to think of a reason why I shouldn't go. "He has been here longer."

"Yeah," I said, not willing to let this go. He was scared for me, but I couldn't just sit back while others went out on missions. I needed to be there. "I've been to the camp. And I do have quite a bit of experience hiding from them."

"That's true," Ariana chimed in. A look of utter dismay crossed my brother's face. "Like, if they have to run or something, Renee would know where she was going."

"Well," Damion said, relenting. "I guess you'd have a partner anyway."

"Exactly," I said with a nod. "Besides, I won't even be going into the camp."

"You can both go on some of the missions," Damion said. "And I'm thinking we need to start right away. There's no time to waste."

The other groups that were still out scouting were expecting to hear from Elliot, so despite Damion's best attempt at protest, I'd been selected for the first mission. Ariana would come as my backup. Her force field could come in handy.

Meanwhile, Damion was going to go talk to all of the people with invisibility powers, to see who could help hide the Base. We couldn't have the Takers stumbling upon us. We would just have to put some sort of mark where the gates were so none of us got lost. Damion would tell everybody else it was a precaution against the gangs.

We all flooded out of the room, and Ariana and I headed toward the training area. We replenished our packs, this time with extra blankets since we probably wouldn't be able to make a fire.

We walked about three quarters the way to the Taker camp before deciding we should set up for the night. It wasn't too dark yet, but we didn't want to be too close to the Takers while we slept. We could make the rest of the journey in the morning.

"I'll take first watch." I propped myself up against a tree. I didn't actually plan on trading. Pulling an all-nighter wasn't a big deal. I'd done it before.

"Okay, thanks," she smiled. "Make sure you wake me up this time though."

Right. I couldn't get away with not waking her up two times in a row and not be forced to talk about my fears. Which I wouldn't do. It would upset her that I didn't trust her enough to keep watch while I slept. I wished I could, but she'd fallen asleep too many times before. I just couldn't take the risk that something would happen while we both slept.

"No problem," I said. "Night."

What was I going to do? It would be selfish to wake her up if I wasn't going to sleep anyway, but I really didn't like lying to her. Maybe I didn't have to say that I'd been able to sleep when Xavier kept watch. She probably wouldn't ask. I'd just tell her the truth, that I had trouble sleeping out here know-ing something could happen. She'd heard all of the scary noises and seen all of the shadows. She would understand.

I explained in the morning, after she scolded me for not waking her, and it seemed like she got it. "To be honest," she said, her tone lighthearted, "I think I just snore so loud that I don't hear many noises."

I laughed, and she followed suit.

Soon, we were packed up and walking. It didn't take us long to arrive at the Taker camp. Only a couple were out of the tents, but I could faintly hear people talking from within them. We crept close to the camp, nearing the front line of trees.

There was a tent in front of us, and I tuned into the thoughts of the Takers inside. Mostly, it was trivial things, such as what they were having for dinner or how hot some-body next to them was. I did catch something important from Bernard.

Those freaks better not screw with us getting the supplies to save Mozaan, Bernard thought, his tone sour. *Why couldn't they just die when they were supposed to? Oh well, they're a bunch of untrained idiots. They wouldn't know the first thing about the RCCs, let alone how to stop us.*

RCCs? Whatever they were, it was probably bad news for us.

More Takers toward the rear of the camp began coming out of their tents.

Renee, we have to go farther back. Ariana thought to me.

We started to move away, but I heard one of the Takers thinking that they were about to send out some people out for a training exercise.

We need to get out of here, I thought to Ariana. *Some of them are coming.*

We both sprinted off into the forest. I kept looking to the side to make sure Ariana was still there as we ran. About a quarter of the way to the Base, I was startled to a stop.

How did I let my gun die? I heard the man think. *I'll have to let it get some sun.*

Ariana stopped too.

"What's wrong?" she asked.

I put my hands over my face, sighing. I wasn't just going to keep silently doubting my sanity. I felt that I had enough proof now that the man was a likely Taker, as I'd suspected all along but wouldn't allow myself to admit, and I wasn't going to just keep it to myself any more.

"I keep hearing this man's thoughts by accident," I finally said. I took my face out of my hands. "I have been since we got here."

"What? Whose thoughts?" She looked at me with a searching expression. "Why didn't you say anything?"

"I don't know," I said. "I kinda of thought maybe I was just hallucinating or paranoid, but then we found the Taker camp. And now I think I might have been right all along." I spoke in a rushed sort of way.

"Wow." She blinked. "Okay, well, I think you're probably cranked for not mentioning it. But, what kind of things have you been hearing?"

"I dunno, like he ran away from something and doesn't want to be near other people. At first, I thought he was from one of the gangs, but something about that never sit right with me."

"And you're just hearing the thoughts by accident?" She pushed her hair back, scratching the back of her head. "Like what you said happened with Xavier?"

I nodded. "Yeah, and I don't get why. Maybe I'm getting rusty or something?"

"Well, I don't know why you're hearing this guy's thoughts," she said. "But you can't be crazy. I mean, the Takers *are* here, and it's not like it's just this guy's thoughts you've been hearing." That had been my reasoning, and her saying it was reassuring.

"Yeah," I said. "It just freaks me out, y'know?" "Have you tried thinking back to him?"

"No." I shook my head. I hadn't been sure if I was cranked, and I didn't think that talking to the voice in my head would help me feel any saner. Besides, I was sure now that this man was a Taker. That could only bring bad things. "Honestly, I've just been trying to ignore it." We started walking again. She turned to me. "You said he didn't want be near the Takers, right?"

"Yeah, but he is one," I said. "Or at least, he used to be."

"Or at least, he used to be. Maybe he'd have information about them!" she said, clapping her hands to together. "You could ask him what's going on with the camp."

"He hates us too." I reminded her. "And we can't take battle advice from some guy in my head. There's still a chance he might be some gang member, or worse, some messed up hallucination in my mind. I don't think we can risk it." I'd expected Ariana to be a bit more doubtful, and I found it weird how confident she was in my sanity because I really wasn't sometimes.

"We don't have to totally hop on board with everything he tells us," Ariana said. "But, it'd still be a good way to get an idea of what's going on."

"Maybe..." I tilted my head and bit the corner of my lip, considering it. It would be nice if we could get some information, but the fear that it might all be a delusion still tugged at me, no matter how I tried to push it away with reason.

"It'll be fine," she said. "And you can stop talking whenever you want 'cause it's your head."

She had a point. Besides that, it would help me confirm once and for all that he *did* exist and he *was* a Taker.

"Alright," I said after a pause. I rubbed the back of my neck. "I guess it can't hurt anything."

Who are you? I thought to the man.

Several seconds passed without response.

"Did he respond?" Ariana asked.

Great, I thought to myself. *The voice in my head is ignoring me.*

"No." I sighed. I waited a few more seconds. "I'll try one more time."

What do you know about the soldiers? Nothing again. I slumped my shoulders.

"It was worth a try," Ariana said.

I didn't think so.

"Let's just get home," I said, picking up my pace. "We need to tell Damion and the others what we heard at the camp."

We'd be walking for about an hour when the voice stopped me again.

What was that? came the man's alarmed thoughts. *Plat, it's some for those freaks. I'd better hide out in the cave. Where did I leave that gun?*

"Renee?" Ariana stopped beside me.

"Stay here," I told her.

I began to sprint in the direction of the only cave nearby. The only one close enough for me to have heard his thoughts. I needed to prove to myself once and for all that he was what I thought he was. I needed to know I wasn't crazy.

"Wait!" She ran after me. "What are you doing?"

"I heard him again!" I swerved past trees as I dashed forward. "He's heading to the cave!"

I arrived at the cave panting, Ariana only a few seconds behind me. I ran inside, only to come to a dead stop. "I don't..."

There was nobody in the cave.

My posture deflated completely. I felt my chin start to tremble.

"No," I breathed. He didn't exist. I'd really lost it. I felt the pressure starting to build up behind my eyes.

"Renee." Ariana seemed to struggle for words but put a hand on my shoulder. I turned away from her and lowered my head, covering my mouth and nose with my hands. Tears pricked at my eyes. How could I have been so stupid?

"It's okay." Ariana patted my shoulder.

"No it's not." I looked up to face her. "I've lost it, Ari."

"No," she said, but she didn't sound so sure. "You've been through a lot, that's all."

"So have you and Xavier," I said. I swallowed. "But you aren't hearing voices."

"Don't move." I heard the man's voice again. I looked up at Ariana, blinking in an effort not to cry.

"Renee—" she started.

"Nothing you say is gonna make me feel less crazy, Ari." I said. She grabbed my arm and turned me toward the cave entrance.

"You aren't crazy," she said.

We both stared at the man pointing a gun at us.

Chapter 20: Control Freak

I knew it." Despite the fact that he had a gun in my face, I started to laugh. "You *are* real, and you *are* a Taker! I was right!" Relief flooded through me. I wasn't crazy.

The man furrowed his blond eyebrows in confusion and tightened his grip on the gun. "Put your hands on your heads and stay still."

Ariana slowly complied.

I clenched my jaw, nostrils flaring. I might have been happy about being right, but no Taker was going to push me around. "No." I spoke in a lower voice, carefully pronouncing each word as I continued. I'd had quite enough today. "*You drop the gun.*"

The gun clattered to the ground. The man's eyes were as wide as saucers. I stared, stunned. He'd actually done it?

"What the hell was that?" He looked frantically between me and Ariana. He had gone ghost white. "What the hell did you do?"

"*Get away from here.*" I started at him, dead in the eyes, and tried not to look as shocked and mystified as I felt. He quickly scrambled out of the cave, casting quick, alarmed glances back at me as he did.

Ariana and I waited in silence as the man ran away from the cave. Ariana was the first to recover and speak...

"Wow," she said.

"Yeah," I said.

She turned to me. "What on Earth did you do to that guy?"

"I wish I knew."

Her guess was as good as mine. I went over to where he had dropped the gun and picked it up. I turned it over in my hands. It looked burnt, and part of the metal was dented. I doubted even Wayne could fix it with his ability, but it was worth bringing back to find out.

"Has that ever happened before?" Ariana came over to where I stood. She was still looking at me with that disbelieving expression.

"No." I shook my head. "At least, I don't think so."

How had I done that? It was like I had overridden his will with my own.

"Do you think maybe that's why you've been hearing thoughts without meaning to?" she asked.

That would make some sense. Had I been slipping up because I was getting stronger and needed to control it more?

"Maybe," I said. "That would make sense."

"We have to tell Damion and Xavier." Ariana's expression was almost excited. She bounced on her feet. "They aren't going to believe this."

"We're not even sure what this is yet," I said with a shake of my head.

But when I had screamed for the Taker in the lab to turn off the electricity, she had. Had it really just been a coincidence?

"What do you mean?" Ariana asked. "You told him to drop the gun and leave. He did. Mind control."

Reading minds was one thing, but controlling them? Who should have that power? Certainly not me.

"Can we just wait until morning?" I asked. I knew we had to tell the others, but I was barely able to tell myself at the moment. "I just need some time to digest it, y'know?"

"Okay," Ariana said, her eagerness fading. "I just thought you'd be excited, that's all."

"It's just weird and kind of a shock," I said. "I mean, with everything else going on, it's a lot."

"No, I get it." She nodded, her tone more understanding. "I won't say anything about it."

"Thanks," I said sincerely. I glanced at the sky. "We should probably get moving again if we wanna make it back tonight."

"Yeah."

We started the walk back to the Base. Once I knew we were close, I sent a message to ask Damion what the marker was. I didn't really want to fumble around all night looking for an invisible Base. He said there was a patch of burned ground just outside each gate. That was smart. Ground wouldn't get moved, and it wasn't that obvious a sign.

"We gotta look really carefully," I said to Ariana as I scanned the ground in the growing darkness.

It took us forever to find a burn mark. By the time we got in the gates, it was pitch black. I told Damion he'd just have to come out and meet us next time.

We set another meeting for bright and early the next day. For now, I skipped over the part where we'd almost been caught, and I definitely didn't tell anyone what I'd done to the Taker. I had to figure myself out before letting Damion and the others try.

Chapter 21: Finders Keepers

"What?" Damion asked the next morning. He blinked. "Save Mozaan? What do you mean?" He rested his arms on the edge of the table and sat straight in his chair.

"The guy thought they needed supplies to save it," I said, pressing my lips together. "I guess that means they're running out?"

"How?" Wayne asked, from across the table. He lowered his reddish eyebrows. "Don't they have renewable systems and stuff?"

"I don't know," I said with a shake of my head. I shrugged my shoulders. "Maybe something happened?"

"Is that all he thought?" Damion asked.

"No," I said. *I have no idea what these RCCs are, but maybe someone here will.* "He said something about RCCs."

"What's an RCC?" Aukai asked.

"No idea." I leaned back a bit in my chair. "He just though that we wouldn't know anything about them, which I guess was right."

"He also thought we'd be untrained," Ariana said. I'd told her everything already. "That's probably a good thing, right?"

"Yes, it is," Damion said. He exhaled, his posture loosening. "That means they haven't found us yet. Did anything you heard suggest they're looking?"

"Not really," I said, glad to have at least some good news. "He was thinking that we'd better not screw with their plans for saving Mozaan, so I think they just want us to stay out of the way."

"So, you think they're just grabbing some stuff?" Thalia asked, her tone hopeful. "Mozaan'll be fixed, and they'll stay away from us?"

"That would be the best-case scenario," Damion said. "But we can't know for sure. If Mozaan is in enough trouble that they need to take resources from Earth, I doubt it could be a quick fix."

"You think they'll stick around?" Xavier asked, from my right.

I would believe it. I'd finally been happy again recently, so why wouldn't the Takers come and try to ruin it?

"They could." Damion ran a hand over his face, rubbing the eye that wasn't covered by his side-bangs. "We still need to know more before we do anything." He turned to Ariana and me. "Anything else?"

"No," I said to him, wishing we had more information to give. "Sorry, it was all we could get before we had to leave. And on the way back...something happened."

"What happened?" he asked, scanning the two of us for any sign of injury. "Are you guys alright?"

"We're fine," Ariana said, giving him a small smile. "But we ran into this man..."

She looked at me, and I nodded. I explained to them about the man, starting with the thoughts I'd heard when I first arrived. By the time I'd gotten up to the point when we encountered him in the cave, I'd received lots of comments along the lines of "you should have told somebody" and "we could've helped".

"How did you get away?" Hamisi asked.

I'd been hoping to avoid this awhile longer. "Something weird happened." I shifted in my chair. "I just told him to drop the gun."

"And he did it?" Xavier turned around to face me.

"Yeah, I don't know." I gestured out with my hands. "I mean, I just told him to drop it, and he did. Then, I told him to leave, and it was the same thing."

"Lucky," Elliot said, but I didn't think so. An ability like that was a huge responsibility, and I didn't even know how to work it. "Wonder if I'll be able to do that," he added.

After taking a few seconds to absorb the information, Damion said, "Well, the important thing is that you're both alright. We can try to figure out what's going on with that later, but we have to get back to talking about the Takers."

Some people still glanced my way, but since everyone respected what Damion said, we got back to talking about the Takers.

"So, what do we do now?" Wayne asked. "Send more scouts?"

"That's the plan," Damion said. "I'm gonna keep sending new teams, and as soon as one gets back, we'll discuss what was learned. We need to know everything we can, especially if there are more camps close by."

All the other resource scout teams had come back. They hadn't come across camps, but they weren't exploring their areas in extreme detail either. There was no way they could have gone over every piece of land, or even most of it for that matter.

"Who's going next?" Aukai asked, moving some of her pale-blue hair out of her face. Her eyes were a shimmery golden colour right now, but I could have sworn they'd been pink when I first met her.

"I was thinking Elliot and Hamisi," Damion said, turning to look at the two guys. "That good?"

"Sure," Elliot said, his hands in his pockets.

"Yeah," Hamisi nodded. "Yeah, I can go."

"Alright, well let's—" Damion was interrupted by a series of fast, hard knocks on the metal door.

"Anybody order in?" I asked, looking around the table with a raised eyebrow. My friends shook their heads, and I saw Elliot roll his eyes.

Damion was closest to the door. Just before his hand grazed the handle, someone yanked the door open from the other side.

Rude. I shook my head in disapproval.

"We're gonna need the mind readers down by the cells," the lady in the doorway said, glancing over at Elliot and me. *She knows we have names, right?* "We found one of *them* caught in a hunting trap not too far from the left gate. Think he might've been looking for us, and a mind reader would be pretty helpful during the interrogation." She gestured in our direction with her thumb.

My eyebrows shot up. "You *have* one of them?"

I'd forgotten there was a jail area in this place. But it was perfect. We didn't even have to go anywhere for the information we needed. He'd come right to us.

"Well, yeah—" She placed a hand on her hip.

"Who else knows about this?" Damion interrupted.

"Just Brett and me. He's my partner," she said. "There wasn't anybody at the gate we came through." Damion had arranged for our shifts to be covered, but maybe the people supposed to be guarding had had some sort of mix up.

"Alright," Damion said, his tone serious. "I need you to keep this between yourselves. We're taking care of it, and there's no reason to freak people out."

"You knew they were here?" she asked, going a bit paler. "How did they get here? What do they want?"

"It's nothing to worry about." Damion lied. "It's just a couple of them. We're figuring out why they're here, but there's no reason to get everybody all stirred up."

"I...guess so," the lady said, frowning. "Nobody else can know?"

"Nobody," Damion said. We had no idea what people would do if they knew. Some might try to kill the Taker, and there would probably be mass panic. "I'm waiting until there's more information before saying anything."

The lady agreed to keep quiet and to pass the request on to Brett, though she seemed unsure enough that I double-checked with her thoughts.

Once she was out the door, I looked to Elliot. "Come on, then."

I got up and started toward the door. Anxiety had started to spread through me as memories of electrocution flashing through my mind, but I reminded myself that the tables were turned this time. I was the one in control; I was the one doing the interrogating. And I was going to get the information we needed.

I smiled. "It's our lucky day."

Chapter 22: Insomnia

The cell was small, just big enough for a cot at the back. The walls were made of steel like the Base's walls. The door that closed off the cell was simple, just metal bars that went from the ceiling to the ground. They had obviously been put in after the first Outliers got here. The spacing in the bars was somewhat uneven, and the lock was crude. A large door latch was locked by sliding a metal rod through a couple metal loops.

The Taker didn't say a word to us. He didn't acknowledge that we were standing outside the cell. He just sat on his cot.

"Why were you spying?" I asked. I narrowed my eyes and kept my voice hard. "Are you planning an attack?"

"You can torture me all you want," he said. His silver eyes flicked up to meet mine. "I'm not going to tell you anything."

"You don't have to *tell* us anything," Elliot said. *They aren't planning an attack*, he thought to me.

I rolled my eyes. *I know.*

"If you aren't planning an attack," I said, furrowing my eyebrows, "then why bother spying?"

"How did you know that?" the man asked. Now he looked back and forth between the two of us, a wary expression on his face.

"Why were you looking for us?" Elliot ignored the man's question.

Because we wanted to scope out your defenses and weak points. We needed to know if you were a threat, which you aren't, the Taker answered.

"Yeah, we'll see about that," Elliot muttered.

"What's an RCC?" I asked.

The man's eyebrows shot up. He didn't think we'd know about them. The other Taker at the camp hadn't either.

"I don't know." He put his hands up in front of himself. "I've heard the word a couple times, but I don't know."

I scowled at him. *Yeah, right.*

I dug deep into his thoughts. He was trying hard to keep them blank, but it didn't matter. *Resource Coordinate Controller.*

"Liar." I stepped closer to the cell's bars. "What else do you know?"

"Nothing," he said. *It tells the guys up in Mozaan where to collect the resources.* Why didn't he realize it did no good to lie? *There's one in all three camps. It's weird I've never seen one actually. But, I guess the less people with access, the safer. Without the RCCs, they would be flying blind.*

That was why the Takers had people on Earth. Without these RCCs, and the Takers to get them here, Mozaan wouldn't be able to suck up the resources.

This was good. We had a target. Something that could bring the Takers down. But all we knew was that RCCs would have to fit inside a tent. That didn't narrow things down much.

Apart from that, all this Taker knew was that something was wrong with the farms on Mozaan and taking Earth's resources was necessary to help sustain things. This was the worst-case scenario I had been dreading. They weren't just getting some stuff and leaving. They would need to keep taking more and more because the problem wouldn't go away. And apparently, it couldn't be fixed.

Elliot and I just stood there in silence for a moment, unsure what to say. The world was ending, at least on Mozaan. It could be ending here too if the Takers kept stealing resources. Eventually, there would be nothing left on Mozaan or Earth.

When we got back to the office, everyone looked at us expectantly. We relayed what we'd learned, and then we all just sat in silence, stewing in the bad news.

"So what do we do?" Xavier asked eventually. "Just sit around, waiting for everything to be gone?"

"What would happen if we could stop them?" Wayne asked. "Figure out about those chip things or whatever?"

"The people on Mozaan would run out of food," I said.

We were really stuck. No matter what we did, there would be serious consequences.

"Couldn't they just be evacuated here?" Ariana asked, lowering her eyebrows. "Why don't the Takers do that if they know Earth is healing?"

"There's not nearly enough space," Damion said, shaking his head. "There's over a million people on Mozaan. Judging by the boundaries reported by the scouts, it would be hard enough for another Base worth of people to survive down here, let alone a million."

"Can't they use some of their technology to, I dunno, make more livable land?" Thalia asked.

"I don't think so," Aukai said. "Terraforming could take hundreds of years. And given what we just found out, I doubt they have the resources to do it anyway."

"How long do the people on Mozaan have if they stop getting resources?" Ariana asked. "Maybe there would be enough time for Earth to heal more. If we had the RCCs, maybe we could convince the Takers to start evacuating gradually."

"I doubt this is going to be a diplomatic situation," Xavier muttered.

I had to agree. The Takers likely would not be convinced of anything.

"By the way the guy was thinking," Elliot said with a sigh, "they don't have that long. Definitely not the hundreds of years it would take to terraform or let Earth heal on its own."

But there had to be something—anything else—that could save the people on Mozaan. Rationing or… Everyone from Mozaan might not be able to survive on Earth, but there were enough resources here for some.

"If we did stop them from taking resources, they might evacuate *some* people though," I said. "Even if it was just the Takers that fled here, as bad as that would be for us, the human race would survive."

But all those people. Was there really no other way?

"That's still a big *if,*" Damion said before pausing for a moment. "We don't understand enough about these RCCs or other camps to know if we could stop them, and we don't know enough about what's happening on Mozaan to really decide what to do."

"We definitely need to know more," I said with a nod. "We might even find something that could save more people."

"I'm going to continue with the scouts as planned," Damion said decisively. "Even if we don't have to go after these RCCs, that camp is still far too close. The Taker we caught could have found us and reported back. Even with the cloaking, it's too risky to have their camp there. We need to take it out as soon as possible."

Everybody agreed. Personally, I couldn't have agreed more. Having a Taker camp so close was making it even harder to sleep at night. I stayed awake worrying that they could burst in at any moment and hurt the people I loved...again.

After some more deliberation, Damion decided to let the captured Taker live for now. Trickles of fear roiled through my gut. One of them was inside the Base. How strong were those metal bars?

By the time we were done, it was late enough that it didn't make sense for Elliot and Hamisi to head out until morning. We all went to the dining hall and had dinner together, though the meal was kind of somber.

After we finished eating, the other girls and I all headed straight to our beds. Thalia and Aukai had beds on the far side of the room, so it was just Ariana beside me. I flopped down onto my bed and stared up at the ceiling.

There was no way I could sleep. The stress about the Taker was keeping me too alert.

I sat up and looked at Ariana. She seemed lost in thought, staring down at her comforter. A small smile played at her lips. What was she daydreaming about? After everything we'd just been dealing with?

Before I could ask, her thoughts came rushing into my head.

Too late, I realized I didn't want to know what she was thinking. My hands instinctively flew to my ears, as if to block the sound out. I shook my head to purge myself of what I'd just heard.

"Agh!" I shuddered. The thoughts had long since gone, but I was left extremely disturbed.

"What's wrong?" Ariana asked. She looked worried, her eyes wide.

"*Ariana,*" I said, my voice filled with my horror. I still couldn't believe what I'd just heard. "That's my *brother* you're thinking about."

Ariana blushed deeply. Mortification was written all over her expression. "That was—That was none of your business," she accused.

"I swear, I didn't mean to." I put my hands up in fake surrender and made a face. "But, just...*elch*. Gross."

"You *promise* you didn't do it on purpose?" She stared into my eyes, looking for any trace of dishonesty.

"Promise." There was an awkward silence for a minute.

"Please, don't say anything," she pleaded.

I sat with her on the bed. "You have my word."

But I was still grossed out. She was kidding herself if she thought I would *want* to talk about it with anyone. Why did she have to like my *brother* of all people? She could have liked anybody else.

"Haven't you ever heard of mind reader/mind readee confidentiality?" I teased.

Like I'd told Elliot, I didn't intrude on my friends' thoughts. I owed them that respect. People's thoughts were intimate, private. Since I had failed to not read Ariana's thoughts, it was my job to keep things between us.

"Oh, of course," she said, rolling her eyes. She looked at me with a serious expression. "But thank you."

"Seriously though?" I asked.

The dumb smile she'd had earlier was back. "Shut up."

She tried to look angry. She failed. I laughed.

I flopped back onto my bed, and Ariana got into hers. Only a few minutes later, I could hear her snoring. I still had no idea how she could get to sleep so fast. I checked with the guys as per usual, and by the sounds of it, they were nearly asleep as well.

But I was wide awake. The Takers were on Earth. If they continued doing what they were doing, it was highly unlikely the human race would survive much longer. Plus, they were only a day's walk away from the Base. And they wanted to find us.

How long would we be able to hide from them? Would we be able to attack them soon enough, or would they find us and join with the other Takers to attack us? If we couldn't get rid of that camp fast enough, the people I cared about wouldn't be safe.

If that weren't enough, I'd forced a man to drop his gun and leave just by telling him to. It was good to know I hadn't lost my marbles, but what *was* happening to me? I couldn't control hearing thoughts all the time, and all of a sudden I was making somebody do things?

And then there was a Taker in a cell, who could only be trouble. What if he escaped? We were risking so much having him here.

I flipped over onto my back to stare at the ceiling again. Most of the people around me had even breathing now; others were snoring.

I spent about ten more minutes looking at the plain white ceiling. Then I couldn't take it any more. Fear was keeping me awake.

I edged off my bed, wincing at the loud creak it made when I finally stood up. I crept out of the sleeping quarters and wandered through the Base. I hadn't planned on ending up where I did. I really hadn't.

But there I stood, face-to-face with the Taker in the cell.

Chapter 23: Nightmare

Come for a chat?" he asked.

I just glared at him. In truth, I wasn't sure what I'd come for. But with all the crazy things running through my mind, he was the only problem I could actually reach.

Only a few feet from me, he tilted his head and arched one of his carefully manicured eyebrows. "Or did you come to be the hero? Huh, little mind reader? Come to finish me off and get a gold star?" Given time to come to terms with our ability to see inside his mind, he'd definitely gotten bolder since the last time I'd seen him.

"*Shut up*," I ordered. There was a twinge of anger to my voice, but it was more than an emotional reaction. It was a demand. A demand that I knew—the way I knew that a thought would leave my mind and reach somebody else's when I wanted it to—he would obey.

And he did. His eyes became as wide as saucers. He put a hand to his throat, opening and closing his mouth.

Was this what the experiment lady had seen on the brain scans that made her think I was lying? That made her stop with the electricity?

"*Take a step forward.*" Again, he complied.

The small strain on my will that typically came with mind reading followed, but it was more prominent than usual. This took more focus. Rather than just listening, I had to override his will with my own. That was how I could be sure the Taker wasn't just pretending.

I wish she'd step closer so I could strangle her through the bars, he thought. *When I get out of here, I'm gonna pump each one of 'em full of burning-hot laser beams.*

I gripped his wrist tight enough to turn the skin around it white. I didn't remember ordering him to come to the bars.

I loathed him. He had taken away my family, and he still wanted to take what I had left.

Hatred bubbled in my blood and seeped through my skin. It exploded through me, rushing through my veins like a tsunami until it broke free and reached the Taker.

His eyes grew wide and wild with fear. A stony, grey colour was spreading rapidly across his skin, and the parts it reached dissolved into tiny grey snowflakes. I snatched my hand away, but it was too late. Those few seconds had reduced him to a pile of ashes on the floor.

I didn't know how I'd done it.

I didn't know if I regretted it.

I rushed out of the cell. My heart pumped fast and hard inside my chest. I was breathing in short bursts.

I murdered the prisoner. I murdered the prisoner.

I wasn't sure how I felt. I wouldn't get caught. It wasn't like there was much evidence. He probably would have been executed later on. But I'd killed somebody without knowing I was doing it. Just by touching him. Like the woman on Mozaan. It wasn't just a one-off any more. It wasn't a fluke. Anybody who touched me could be at risk of dying.

Damion was a healer. What was I?

Mind control, the ability to murder in an instant... When had those ever been good guy abilities?

I went back to my bed, but I lay there, restless. Maybe I had been right a couple years ago. I could leave and protect my friends from whatever I was. Did they really need me now? They had this whole Base and my brother. Elliot could do the scout missions.

Somehow though, I couldn't bring myself to leave. It was selfish, and though I hated myself all the more for it, I didn't want to be away from my brother and friends. I still wanted to believe that we could get rid of the Takers and finally have some peace. One day, we would all have a life together. Despite everything we had suffered, we would find some happiness.

So I didn't move. I just lay there, waiting for morning.

Around six thirty, I couldn't take it any more. I got up and changed into my guard clothes.

Ariana woke up as I was pulling on my shoes. She got ready as quickly as she could, but she was still just as slow in the mornings. We were heading out to the training area when Elliot messaged me to say that Damion was calling an immediate meeting.

"Wonder what it's about," Ariana said as we headed to the office room.

"Yeah," I said, even though I knew. My voice sounded a little far away, but she didn't seem to notice.

I sat in my usual chair when we arrived, fiddling anxiously with my fingers under the table. I wasn't letting myself touch anybody after last night.

"Alright," Damion said, glancing around the table. His expression was serious. "We're all here. Let's get down to business."

"Did something happen?" Ariana asked, looking concerned.

"Yes, it did." Damion's back was straight, and he took the time to look at everybody. It was hard for me to not just come out with the truth right then. "And I need you all to be completely honest. Did any of you mention the prisoner to somebody?" There was a chorus of "nos" and "whys."

Xavier asked, "Have other people been talking about it?"

"The prisoner is dead," Damion said. Everybody seemed surprised, but not so much so that they couldn't believe it. "So either somebody here killed him, or somebody else found out and killed him."

My heart had started to beat a little faster. What would Damion think if he found out it was me? He knew about the Taker I'd killed on Mozaan, so there was the chance he could piece it together. Would he be as understanding now that it had happened a second time? Would Ariana and Xavier? Or would they look at me like…like a murderer.

"None of us would do that," Aukai said, shaking her head. "There's just no way. How did he die? Maybe he did it himself, so he wouldn't give us more information."

"It would've been pretty hard for him to do that himself." Damion paused. "All I found was a pile of ash."

Everybody turned to look at Xavier, but he glanced at me. "Wasn't me," he said, putting his hands up in mock surrender, his expression sincere. "I swear it."

I hadn't even considered that they would think it was him.

"You're the only one in this room with a fire ability," Wayne accused.

This was bad. I had to get Xavier out of this.

"It wasn't him." I said, avoiding looking at him. "I just checked his thoughts."

Xavier probably knew that was a lie, but he wasn't going to argue with me. If he knew I was lying though, he would know it had been me who had killed the Taker. I didn't want to look at him, in case he was looking at me differently.

"Well, if it wasn't Fire Hands over here," Thalia said, raising a light eyebrow, "then who was it?"

"Does it really matter?" Elliot asked. "I mean, it probably would have happened eventually." *That's true, isn't it?* I tried to convince myself. *The Takers have done so much awful stuff to us...* I had protected my family, hadn't I?

But I hadn't known what I was doing. This time it was a Taker, but what if there was a next time? Who would it be?

"It does," Damion said. He looked more disappointed than angry. He was supposed to be able to trust us, and now he must have felt betrayed. "Because somebody here doesn't give a damn what was decided, so who's to say there aren't going to be any future incidents?"

All of this was my fault. I wanted to tell him, but... I was afraid of what he would think.

"What about that lady and her partner?" Ariana asked. "The ones who found him? Couldn't they have done something or told someone?"

"That's possible," Damion said, his tone seeming to shift away from disappointment a little. "I don't know Gina and Brett very well."

"And it doesn't make sense that somebody here would do that," Aukai said. "They would know you'd find out."

"That's true," Damion said, nodding. The disappointment vanished from his face, a hint of guilt taking its place. "I'm sorry, but I had to be sure."

"We understand," Hamisi said.

"Yeah, no issues." Ariana's body was angled toward him, and she played with the ends of her hair.

"I guess there's no way now to know who did it," Damion said. "I mean, those other guards could have told any number of people. We'll just have to hope it doesn't spread and turn into panic."

We left soon after that. Most of us had shifts to do, and Elliot and Hamisi had to leave for their mission. I kept my head down and my hands stuffed deep inside my pockets.

My brother matched my pace. He looked over at me. "You alright?" he asked, his tone concerned. "You were quiet the whole meeting."

"I'm fine," I lied. I looked up and gave him a false smile. "Just tired, I guess. Didn't get much sleep."

"Y'know, it's okay to be a bit upset," he said. "I mean, the last couple days have been hard." He moved to put a hand on my shoulder. I flinched away. "Renee, what's wrong?" He looked much more worried now.

You were right, I thought to him. *It's just the last few days have been rough, and I haven't gotten much sleep. I'm just not really feeling like myself today, that's all.*

"Are you sure?" He seemed skeptical.

"I'm sure." I gave him a tight smile.

"Okay," he said, his tone still suspicious. "But if you aren't, we'll talk. Right?"

"Yeah," I said. "Of course."

The rest of the day was a blur. Before I knew it, I was lying on my bed again, staring at the ceiling after checking with Xavier and Damion.

What was I going to do? I had no idea why all of this weird stuff was happening with my abilities. Could I avoid touching and speaking to people for the rest of my life? That seemed the only way I could be sure I wouldn't use my abilities by mistake. Maybe the Takers had been right to want to kill me.

If only I could go back to when I was younger, when things were simple. Before I got my abilities, before I knew what it felt like to lose people. Back to when my mom and dad took care of me and I didn't have nightmares about them being killed. When the thought of killing somebody was completely abstract. Before I became a monster.

After not sleeping the night before, my brain eventually gave in and let me drift away.

~

I was at the Taker's cell again. My hand gripped his wrist tight enough to turn the skin around it white. He had taken away my family, and he still wanted to take what I had left.

I loathed him.

A stony, grey colour was spreading rapidly from where I held him, and all the parts it reached dissolved into tiny grey snowflakes. He was crumbling away into ash. His eyes were wide and wild with fear.

But they weren't his eyes any more.

They were dark, covered by long side-bangs. I tried to take my hand away, but it was too late. My brother crumbled away before me, his last look afraid and betrayed.

"No," I sobbed. "No, no, no. Not again. Not you."

~

"Renee." It was Ariana's voice.

Not her too. Please, not her.

"Renee." Someone shook my shoulder.

I startled awake and jumped away from her. I'd clutched my blanket tightly, and my cheeks were wet.

"You were talking and turning a lot in your sleep."

I dropped the blankets onto my lap, calming down a bit, and sat up more.

"Are you... Are you okay?" Her tone shifted into a softer, more concerned one. She could probably see that I had been crying in my sleep. I hadn't done that in almost a year.

"Yeah," I said, trying to make my voice normal. I wiped at my eyes. "I'm fine."

"Are you sure?" she asked as I got up to change into my guard clothes. I was almost late for my shift. Thankfully it was just me today because Elliot was out scouting.

"Yeah, it's nothing," I said, shoving my feet into my shoes. "I'm fine."

"You don't seem fine," she insisted.

"I gotta go," I said, already starting to move. "I'm late."

"A couple minutes can't hurt too bad. Come on, don't you wanna grab something to eat first?" She reached for me, but I flinched away from her.

"You go on ahead," I said. I struggled to keep my body relaxed and my breathing normal. "I have to be there. Elliot isn't here today."

She wasn't fully ready yet, so I left without her and headed straight to my guard post. I managed to avoid touching anybody all day and was as careful as I could be with speaking. I avoided Ariana's questions about the morning too. I didn't see her alone all day, and I made sure I got to the quarters before her. When she came in, I pretended to be asleep so she wouldn't ask.

You can't do this forever, I told myself.

Well, I could try. Short of leaving, it was the only choice I had.

Chapter 24: Petrichor

When Elliot and Hamisi came back, we all met again before our shifts. They'd been able to figure out quite a bit about everything happening, and it wasn't good news. Mozaan didn't have long.

"Basically," Elliot said, "there were these fish tanks on Mozaan, and they produced all of the nutrients for the plant farms. They were super genetically modified to be perfect for supplying nutrients into the water because it's so pure up there. But a few years ago, somebody with heat vision accidentally destroyed them all."

"That's why they've been gettin' rid of us," Hamisi added. "They're worried something'll happen again."

Huh. I had figured they just outright didn't like us. I could almost see where they were coming from, if they hadn't been murdering children.

"Why not just make new fish?" Thalia asked, though I had a feeling it wasn't that simple.

"They tried," Elliot said. "But there was nothing left of the old ones to go on. That's why they only started stealing resources now. They had some different kinds of fish they were trying to make work, but there weren't enough DNA similarities or something. There was a stock of nutrients as a backup, but now that's running out too. Food pricing has already gone through the roof."

Trying to afford food back on Mozaan had been hard enough when we were there. People in poor regions must have already started starving to death.

"Sure," Xavier said. "But why steal a river?"

"Water here has more nutrients," Hamisi said. That made sense. All the bacteria, dirt, and bugs we had to boil out of the water here would give it more nutrients. "It's helping sustain the farms for now, but it'll run out eventually if they keep taking it."

"I don't get it," Ariana said with a shake of her head. "Like, I get that they can't evacuate everybody onto Earth, but how come they haven't just fled here themselves?" she added, echoing my own thoughts.

"From what I gathered," Elliot said, "they're afraid now that they know we've been surviving. They wouldn't be able to get their weapons as easily, and since they can't transport buildings, genetic modification would be gone for a while. They wouldn't be able to immunize themselves against any new diseases on Earth that we don't know about yet."

It was weird to think of them being scared. They definitely hadn't been scared when they were electrocuting me. Only that lady in the lab had been, and I still wasn't sure how much of my time in there might have been a nightmare.

"And the people they left behind could find transports and follow," Hamisi said, his tone growing more grave. "Which is why there's no way they'll evacuate anybody. If the rest of Mozaan found out, they could all come and overpopulate Earth. There'd be the same resource problem, except there would be no going back to Mozaan when things got bad."

At that, we fell silent. People from Mozaan couldn't be saved if we stopped the Takers because then we would risk dooming everybody.

But something still didn't make sense to me. "So, the transports can't work from here to Mozaan? Then how are they getting stuff up there?" Whatever that was should have been able to transport people back if things got bad.

"It wasn't too clear," Elliot said. "But I don't think they're using the regular transports for the water. It's something else."

It must have had to do with the RCCs telling them where to get stuff, but I couldn't see how.

"So, there's no way we could save some of the people on Mozaan?" Wayne asked.

"It doesn't look like it," Elliot said. "It would be impossible for us to actually get back on Mozaan. It's possible that if we stop them from taking resources, they might realize it's over and send some people down, but I doubt it. The government would have to stay behind and cover things up so the people on Mozaan don't figure things out and all come down here. I don't think they'd be willing to do that."

"But there's still a chance they could, right?" Ariana asked, ever the optimist.

"Yeah," Elliot said, seeming to appreciate her optimism. "There's still a chance."

"Did you two get any information on the RCCs?" my brother asked. He hadn't said much since the beginning of the meeting. I turned to look at him. I shoved my hands deeper into my pockets as painful flashes of my nightmare assaulted me.

"No." Elliot shook his head. "We stayed as long as we could, but nobody was really thinking about it."

"Alright, I'm going to need to send out another team," Damion said. He sighed, his eyes downcast for a moment. "These RCCs are going to determine a lot. As horrible as it is, it looks like we're going to have to try and stop them from getting more resources, or the whole human race will die off in a couple years. But we need to know if it's actually possible to stop them, and if so, how to do it."

So, it was official. We were going to try and stop them. Silence came over us for a few seconds. There was such a heaviness in my stomach that thought I might throw up. It was so horrible and sickening and unfair. So many people, innocent people, dying... How could it come to this? And why was it up to us to make it happen?

"Who's going?" Wayne asked, his voice small. His words sounded strange as they cut through the blanket of guilt and misery that now covered the air. It probably wouldn't be him. He didn't look super fit, and his ability just pertained to fixing things. The idea was to have somebody that could help protect the mind reader.

"Renee and I will go," Damion said, looking to me. I nodded, though I thought it was odd he was going. *Don't they need him here?* "I need to see this camp for myself." Was that really why? He turned to Elliot. "The advisors should be good to run their job sectors for a couple days, but could you contact me if anything comes up?"

"Uh, yeah," Elliot said with a nod. "Sure, I can do that."

"If people ask," Damion said, "I went out on a normal scouting mission to check something out, okay?"

"Alright," Elliot said.

After the meeting ended, Damion and I headed to the training area to gear up. We packed our bags and grabbed a bit of food before leaving. I'd been trying to avoid the dining area because of all the people, but luckily, it was relatively empty this early in the morning. After we ate, we had no reason to delay. We pushed open the thick, metal doors of the Base.

There was no break in the clouds. Fat and grey, they stretched across the sky as far as I could see. I could already smell the rain in the air. It was damp and clean. The moisture cooled my hands and face. The trees seemed to feel it too. They stretched toward the sky, eager and thirsty for the rain they knew would soon fall. The birds had ceased their songs, tucking themselves away for cover. The air was still.

"Not a great sign, eh?" I asked Damion, trying to appear like I was fine.

It wouldn't take a lot for him to figure out what happened with the prisoner. I was sure Xavier had, but he hadn't said anything to the others. And I'd managed to avoid talking alone with any of my friends since it happened. I'd tried not to even look at Xavier much, too scared to see how he would be looking at me now. And on top of that, now we had made this decision about Mozaan. I still felt queasy just thinking about it. In what cruel universe was any of this fair?

"What?" Damion tilted his head.

I breathed in the fresh air. "The calm before the storm," I said, managing to smile.

"Well," Damion said, still with a sombre tone. "Let's hope the rain's the only storm we get."

We went through the gate that Elliot and I normally guarded so we wouldn't have to explain to other guards where we were going. He wished us good luck and reminded us to be careful.

The sky grew greyer as we walked. The whole forest seemed to be holding its breath. Everything was waiting for the rain to cut through the heavy air. But it still hadn't rained by the time we got halfway to the Takers' camp. I was starting to think that Damion hadn't noticed that I was acting different at all because he hadn't said anything.

Until he did. "What's wrong?" he asked, as we walked on. "You seem really off lately."

I avoided his worried gaze. "Nothing," I said, trying to shove my hands even deeper into my pockets.

"Seriously?" he asked.

I could feel him rolling his eyes. I didn't say anything. He made an annoyed sound but didn't press.

The silence between us was heavy, weighing down on my shoulders. I couldn't take this any more, the lying and pushing him away. He deserved to know what I had done. If he was going to be angry, or scared, or disappointed, then he had the right.

"Do you remember the tree? When we were little?" I asked. Part of me wanted him to be angry, to kick me out of the Base and say all the horrible things I thought about myself. I deserved it. Maybe the peace I found always ended up ruined because I didn't deserve to feel peaceful.

"Yeah," Damion said. I looked back up to him as he nodded. "When the branch died?"

I nodded. "It's like that." I focused on the dark clouds that covered the sky. "There was this Taker, on Mozaan, and..."

"The prisoner?" he asked.

I nodded, still not looking at him. I was determined not to cry, but I wouldn't be able to help it if Damion looked at me differently. Anxiety swelled like a balloon in my chest. "I don't know what's going on." I chewed the inside of my lip. "I can't...I don't know how to stop it."

"Renee," he said. We stopped walking. "Look at me."

I took a deep breath and met his eyes. "What?"

He didn't look angry, or scared, or disappointed. He looked understanding. "We'll figure it out," he said. "Promise."

"How?" My voice was small as I tried to prevent it from cracking. I *wasn't* going to cry. I had done enough of that lately.

"It's like any other power when it develops." Damion's voice was calm, as if all of this were completely normal. "You couldn't stop mind reading at first, right?"

"Yeah," I said. I started to relax a bit and slowed my breathing. He sounded like he was going somewhere with this.

"This and the mind control thing, they're the same," he said.

"Okay," I said, nodding. "So, what do I do?"

"You gotta control it." One of his shoulders shrugged upwards. "So, we practise."

I stared at him, taken aback. "I'm not gonna practise dusting people!" How could I control something if I couldn't practise without hurting people?

"Not people, stupid." He rolled back his one exposed eye. How was he so calm about all of this? "Try a plant or something."

I tilted my head, unsure. He sighed and grabbed me by the shoulders. I'd at least calmed down enough that I didn't flinch away from him. He brought me over to a tall, yellow-petalled flower. He gestured to it with both hands. "Go."

"Alright," I said, still uncertain. I touched the plant, doubtful it would work.

Die. Nothing.

Ash-ify. Nope.

"I feel stupid."

"You aren't trying." Damion crossed his arms.

"How would you know?" I asked, narrowing my eyes. I wanted this to work more than anything. I wanted to believe that I could control this—that I wasn't just a ticking time bomb. "Are you in my brain?"

"Try again."

I sighed and turned back to the undamaged plant. I focused entirely on turning it to ash. Still nothing.

"It's no use," I said. As much as I wanted to control this, I just couldn't.

"Why're you giving up so easily?" he asked. "Keep trying."

"I *am*." I shot him an annoyed look.

"Try harder," Damion pressed.

A bubble of anger formed in my chest. I didn't want to have to control this. I didn't want this stupid ability. I hated it. I hated that I was such a danger to the people I wanted to protect.

"There you go," he said.

"What?" I asked.

He nodded to the plant. A single petal had crumbled away, now a tiny dusting of ashes on the forest floor.

"What'd you do?" my brother asked. He stepped closer to look.

"I dunno." I didn't know how I'd done it any more than he did. "I wasn't even trying. I just..."

"What were you doing the other times?" Damion asked. "What happened?"

A realization hit me. "I was mad. Both times."

"Ouch," Damion said. His mouth twitched up into a smirk.

"Yeah, but I wasn't *that* mad this time." I shook my head. "I mean, I was just a bit annoyed."

"Maybe that's why you only turned one petal," he said. "Still, it's progress."

I smiled at him. "Thanks."

Now there was at least hope of controlling this. I knew I only had to worry about destroying things if I was mad. Damion always knew how to fix things.

"Fifty creds," he said, ruining the moment.

"Yeah right." I pushed him, feeling free to do so for the first time in days.

"Wanna try again?" he asked.

"I'm sorry I didn't tell you before," I said. "I should have, but I was scared. I...I didn't want you to see me differently, and I knew you'd decided to keep him alive. And..." When I trailed off, Damion hugged me.

"It's okay," he said, then paused. "We've all done things, Renee. The best thing we can do is try and become better from it."

"Have you..." I asked.

He pulled away from the hug, nodding soberly. "Yeah. Most people wanted me to run things on the Base, but not everybody. I've had to defend myself a few times, and it hasn't always ended well." He'd had to kill people to defend the Base, and now we were talking about killing people, a lot of people, to defend Earth. On his face, I saw how much he regretted those earlier deaths, so I couldn't imagine how heavily this Mozaan decision weighed upon him.

I'd had no idea about people attacking him though. I'd just assumed things had gone smoothly on the Base once he took charge.

"I'm sorry," I said. "I didn't know."

"Don't be." He closed his eyes for a moment. When he opened them again, he raised his eyebrows. "Did you want to try again?"

"Uh, yeah." I took a breath in and nodded. "Sure."

I managed to do another flower petal after about ten minutes. We decided I would practise more on the way back because we wanted to at least get three quarters of the way to the Taker camp before nightfall.

"What about the mind control?" Damion asked just as we were starting to walk. *That* I could not practise on a plant. "Did you want help with that?"

"What? No," I said, taken aback a little.

"It's okay," he said, his tone assuring. "I trust you."

"No. No way." I hated the idea of anybody controlling me, especially since the electricity. I'd felt so out of control, like I couldn't use my own body, so the the mere idea scared me. There was no way I would do that to my brother. "Absolutely not."

"Alright," he said, seeming to understand. "That one isn't really urgent anyway. I mean, if it starts to get out of control, you'll just have to be careful about the way you talk."

"I have been," I told him.

"You know," he said, and I had a feeling I wouldn't like what came next. "You should tell Ariana and Xavier about the other ability."

"They already know about it from back on Mozaan," I said with a sigh. "I'm pretty sure Xavier's figured out I'm the one who killed the prisoner, and Ariana knows something's up. I've just been avoiding them."

"Yeah, it's not cool to shut them out," he said. "I don't care if you tell the others, but Ari and Xavier deserve to know."

"Yeah, I know." I wasn't looking forward to telling them, but I did have to. "I'll tell them when we get back."

When we got close enough to the camp, we decided to set up for the night. Would I be able to sleep when Damion was on watch? In all the time I'd known him, we'd never had to take shifts sleeping. Then again, if he could keep a community of a couple thousand together, he could watch carefully enough for one night.

"I'll take first watch," he offered.

"Are you sure?" I asked. "I don't mind."

He looked me dead in the face. "You look terrible and exhausted. Sleep."

I rolled my eyes. "Fine." I took my blankets and lay down, arranging my pack under my head as a pillow. "Love you. Night."

"Love you too," he said. "Night." I had Elliot check on Ariana and Xavier—the only solution I could think of, having exceeded how far I could hear them from—and they were both safe. The crickets' melody was softer this time, pleasant even. The howling seemed more distant. My brother was here, watching out for me. I found myself drifting off without too much trouble.

~

Something wet had landed on my cheek, but I wasn't crying. *Drip.* I blinked my eyes open, only taking a few seconds to adjust to the mild light. I put my hand to my cheek and sat up. *Drip.* There was a new drop of water, on my arm. I widened my eyes and jumped up.

"Is this rain?" I asked my brother, who was standing up near the tree instead of sitting against it. "Real rain?"

I looked at the cloudy sky. A fat droplet landed on my forehead. The cool water slid down my nose.

"Yeah," he said. His lips quirked up. "This is your first rain?"

"Yeah." The drops started coming quicker. I grinned as it became a downpour, and I stretched my arms wide. Damion was shielding himself with his blanket. It was a bit cold but totally worth it.

"You got your storm," he said, laughing.

The water had already soaked my clothes and now dripped down my face and hair. "Come on," I said, pulling him by the arm. He gave up on the blanket. "Dance with me."

He shook his head, laughing. He was soaked. I was soaked. It was absolutely wonderful.

His hair was flattened by the rain. His bangs split into several large, wet sections and stuck to his face. He shoved his blanket into his pack and was nice enough to put my blanket in mine.

"This is amazing," I breathed. I licked my lips, tasting the sweet water. "Real rain... Real *worms*!" The small, beautiful, brown creatures were digging themselves out of the soil.

"It is, isn't it?" he asked.

I crouched down and scooped a worm out of the wet soil. It wriggled in my hands, its nearly see-through body curving left and right as it tried to escape over my fingers. Bullfrogs croaked nearby. It wasn't as cold out today, but goosebumps rose on my arms.

"Dad would've loved this," I said. I set the worm on the ground, my fingers brushing the wet soil, and stood back up.

"Yeah." Damion pressed his lips together. "He really would've."

"Do you think about them a lot? Mom and Dad?" We started walking again.

"All the time," Damion said. "I wish they could've seen all this."

"Me too," I said. "Dad wouldn't know what to study first."

"I wonder how many 'pets' he would've tried to bring home," Damion said.

I smiled. "We definitely would've had a frog."

"Yeah." Damion shook his head, a smile appearing on his face for a few moments. "Can you imagine all the fishing he would do?"

"Man, can I ever."

There had been no fishing on Mozaan, but Dad had read about it and had always wanted to try. My mind started to wander to Mozaan, and the choice we had made. How many families were there? How many children would have hungry bellies if we succeeded? A lump formed in my throat. I thought of Aunt Liz, who already struggled to afford things. How long would she last?

"What about Mom?" Damion asked, bringing me back to the conversation.

I thought for a few seconds as rain droplets fell into small puddles. "She would've tried to paint the whole place."

I pointed to the trees, but their vibrant colours were barely visible in all the rain. Damion was barely visible, and he was less than a foot away from me. Still, I was sure my mother could have made a beautiful scene from it.

"I don't know how she painted like that," Damion said. Mom had always had a way of making the colours and places come to life. Her paintings had felt like windows to somewhere else.

"Yeah," I said. "I used to try, but nobody's as good as Mom was."

"No," he agreed.

"I miss her," I said. "I miss Dad."

"Me too." Damion pulled me into a hug. I hugged him back. We held onto one another for several more heartbeats before we started walking again. "I missed you a lot."

"I missed you too. I missed your stupid bangs and your stupid face." I tried to lighten the mood or, at the very least, provide the illusion of it.

"Thanks," he scoffed, but he bumped my hip with his in a way that let me know he was smiling internally.

"And your *pointy attitude*," I continued.

"Hey!" He feigned seriousness. "You can insult my face and my bangs all you want, but I do *not* have a pointy attitude."

~

The novelty of the rain wore off pretty quickly. After four hours of walking through cold puddles and eating a lunch of wet food, I was ready for it to be over. We crouched in the line of trees bordering the Takers camp, and I hoped that we would get the information we needed soon because the rain showed no signs of stopping.

For about an hour, almost all I heard from the Takers was whining about the rain. They missed Mozaan. They'd volunteered to stay permanently, and it seemed like they were regarded as "heroes" by the other Takers back on Mozaan. Eventually there came some more information about how the transports worked.

Basically, from what I'm getting, I thought to Damion, *they only work one way because of how Mozaan is suspended above Earth. Mozaan stays fixed, but Earth spins. It's like if somebody stood still and somebody else was spinning. It'd be a lot easier for the still person to hit the spinning person with a ball than vice versa.*

We didn't get the explanation of how they sent the resources up to Mozaan until a half hour or so later. I almost missed it because I was distracted by the cold.

That's why the Takers have to be here with the RCCs, I thought to Damion. *They need the precise location of the water so people on Mozaan can make the calculations. They have to time it when the stuff has spun in reach, and then they scan it and transport it back. I think that's why people can't go back. There's still a bit of time between the scan and the transport, so their atoms could be all scrambled or something.*

It was good to know, but we still needed more on the RCCs. Which meant more time in the cold rain. Even my socks were wet, and I didn't have a spare pair of those.

We're going to have to leave soon, Damion thought to me after a while longer. *We have to make it back tonight because I don't think this rain is stopping.*

But we also needed this information. We needed to know if we could stop them. The minutes sped by, and I was getting nothing.

Come on, I thought, growing more anxious. *We can't leave before we know. It's too important.*

Finally, in a stroke of luck, I heard a thought mention the RCCs and focused on that person right away. *It's stupid they put our camps all so far away. I mean, sure, if the RCCS were put together, we'd be screwed, but who's gonna do that? Those freaks wouldn't stand a chance if our camps were together. And the RCCs are secure inside people's heads, especially with five soldiers constantly on guard.*

I put a hand over my mouth, not sure whether to be relieved or disgusted.

What is it? Damion thought.

I think we can stop them, I thought to him. *But they've used human containers for the RCC chips. They've hidden them in people's heads. The one for this camp is inside a tent, with five guards.*

Damion seemed just as disgusted as I was, but he focused on the other news—although we could hardly call that *good* either considering all of the lives that would be lost on Mozaan.

How could we stop them? he asked.

He just thought that they'd be screwed if we put all the RCCs together. I don't know how yet. I was still listening. The man thought that putting them together would shut down the machine responsible for scanning Earth.

Why do that? Damion asked.

I think it's like a backup plan, I thought to him. *In case the teleport starts malfunctioning and destroying both places. Apparently the design is more of a prototype, but they had to use it before it was really ready because of how quickly Mozaan is deteriorating.*

I was trying to figure out why they would be so screwed if the RCCs all got together, but a more important thought entered my head.

Crap. We gotta go, I thought to Damion. Someone moved within the closest tent. *Somebody thinks they saw something.*

We booked it from there. Luckily the rain and trees were thick enough to hide us well. It actually felt good to be running. It returned a bit of the warmth to my body.

We have enough, Damion thought to me. His next thoughts sounded thick with remorse. *We're gonna discuss this at next meeting, and I want to start planning an attack.*

We got about a quarter of the way before slowing down.

It was dark when we got to the Base, but at least we got there. Hamisi and Thalia must have seen us coming because part of the gate was open and became visible to us. We rushed over, eager to be out of the rain.

"How'd it go?" Thalia asked. They were both soaked too and had blankets wrapped around their shoulders.

"Found what we needed," I said, looking to the doors. We were so close. I just wanted to be inside and to take these awful, freezing shoes and socks off.

"We'll talk tomorrow morning," Damion said. "Meeting first thing like usual."

Ariana was asleep when I got in, so I would be spared from talking to her until before the meeting tomorrow. I probably wouldn't get the chance to talk to Xavier until after the meeting, which I was perfectly fine with.

Now that I knew it was possible to control the ability, I wasn't quite as terrified of telling them, but the anxiety hadn't vanished either. Sure, I hadn't thought I would kill the man, but why had I gone to his cell? What else had I been hoping to accomplish? And even if the ability could be controlled, what kind of person had an ability like that?

~

"Did you wanna hang out for a bit at training or something?" Ariana asked me the next morning. Guilt twisted inside my stomach. She always tried to be such a good friend, and I'd been so crappy to her lately. She sat down on her cot and pulled out her box of things from underneath it. "Or we could, like, go trading at the stands." She dug through the box and plucked out a small, wooden container that held lip gloss. I had no idea how she'd gotten lip gloss on Earth, but then, she never ceased to amaze me with her determination.

"Actually, I was gonna tell you, I'm going back out for a bit," I said. *Deep breaths,* I thought to myself. *You have to tell her. Just rip the bandage off.* "Not to the camp or anything though."

"Are we... Are we okay?" she asked, concerned. "Because I don't know what's been going on with you, but I know you've been avoiding me. Xavier says you've been avoiding him too. Plus, you've been pretty quiet at the meetings, and I just... I don't know if we did something that upset you..."

"You didn't do anything, Ari," I said with a shake of my head. I sat down on my bed. It wasn't fair that she was worrying when all of this was my fault. I just had to come out with it. "I did...I... Something happened—something I did—and I was scared to tell you."

She sat down beside me. Her eyes were warm when she looked at me. "Whatever it is," she said. "I promise you can tell me. We've always been there for each other, right?"

"Yeah," I said with a nod. "Yeah. It's..." I took a breath in.

"Renee, whatever you've done," Ariana said, her tone reassuring. "We'll get past it."

"You remember the parking lot on Mozaan?" I asked her, lowering my voice a bit. I scanned the room for any sign somebody was listening. Most people seemed to still be sleeping, and those who weren't paid no attention to us. But there was still a chance somebody could hear.

"Yeah," she said, lowering her voice too. "When we were trying to get away from *them*?"

That's what happened to the prisoner, I thought to her. I couldn't risk somebody overhearing.

Her thin, dark eyebrows shot up. "What?" she asked. Her voice was louder than I would have liked. "What did you—"

"Shh," I said, looking pointedly around the room.

"Right, sorry," she said, lowering her voice again.

It was an accident, I thought to her in a rushed sort of way. *That's why I'm going tonight. Damion's trying to help me figure out how to control it.*

"Why didn't you tell me? When it happened?" she asked, her eyes narrowed.

"I'm sorry, Ari," I said. "I just... I was freaked out. That's all."

"Is that why you've been so flinchy?" she asked. "Like when I woke you up?"

"Yeah, I didn't think I could control it," I said. "I was worried that if I touched somebody..."

"Look, I don't like what happened," Ariana said, her tone understanding. "But you said it was an accident, and I believe you."

"I don't even know why I went there," I confessed, hiding my head in my hands. "I just couldn't stop thinking about how close he was to all of you, and..." I didn't mean to kill him, but I had wanted him dead. Did that still make it an accident?

"I...It's okay," she said. "Are you alright?"

"Yeah," I lied. I slowly brought my head up and gave her a tight smile. "Always."

But accident or not, I would never be completely okay with myself. Sure they were Takers—maybe even monsters—but at the end of the day, when I closed my eyes, I saw people. People I'd killed. And now, there were the innocent people on Mozaan. Old neighbours, friends, anybody I had ever known there, and I was going to be part of them dying. How could anything ever be alright?

Chapter 25: The Drawing Board

The next morning, each of the nine chairs in the small office room was taken as we sat around the long black table in the center.

"So?" Wayne asked, his red curls messier than usual. "What did you find?"

"You remember how there's two more camps? With an RCC in each?" I received a chorus of "yeahs." It was almost all we talked about these days.

"Do we gotta find those and blow 'em up or something?" Thalia asked, scooting her chair closer to the table.

"No," Damion said with a sigh. "That's the problem. We can't destroy them."

I wished it could have been as simple as just destroying them. It would have been easier and less risky than collecting all three to put together.

"What?" Xavier asked. He ran a hand through his thick, brown hair and scratched the back of his head. "Why not?"

"If we put them together," I said, "they'll shut down the Takers' ability to teleport stuff." I met Xavier's eyes for the first time in days.

Can we talk after? I asked him.

Yeah, he thought. *We should.*

"Why would they have things that could foil their whole plan?" Aukai asked, looking perplexed.

"I think it's a precaution," I said. "In case things start to go wrong. And by the sounds of it, they can't just send down more RCCs and Takers and try again. So, this is how we stop them."

"Do you think we can?" Hamisi asked. There was a certain and reasonable uneasiness to his tone. "I mean, with all of their weapons..."

"We're going to have to try," Damion said. "This is the human race we're talking about. And they're so close to us. We don't know how long we have before they find and attack us."

"So are we going to get the guards to fight?" Xavier asked. "We'd outnumber them by a lot." There were some murmurs of agreement.

"How do we get these RCC chips anyway?" Elliot asked. "Where do they keep them?"

"That's the other thing," I said, pressing my lips together. I hated the other thing. "They don't just have the chips in a box or something. They're using people."

"What?" Ariana asked, appalled. "Like, *inside* them?"

"Yeah," Damion said with a small, thin frown. "It sounds like they've implanted them in their heads."

"That's sick," Thalia said. Disgust contorted her expression and made her posture go stiff. "In their own people's..."

"Oh my god," Aukai said, her expression grave. She shook her head. "How...how could they do that?"

"So, we what?" Elliot asked. He grimaced. "We have to get to this person and just dig it out?"

"Pretty much." I nodded, pressing my lips together. I leaned back in my chair and crossed my arms. It wouldn't be pretty, that was for sure.

Elliot's lip twitched up in disgust. Thalia and Aukai had both paled considerably, and Ariana brought a hand up to cover her mouth. Wayne and Hamisi looked at each other with widened eyes.

"Back to the guards thing," Thalia said, swallowing. "Are we gonna ask them?"

"I don't think so," Damion said. "I still want to keep this quiet if we can, and judging by the numbers at their camp, I don't think we need that many people."

"Everybody here is willing to fight, right?" I asked. Damion had already tried to talk me out of going, but there was no way I was staying behind. Everybody else agreed to fight too. "There's nine of us. They only look like they have about the same, maybe a couple more."

"They still have really advanced weapons," Wayne said. "I don't see how we can attack them with knives and arrows."

"They also don't have abilities," Damion reminded him. "If we play to our strengths enough, there's no reason we shouldn't be able to win." We would also have the element of surprise on our side.

"So where do they keep this person with the RCC?" Xavier asked.

"In a tent," I said. "With five guards."

"It's on the edge of the camp though," Damion said. "So, we might not need to take out all of the Takers if we're fast enough."

Wayne and Hamisi were talking quietly to each other about it from across the table, and Elliot was leaned back in his chair, looking up at the ceiling. Aukai had drawn inward, curling into herself. Damion looked around and waited for everyone to consider. Ariana tightened her ponytail on my right, and to my left, Xavier was tapping his fingers lightly on the table and tightening his jaw with resolve.

"But then wouldn't the camp still be close by?" Wayne asked, several seconds later. "Yeah, we'd have the chip, but I thought the main reason we needed to attack so soon was to get rid of the camp."

"I've thought about that," Damion said. "It would be good to get rid of all of the Takers, but the longer we're there, the higher the risk for all of us. I can't see any reason the remaining Takers would stick around if we have the chip. That's their whole purpose for being there. They'd probably have to move to another camp, farther away. We'll take them all out if we have to, but if the battle starts getting rough, we have to prioritize the RCC and get out of there."

"What if we drew away all of the nearby Takers?" Aukai suggested. "Create some sort of diversion to get them out of the RCC tent?"

"That could be good," Ariana said, nodding. "I mean, you said they'd probably abandon the camp if the RCC was gone, right? This way, we might not even have to fight too many of them."

"It could work," Damion said, considering it. He sounded a bit reluctant to think about it, probably worried about us getting hurt...or worse. I was worried too, but as awful as this whole situation was, it was up to us to stop the Takers. If we didn't, we'd all be dead anyway, and eventually, the whole human race would be too.

"But what would we use?" Damion asked.

"You said the tent is on the edge of the camp, right?" Xavier leaned forward and rested his elbows on the table.

"Yeah." Damion nodded. He tilted his head to the side. "What are you thinking?"

"I could start a fire at the other side," Xavier said. "They'd all run to the fire, and a couple people could sneak in to grab the chip person."

There were enthusiastic hums and mumbles of "yeah" around the table.

"That's a good idea," I said. "And a fire probably wouldn't make them suspicious of an attack either."

It was going to be better that we weren't taking the other guards too. If we only had a few people, the Takers would be less likely to see us coming.

"That could really work," Ariana agreed, nodding. "We'd be gone before they even knew it was a fake-out. "Let's start drawing up the plans," Damion said.

We found some lined paper and a pen in the small black cupboard in the corner of the room. We laid one of the sheets down in the middle of the table.

"So, let's say the tent with the RCC is here..." I drew a messy triangular prism at one side of the paper. I coloured it in with blue ink. It was not a good testimony to my artistic skills. "And these are the rest of the tents." I drew what I remembered of the layout, making a large circle of tents with more filling the middle. "Trees..." I drew some horrible stick trees around the perimeter of the camp.

"We'll wait here," Damion said, pointing to the trees around the RCC tent. "For the signal." I coloured in a dot where Damion had pointed.

"Let's say I set the fire on this tent." Xavier pointed to a tent at the opposite side of the page. I made an uncoloured dot.

"Okay," I said, looking up at everybody. "So, what's the plan once we're actually inside the tent?"

"We can bet there's gonna be some guards that stay behind," Hamisi said. He was right. They wouldn't all leave the RCC unattended to help with the fire.

"And they have guns," Thalia pointed out. "How can we fight without them shooting us in two seconds?"

That was a good question. Was this whole plan a waste of time?

"I can put up a force field," Ariana said, brightening at the opportunity to contribute. "That'll stop anything from hitting us when we go in."

"Good idea," I said, relieved that our plan could still work. "We'll just have to make sure we're as quick as possible." Ariana could only hold her force field up for so long. The most she could usually do was a couple minutes.

"But how are we supposed to shoot at them from behind it?" Wayne asked her. "We'll have to drop it to take the RCC person too."

Ariana's face fell. "Oh," she said, disheartened. "I didn't think about that."

I shot a sharp look at Wayne, but then I got an idea. "Well, I can make the RCC person come with us," I said, forcing confidence into my voice. I wasn't 100 percent sure I could do it, but we needed this plan to work. I drew stick figures of Ariana and me inside the RCC tent. I made a curve to show the force field, and then drew the Takers at the back of the tent. "And if we have a few more people behind the force field..." I drew three people around Ariana and me. "They can jump from the sides and throw knives at the guarding Takers."

"That would work great," Ariana said, uplifted again.

"Are you sure you'll be able to make the RCC person come with us?" Damion asked me. "You don't have too much experience with it yet."

"I'm sure I can," I said, my tone reassuring. "And if for some reason I can't, we'll just make sure we've taken down all of the others, and then we'll grab the guy."

"Alright," he said, but I sensed from his tone that it wasn't the end of it.

"And Damion should come too, in case anyone, like, gets shot," Ariana said. We looked at Damion for his approval.

"Draw me in," he said, the corner of his lips quirking up. I drew a little stick Damion, making his bangs dramatically long. "Real mature." He rolled his eyes. Or eye. I couldn't see past his long bangs.

"Whoever's left should go with Xavier," Aukai suggested, her voice so quiet I strained to hear what she was saying. "It might work better if the Takers think they're fighting us, or that there's more of us in the woods."

She wasn't wrong. There was a chance the Takers could be suspicious if there was just a spontaneous fire, so if we had a couple of people there to fight, they would think that was our attack.

"That could work." Xavier nodded.

"It might be good if Hamisi was one of the ones over here." Elliot pointed to the side of the drawing I was on. "We could use telekinesis and actually get one of their guns to shoot. It'd be better than only having knives."

"Sure," Hamisi said. He shrugged his broad shoulders. "That works."

"Alright, done." I wrote an *H* over one of the stick people after Damion gave his stamp of approval, then sat back, looking around. "So, who else?"

"Well, if Hamisi's going, I'm going with him." Wayne said. His tone made it clear he was ready to argue if it came to that. He made a point of taking Hamisi's hand.

"That's fine," Damion said, nodding. I scrawled a *W* over the other stick person.

I understood Wayne's insistence. I always wanted to protect the people I cared about. *Xavier's going to be on the other side of the camp. What if something happened to him?* I pushed the worry aside. He would be fine. They wouldn't be able to get to him past the fire.

"The third?" I asked, refocusing.

"I'll go," Thalia said, gesturing to the paper. "I'm pretty good with knives."

"Damion?" I asked, and he nodded. "Okay." I added a *T* over the last stick person.

"So," Damion said, sitting back in his chair. "That leaves Elliot and Aukai here." He gestured to the other side of the camp. I wrote down *X, A,* and *E* over the uncoloured dot.

How good of a fighter would Aukai be? She looked opposed to hurting a fly. Honestly, I was surprised she had agreed to fight with us at all. Hopefully she was better prepared than she let on.

At least from what I'd seen, Elliot had good combat skills. "That might be good," he said. "Each group will be able to communicate back and forth through Renee and me."

I hadn't thought of that. It was a good idea. "So, is it settled then?" I asked, looking around the room for any objections.

"Alright," Damion said, after nobody spoke up. "Looks like we've got a plan."

Everybody left the office room, except for Xavier and me. We sat down beside each other at the table, a strange silence overlapping us.

"I know it was you," he said after a while, but his tone wasn't accusing.

"I know," I said, meeting his gaze. He was looking at me, but not like I was a murderer. "Thanks for not saying anything."

"You'd do the same for me." He shrugged. And I would have. "You didn't have to avoid me."

"I know, I just..." This was the third time I was talking about this, but it hadn't gotten easier. "I thought you would look at me differently."

"Well, I'm not. Whatever happened, he deserved it." His callous tone told me that he believed what he was saying. He wasn't just trying to make me feel better.

"I didn't mean for it to happen. It was like on Mozaan." I pressed my lips together. "But I didn't want him alive, and I went to his cell. Do you think that's any better than if it wasn't an accident?"

"Whether you meant it or not, it needed to happen." There was a slight pause. "To be honest, if it hadn't happened, I might have done it myself."

"You would've?" I asked.

Maybe it was good I'd done it then, if it saved him from having to. He wanted the Takers dead, and with good reason, but he didn't know what it was really like to have killed somebody. "Yeah," he said. "Me and probably half the others who knew."

"Anyway," I said, shifting around in my chair so that he was in front of me. He did the same. Our knees almost touched. I looked him in the eyes and rested my hands in my lap. "I'm sorry I was avoiding you. I was just scared of what you'd think, and I was terrified that I might hurt somebody if I couldn't control it."

"Do you think you can control it now?" he asked, and I explained to him about practising with Damion. "Well, that's good."

"Yeah," I said. "We're gonna practise some more in a few hours, after lunch."

"Speaking of food," Xavier said, "the others are probably wondering where we are. And I'm starving."

"Me too," I said, smiling at him. It hadn't been that long, but I'd missed talking to Xavier. "Let's go."

Chapter 26: Practise

So, let's say by five, we meet at weapons?" I asked, stabbing my fork into a couple carrot rounds. All of us sat around one table in the dining area at lunch, squishing our chairs beside each other and overcrowding the square four-seater with our nine plates. All the nearby tables had been taken, so we couldn't even put two together to make room.

"Five?" Ariana asked. She frowned, her shoulders sagging. "That's really early, isn't it?"

"Not really," Damion said. "We want to be about three quarters of the way there by dark, and five will give us a bit of extra time in case something comes up." Everybody other than Ariana mumbled their agreement.

"So, five then?" Thalia asked. She leaned back in her chair and let out a long breath. "Guess I better start sleeping, like now."

"Seriously though," Ariana agreed. She turned to look at me. "You're gonna have fun waking me up." I groaned, stuffing a piece of dark mystery meat into my mouth.

"Sucker," Xavier said, his shoulders rising up with a short laugh. We'd taken turns forcing her to wake up when we first started working at FitHub. He knew the struggle.

"So," Elliot said. "What'll we do till then?"

"Whatever you want," Damion said, glancing around the table. He and I planned to practise my death ability, but I didn't want anyone beside Ariana and Xavier to see that. I wasn't sure I trusted the others to know.

"Just don't go getting high on oranges, and it should be fine," he added. This earned him a couple laughs. I doubted anybody here would be dumb enough to party before the attack tomorrow. We all knew everybody had to be at the top of their game, and nobody was going to risk something this important.

"Sounds good," Elliot said, scooping some food into his mouth.

After lunch, I walked down the halls, stopping in front of the large doors that led out to the main gate.

I pushed them open and breathed in the moist air. It had stopped raining, but grey puddles lined the gravel path to the gate. The wooden fences were a much darker shade of brown. Raindrops rested on tops of the blades of grass on either side of the path, with thick mud underneath them. The sky was a pale bluish-grey, but the clouds had returned to white.

I looked around for Damion, but he wasn't out here yet. Plenty of others were out and about doing a variety of activities, from a couple collecting snails to daycare kids jumping in puddles.

Someone pushed open the doors behind me. I turned around to see my brother just behind me.

"Hey," I said. I raised my eyebrows. "You ready?"

He nodded. "Yeah. Let's go."

We walked down the wet gravel path, thanking the guards on shift when they opened the gate for us. We didn't go too far into the forest, only far enough that we were out of sight of the Base.

"Here's probably good," I said.

We stopped. Different trees surrounded us, some with normal green leaves and some with strange colours that I was sure trees weren't supposed to be. A variety of flowers had sprung up, many of them up to my knees.

"Alright." Damion looked around. "Where d'you wanna start?"

"Let's try this one." I put my fingers against the petals of a flower that grew right next to the tree I stood beside. Its petals were a deep red and opened in a cup shape. A tulip, maybe? I couldn't be sure, and it didn't really matter since I was about to kill it. I wished I could have been with the farmers, helping plants grow rather than destroying them. "I guess I just try and be mad?"

"Guess so," Damion said. He stood back to watch.

I nodded and then turned my attention the plant in front of me. *I hate you,* I thought to the flower. *You're the worst thing that's ever happened to me.* I tried to imagine being mad at the flower, wanting it to die, but it felt ridiculous. The flower was beautiful.

I tried for a few minutes before getting fed up. "I don't think it's working." I rubbed my hands over my face.

"How are you trying to be mad?" Damion asked.

"I dunno. I'm trying to hate it, like I did with the Takers, but..." I sighed.

"But you weren't mad at the flower earlier, were you?" Damion asked. "You were mad at me, and you were mad you couldn't make your power work."

He had a point. "So, maybe I should just think about stuff that makes me mad."

It was worth a try. I pinched the petal in my fingers and concentrated on what the Takers had done to us. Throwing us down here, destroying our lives.

The flower didn't change. I frowned, closed my eyes, and thought harder. I thought of how they took my parents. The woman in that van who tortured me. How they sucked up the resources in a futile attempt to preserve their gluttonous lives for a couple of years longer.

The petal crumbled away in my fingers. I opened my eyes to see almost all of the flower gone, the rest faded.

"Yes!" I pumped my hand up in a fist, grinning. I could control it.

I turned around to face Damion. The corner of his lips twitched up. "Told you."

I rolled my eyes but wrapped him in a hug.

"Thank you," I whispered after a couple seconds.

"Yeah, well," he said, his tone casual. "What're big brothers for, right?"

I stepped back from the hug, looking up at him with admiration. "Yeah."

Damion nodded over to the flowers. "Bet you can't do a whole one," he said, a lopsided, teasing smile on his face.

"Challenge accepted," I said, lifting my chin up.

We kept practising for a little over an hour. I didn't make a lot more progress. I only managed to do one complete flower, and the effort tired me. But a little progress was still great and gave me more and more confidence.

"Now," Damion said, in a tone that suggested I wasn't going to like what came next. "You have to practise mind control."

"For the last time, no." I crossed my arms. I should've known he wasn't just going to take my word that I could do it. "I'm not messing with your brain."

"Renee, I need to know this plan is going to work," he said. He stared into my eyes and gave me his no-nonsense frown. "I need to know you can actually do this."

"I don't even know if there are side effects." I shook my head. "What if this permanently screws up your mind or something?"

"Plenty of people have tried," he said, attempting to lighten the mood. "I'm still fine."

"Forget it. It just wouldn't be right. This would be ten times worse than reading your mind, and you hate that."

I hadn't always had such strict rules about reading friends and family's minds. I'd been eight years old and had developed superpowers, and I'd been pretty excited to try them out, especially on my mysterious older brother.

"We're not little kids any more. We're going into a life-or-death battle tomorrow, and I need to know you can do this."

"I can do it," I assured him, but it was fake. "I don't need to practise." I was risking a lot for all of us by not practising. *I can practise on somebody else,* I thought. *Just not Damion.*

"Then prove it," he said. "Just make me raise my arm."

Like it or not, he wasn't going to let it go, and I doubted strangers would volunteer for me to practise on them. Besides that, he was right. I needed to be sure I could do this tomorrow.

"Raise your arm," I said.

Nothing happened.

"Are you actually trying?" Damion asked.

No, not really. I took a deep breath, and focused.

"Raise your arm." I repeated, and I could feel his willpower conflict with my own.

His arm started to rise. I hated the feeling, like I was a bully, pushing his will aside and putting mine in its place. I tore myself away from his mind, and he dropped his arm.

"That was weird," he said, staring at his arm. He looked back to me. "But I'm fine. See?"

"I'm not doing that again."

"You don't have to," he said. "I'm sorry, I just needed to be sure."

"I know," I said. I understood why he couldn't just let us go into battle not knowing if I could actually do it, but it didn't shake the rotten feeling in my gut.

Even though I hadn't made too much progress with the death ability, and I was still ticked off about having to use the mind control on Damion, I did feel better overall. The powers didn't feel so out of control any more.

Now I just had to worry about the battle that might very well kill us all.

Chapter 27: Prepared

We left early the next morning with extra food and blankets in our packs so we would be at our strongest for the fight. Luckily there was no rain, but when we got far enough and decided to set up for the night, there was still the problem of the soaking wet ground. After we searched awhile for a dry spot and all came up short, Xavier ended up heating up some spaces enough to dry them. There was a small accidental fire, but we put it out quickly.

Sleeping wasn't optional tonight. I had to be strong for the morning, and that would be difficult if I was half asleep. My friends and brother were there, and I was going into battle with all these people in the morning. I had to be able to trust them enough to sleep. Still, it took probably an hour of debating with my mind before I eventually allowed myself to drift off.

~

There was screaming around me as I opened my eyes. The Takers had found us camped out on the ground. They were shooting. Wayne and Thalia were already dead.

"Run!" Ariana screamed. I jumped up and frantically looked for my brother and Xavier. They were running with everybody else, and I felt a slight relief that nothing had happened to them.

The relief was gone in an instant. Aukai and Hamisi dropped where they had been running, eyes open and unblinking. I was running alongside Ariana, and she dropped too. Her head was bleeding, and there was no light in her eyes.

"Ariana!" I shouted. I started to turn around, but my brother dropped next, just ahead of us. "Damion!"

Xavier was almost to the trees. "Run, Xavier!"

It was a mistake, shouting that. He turned around, and the next beam shot straight into his chest. As I ran to him, the lasers somehow never hit me. Blood poured from his chest, and he stared up at me.

"You fell asleep," he said weakly. "We didn't hear them coming."

~

My breathing was heavy when I awoke, and my heartbeat quick. I sat up and gazed around the dark campsite. The light of the fire illuminated seven sleeping forms. Everyone except Xavier. I searched for him but couldn't see him from where I sat.

I got up, desperate for any sign of him. Faint muddy footprints led toward the trees, and I headed that way.

"Xavier?" I called out in almost a whisper. I couldn't really see much as I got farther from the fire, but I didn't really care either.

Xavier?

"Renee?"

Footsteps smacked in the mud, growing closer. I breathed a sigh of relief.

"What's wrong?" Xavier asked.

It was too dark to see, but I could hear that he was in front of me, within arm's reach. I wrapped my arms around him, and he hugged me back for a moment before pulling away slightly.

"I had this dream," I said.

Our voices were hushed, so we wouldn't wake anybody else. He put a small bit of fire in one of his palms. We were still close enough to almost be touching, so I could just barely make out his face in the dim orange light.

I sniffled. "I woke up, and you were gone. I thought..."

"I'm fine," he said. "I just went out to find some more firewood."

"Sorry," I said, feeling a bit silly for worrying so much. "I guess I just panicked a bit."

"I get it," he said, and I knew he did. "Especially with the battle tomorrow."

"Promise me," I said, looking him in the eyes. Streaks of orange light flickered around the chocolate-brown. "Don't die tomorrow, okay?"

"I promise," he said.

But Xavier had always been a risk-taker, and while I loved that about him most of the time, it was worrying me a lot right now. *He's going to do something reckless. He's going to get himself hurt.*

"No heroics," I insisted. "No taking a hit for either of your team members, if it comes to that. Keep yourself safe. Promise?" I liked Aukai and Elliot, but I cared about Xavier more.

It took him a second longer to respond this time. "I promise," he said. "Do you promise?"

I didn't think I could. Ariana and Damion would be with me. "I..."

But I couldn't make him the same promise.

Fire appeared in his illuminated eyes, the same fire he had whenever he was about to do something risky or exciting. He drew me in by the waist and crashed his lips down on mine.

I was too startled to respond. A deep tingling sensation ran through my body. As he went to pull away, I tangled my fingers in his thick, plush hair and returned the kiss. The feeling of his lips on mine spurred a kind of adrenaline high that nothing else could have given me. Goosebumps tickled my skin as he held me closer. I'd been wanting this for so long, and I hadn't even known it.

We moved backwards as we kissed until I was backed up against a tree. A stick cracked under my feet, but I wasn't thinking about being quiet any more. He'd overloaded my brain with new sensations.

It was just us in that moment, unplagued by the outside world.

Until my brother's voice cried out, "Agh! My eyes!"

We immediately jumped apart like we'd been shocked. Damion was holding a large torch, his disbelief and disgust illuminated in orange.

"Any chance it was too dark for you to see that?" Xavier asked.

At least the darkness made it easier to avoid making eye contact with either of them.

"I wish there was," Damion said. Another bonus of the dark, he couldn't see my cheeks, which would have been bright red.

"What are you... What are you doing out here?" I stammered.

"I heard a noise," he said pointedly. He was not the one here with explaining to do. "And you two were gone. I came to see what was going on."

Well, he had succeeded.

An awkward silence blanketed us as Xavier and I went back to our designated sleeping spots, far apart from each other. Damion had decided that he would take over Xavier's watch, which probably had to do with making sure there was no repeat of what had just happened.

I lay back down, my heart pounding. That kiss had been like bliss and hunger and fire. Was that just a "we're gonna die tomorrow" kiss, or did it mean something real for him?

Did it mean something real for me? I couldn't deny that it felt good being close to Xavier, but what about our friendship? How could we risk what we had? I couldn't deal with any more heartbreak.

But I also couldn't help thinking of him differently after what had just happened. I'd only ever let myself think of him like a friend, but now the floodgates were open. He'd tossed everything up into the air.

Did he like me that way? Surely our kiss couldn't have been like that if he didn't, and if I didn't like him too. But then, what did I know? Having fled normal life at fifteen, I didn't exactly have any romantic experience. What if it had been just the heat of the moment? I wanted to be furious with him for risking our friendship, but that feeling...when we touched...I couldn't help but want more of that.

Had he felt it too? That calm ferocity?

My thoughts were racing, as well as my heart. How could I sleep after what had just happened?

I couldn't. But luckily it didn't take long for morning to arrive. As we all got ready, a noticeable awkwardness lingered between Damion, Xavier, and me. Although, it was masked by the unspoken fear of what we were all about to do. The closer we got to the Taker camp, the thicker the fear seemed to be.

The tree in front of the Taker camp was becoming a regular place for me. I rested my fingers against the damp bark. The sun hadn't come up yet, but the lights surrounding the camp were bright enough that I could see the others. The ground was upturned and riddled with puddles. Mud slurped under my feet whenever I moved. The air itself felt dense with moisture, and a light breeze blew across my skin.

I watched intently for the signal, due any second. Behind me, Ariana, Damion, Wayne, and Hamisi also looked out in anticipation.

Whoosh. A tent at the other end of the camp went up in flames.

Several Takers ran out of the tent closest to us, guns ready in their hands. At least seven of them ran away from us, toward the fire. So far, things were going even better than planned. We had assumed more of them would stay to watch the RCC, but it looked like there would only be a couple left for us to deal with. A cluster of Takers had now surrounded the blazing tent.

We didn't have time to waste. I gave the mental signal for us to move forward. We ran into the tent, shielded by Ariana's force field.

The RCC person wasn't there.

And they were waiting.

More than ten Takers fired their lasers at us. More Takers thumped through the mud on their way from nearby tents.

"*Stop shooting!*" I shouted, but there were too many. Only two ceased their fire.

A gun flew across the room and into Hamisi's palm. He, Wayne, Thalia, and Damion tried desperately to take down the Takers who were advancing on us. Wayne jumped half out of the force field to take a shot with his knife. It missed, and a red beam struck him in the shoulder. He fell backwards inside the cover of the force field.

"Wayne!" Hamisi stopped shooting and ducked down beside his boyfriend. The Takers had begun to make us stumble backward.

"I've got Wayne," Damion yelled to Hamisi over the firing. "You shoot." Hamisi did as he was told, and Damion reached a hand down to Wayne.

Ariana's force field flickered. She was sweating and panting heavily. She couldn't keep it up with the constant firing. This was supposed to have been a fast operation.

The Takers shot red beams at Wayne's exposed feet, kicking up chunks of dirt, mud, and grass. He cried out and scrambled back so he was fully covered by the force field.

"Outta knives," Thalia said, giving a panicked shout over all of the noise.

"*Shoot each other*," I tried commanding the Takers. Pinpricks entered my temple as a couple of them complied. It didn't last long. They were gunned down by the other Takers before they could do any more damage.

Damion stood up from healing Wayne just as we were forced to stumble another step backwards.

The force field flickered.

"I can't," Ariana panted. A red beam whizzed past, skimming the arm of my jacket. The protective material burned away, and my skin seared with heat.

More and more Takers were closing in on us.

"What're we gonna do?" Thalia asked, looking around as if she might find some sort of answer.

"*Shoot each other*," I tried again. Sharp pain shot through my head, but it was no use. There were too many Takers for it to do any damage. We were being forced further and further back.

"We have to run," Damion yelled. "It's no good."

None of the attacks had worked, and the knives were spent. We moved backward, going as fast as we could while staying shielded behind the force field.

"We can't." I struggled to stay where I was.

The Takers had been ready. Our friends were supposed to clear out once we told them we had the RCC. We'd never told them.

Our friends had either been caught or killed.

"Renee, we have to go!" Damion took a tight hold of my arm, tugging me backwards. The force field flickered again. His voice and expression were stern. "*Now*."

"We can't leave Xavier!" I tried to jerk my arm out of his grasp. He took my other arm and started to pull me back. "Damion!" My feet skidded on the muddy ground as I tried to hold my place. He stopped trying to drag me for a moment and spun me around to face him.

"They either got out or they're caught. There's nothing we can do right now except get caught ourselves. "Now, *run*."

As I obeyed, beams of red flew past, searing holes in the trees ahead of me. We had to make it to the trees. Sweat stuck to my face and neck. The taste of metal filled my mouth as I ran faster, harder. Bits of my jacket fell off. A laser flew low, searing the skin of my calf raw. I ignored it and pushed on.

The dark forest was our escape. The shots kept coming, forcing us to split up and weave through the trees. My friends were still in sight, barely visible under the dim light of the rising sun. We kept running long after the beams stopped chasing us.

I drank in air and leaned against a tree for support.

Xavier? I called out, panicked. I'd been trying to contact him while we were running, but he hadn't gotten back to me. Seconds went by. *Please. Answer me.*

I looked over at Damion. The fear must have been plain on my face. He came over to me and wrapped me in a tight embrace. I hugged him back, my breathing ragged.

Xavier? Please. Come on. I was almost hyperventilating. He *had* to still be alive.

"Did you try Elliot?" Ariana asked. She looked like she was about to cry. I was ready to cry too.

Alive, Xavier thought.

"Xavier's alive," I breathed, smiling with relief. "He's okay. He answered."

You scared me! Where are you guys?

"Ask where they are," Damion said, pulling out of the hug. He looked behind us as if he might see them already.

Renee... I'm sorry, Xavier thought. *We didn't make it out.*

My face fell in an instant. My shoulders slumped. *No.* The Takers couldn't have him. This couldn't be happening. Not Xavier.

"What's wrong?" Damion asked.

"They didn't make it out." I tried to breathe, but my throat felt like it would close over. The tears were coming now. For me and for Ariana. *No.*

Xavier's next comment delivered a new wave of shock. *They took Elliot and me. I'm in some sort of tent. Aukai...they shot her.*

"What?" I said aloud.

What? I asked him. This wasn't how it was supposed to go. Our plan had been perfect. It wasn't fair.

She's dead, he thought. *They killed her.*

I slid down the tree until I hit the grassy, muddy ground. I rested my arms on my knees. *We're gonna come for you,* I thought. Even my thoughts were shaky. *Are you hurt?*

"Renee, what's he saying?" Ariana asked, coming closer. Her eyes were filled with tears. "Are they all okay?"

I shook my head.

I'm fine, he thought, trying to reassure me. But how could he be if he was with the Takers? Nothing could make me believe it. *I'm fine, just get far away from here.*

"Aukai," I managed to say to those around me. I tried to blink the tears away. I wiped furiously at my eyes with my jacket sleeve. "They killed her."

I hadn't known her well, but she had always been so kind. She had reminded me a little of Ariana personality-wise, which only made it harder. I had seen her living and breathing only this morning, and now she was gone. With a single shot, her life was over.

The reality of the situation slammed me in the chest. Guilt stabbed at me for being relieved that it wasn't Xavier or Elliot.

"What?" Ariana's voice broke.

Damion's jaw set, and he looked away. He would try and be strong, but she had been his friend before I even got to Earth. He shouldn't have to be the strong one. He'd dragged me away from certain death at the camp. It was my turn.

"We have to go home," I said, trying to keep my voice even as I stood up. My tears were dried. I could be upset later. Xavier was alive. Elliot was alive. I had to focus on that for the moment. We couldn't help them if we stayed out here and risked getting caught too. "The Takers could come."

We trudged back to the Base, all too tired to even think about running. Everybody in the Base was under the impression that we had set out to take care of something important, and most of them probably assumed it was a gang. Since people would notice so many guard shifts being changed around, as well as the absence of their leader and only healer, we'd had to tell them something.

When we arrived at the Base, the two guards saw our faces and our diminished numbers and didn't bother ask us how it went.

"I'm sorry," one of them whispered. Somehow, that was harder than if they had just ignored us.

Somehow, it solidified our defeat.

We headed straight for the office room. Our steps were slow and heavy. The hope of winning had drained right out of me. When we'd set out, I'd thought we stood a good chance. But we'd come back without three of our friends.

One of them was dead.

The others could be killed at any moment. How stupid were we thinking we could do this? The Takers had an army and weapons. We were kids with knives and superpowers. We'd been dreaming thinking we could win.

And our friends had paid the price.

Chapter 28: Hopeless

W hat are we gonna do?" Ariana asked, panicked and tearful. "We have to go back. We can't just leave them there."

I leaned against my chair, and my shoulders sagged.

"We can't go back," Wayne protested, his expression and tone alarmed at the idea. He sat up straight in his chair. "They'd just get us too."

"He's right." Hamisi sighed. "It'd be suicide." Thalia mumbled in agreement.

I heard their words, but it didn't matter what they said. Xavier was in the Taker camp. He was probably being hurt. He could be killed. And there was nothing I could do about it. He was suffering and afraid, somewhere far away, and I was powerless. What good were all of these abilities if we couldn't save our friends?

"But, we *have* to do something," Ariana said. "We can't leave them there. The Takers will hurt them. We don't know how long they'll wait before..."

Death.

Xavier and Elliot could be killed in minutes, hours, days, or months. All the while, the Takers would be doing horrible things to them. I knew what was in store for them. I'd gotten a small taste of it before we fell.

The Takers would want information, and they would—they'd probably already begun to—try to get it out of Xavier and Elliot using whatever means necessary. If either one gave up the information the Takers needed, probably our location, they would likely be killed right away. If they didn't, there was no telling how long the Takers would try to get it out of them. With enough time, the Takers could figure out what they needed, even without Xavier or Elliot.

"We wouldn't even have surprise on our side this time," Damion said, pushing a hand through his dark hair.

We hadn't surprised them this last time either. The Takers had been ready; they had known we were coming.

"I can't stand the thought of not doing anything... But I don't think there's anything we can do," Damion added.

"There's always something," Ariana insisted. She moved her chair forward. It grated against the cement floor. "We…we could go at night and wait for the Takers to, like, not be near them." She chewed on her rosy lip and picked at her already chipped nails.

"The Takers will take shifts," Wayne said. He raised his brownish-red eyebrows. "Even we do that."

"Well, we can do something else," Ariana said. Her violet eyes were glazed, and she tripped on her words a little. "Anything."

I had been just watching everybody else, digging the nail of my middle finger into my thumb to create a crescent-moon indent and keeping my mouth firmly shut. I clenched my jaw because I was afraid I would cry. Ariana turned to me. "Renee, tell them. We have to...to make a plan. Do *something*." Her eyes met mine, pleading with me.

"Look where our plan got us," I murmured.

We'd thought our plan was perfect. It had sounded perfect. And what did we have to show for it? One of our friends was dead. Two of them were probably wishing they were. It was my fault. I couldn't be responsible for losing anyone else.

This seemed to be the last straw for Ariana. A fresh stream of tears escaped from her eyes. "So we just sit here?" Ariana raised her voice. She sniffed, and her stammering got worse. "We just leave our friends to be hurt and sit here, waiting until the Takers come for us or take everything?"

"Ariana," Damion said, turning his chair to face her. "We either wait here, or we die out there."

"You don't know that." She shook her head. "You're all just too afraid to try. Well, I bet Xavier and Elliot are scared."

I'd told Xavier we would come for him. I wanted to go for him, but what would be the point? It didn't matter how carefully we planned, and the Takers were expecting us now. Going anywhere near that camp would just be slaughter.

"It's not that we don't wanna try," Hamisi said. He'd slumped his bulky frame in the small chair, his hands hanging over the armrests. "But there's just nothin' we could do to help 'em."

"We thought there was nothing we could do to stop the Takers," Ariana claimed.

"And there wasn't," I said.

They always won in the end.

"And are you gonna tell *him* that?" Ariana's voice had a sharp edge to it, like she was trying to slice into me with her words. She leaned forward. "Are you gonna sit here, safe, and tell

Xavier you're not coming because you don't think there's anything you can do? Are you really going to tell him that you're not even gonna try while he's there being hurt? We came for you, y'know."

When I stood up, my chair slid backwards until it hit the wall.

I strode out of the room, wiping away the tears before they could even leave my eyes. I hadn't talked to Xavier since we were in the forest because Ariana was right. How could I tell him we were leaving them to the Takers? That there was no hope to hold onto? My pace turned into a run. I wasn't sure where I was running to. I just needed to be alone.

I ended up peering through the thin, blurred windows of the sickrooms. I found an empty one and locked the metal door behind me. I slid down it, pressing my knees tightly against my chest. My breathing hiccupped as I tried to brush away the tears. What right did I have to be crying right now? My friends were being tortured.

It was my fault.

I was here, safe. Xavier wasn't. Elliot wasn't. And I wasn't doing a thing to help them.

I could faintly hear my brother calling me from the hall, but I ignored him. I didn't want him to make me feel better. I didn't want him to convince me it wasn't my fault or that I shouldn't feel like a terrible friend for not trying to go back. Because it was and I should.

The door handle clicked as it failed to open. *Knock. Knock. Knock. Knock.* A fist rapped on the metal.

"Come on," Damion said. I looked up to see him staring down at me through the window, only a single charcoal eye, some dark tufts of hair, and his nose visible through the small window. "Let me in."

I sighed and picked myself up off the tile floor, reluctantly twisting the silver handle to unlock the door. Damion pushed it open and stepped inside. "Hey." He let the door fall closed behind him.

"Hey." I sat back down. He joined me, pulling his knees up, as I did, and loosely flopping his arms overtop them. We were quiet for a couple minutes.

"If you're gonna try and make me feel alright about staying here, you shouldn't bother," I said.

"Good thing I'm not then." *He isn't?* I turned to him. "I'm going to talk to the guards," he said.

"What?"

The Takers had much bigger numbers now, at least forty, and they could send more down at any time. How could we hope to beat them or even convince the guards to try?

"It would be a long shot." Damion nodded "But I think Ariana was right. We can't just sit here."

"You think we could do it?"

I was not going to let myself hope. I'd had hope for the Base, hope that I was done losing people and that I could protect them. I was stupid. The Takers were always going to be stronger. They were always going to ruin any life we pieced together. How could we win now, even if the guards agreed? We didn't have the numbers, the weapons, or the element of surprise on our side.

"I don't know." Damion leaned back his head on the grey door, letting his long eyelashes rest on the skin of his sharp cheekbones. "But we have to try."

"What if they get you too? What if they get Ari?" I asked. "They already have Xavier...I can't risk losing you too."

"We're at risk as long as the Takers are nearby. As long as they have those RCCs," Damion said. "None of us will make it long if we don't stop them."

If we fought, I risked losing Damion and Ariana sooner, but if we beat the Takers, I wouldn't have to lose them at all. I wouldn't have to lose Xavier. I didn't think I *could* lose Xavier.

I'd had enough loss in my life, and I didn't think I could stand to lose anybody else. I needed to get Xavier back, or I needed to die trying.

"Did you talk to the others?" I asked, sitting up straighter. "They'll do it?"

"Yeah." He nodded. "You're in?"

"I think I have to be," I said after a moment. I got up off the ground again. "Can we go talk to the guards now?"

"Sure," he said. "Don't see why not."

I offered him my hand and pulled him up. We walked quickly to the training area after I had called all the guards to meet there. I made sure to tell them it was urgent. I didn't want to waste a minute.

I waited at the side of the training area, just in front of the weapons racks, fiddling with the handle of a knife hung on a lower ring. The guards' feet seemed to be slabs of cement, but they arrived eventually. I nodded to Damion beside me, signaling him to start.

"So, we've got some information for you." Damion paused. "As you know, the river disappeared a while ago. The Takers were behind it, and they're going to keep stealing more. We've discovered they have a camp only a day's walk from here."

Everybody had wide eyes, and people whispered to each other in shocked tones.

"This meeting's off to a feel-good start," somebody muttered.

"But we've found out how to stop them," Damion continued. "There are chips that control the teleport, which is taking everything. If we get the chip, they can't take anything else. And we need to get rid of this camp because it's too close to us. If we don't attack them, they might attack us."

"And you think we can actually stop them?" a boy, Ruben, asked.

If Damion straight up said yes, most people would probably go along with it. The people here respected him, and he was basically their leader. "There's a chance," he said.

"And we need to take it," I spoke up. "They have two of our friends, Xavier and Elliot. They've just murdered another. If we don't stop them soon, it'll only get worse."

"Well, how much of a chance do we have?" a man, who looked to be in his thirties, asked.

"What would we have to do?" a girl asked, raising her hand like a child in school.

"We would have to attack their camp," Damion said. "Win against their army and get the chip."

One of three chips that we need. But I didn't add that little tidbit.

"Army?" somebody asked. "How big of an army are you talking?"

"We can't know for certain," I said. "There are at least forty, but it's possible they could bring more down."

I took a deep breath as the outbursts started in the crowd.

"Forty at least? With their weapons?" somebody asked, stunned. "Well, we're dead. "That's suicide!" another exclaimed among many shocked, angry, and frightened responses.

I was starting to think it wasn't a good idea to even confirm that the Takers were here. What if we'd started a mass panic?

"We know the numbers aren't the greatest." Damion leveled with the crowd. "But we need to eliminate such a close threat. We have training—"

"Right," the man from earlier said, his arms crossed. "Because training will help us not die when we're shot with their *guns.*"

People agreed, raising their voices again.

"Yeah," somebody shouted. "How the hell can you even ask us that?"

"This has to be a joke..." a girl muttered nearby.

I wished it were a joke. "We might not have guns, but we do have abilities. We could plan, play to our strengths," I said, not letting my tone betray how desperate I felt. "They've got our friends, and they're gonna keep taking everything. Not to mention, they could attack us at any moment. We need to take the chance."

"It doesn't matter if they take everything if we're all dead," somebody said. "We had abilities on Mozaan and look what happened."

"You can't think we'll let a lot of us die to fail at getting two people." A woman shook her head. "It's cranked."

"It's not just about two people," Damion said. "This is about all of us. The whole Base is at risk the longer we let their camp stay there." This didn't seem to sway too many people.

Out of ninety guards, only about twenty stayed behind. Five more left once they realized how few people were fighting. They walked away, back to their shifts. Fifteen wasn't going to be enough to beat all of those Takers.

Gray, who I hadn't known was a guard, had stayed behind too. "Hey," he said to Damion and me. We turned around to face him. He pushed his light-brown hair to the left side of his head.

"What is it?" I wasn't in the mood for his flirting and jokes. Damion wouldn't attack with only fifteen extra guards. They were right. It *was* a suicide mission. I might have been fine with that, but I couldn't ask everybody else to be.

"I just wanted to let you know," he said, no cheesy or suggestive smile plastered onto his face, "that I'll help. Whatever you guys need me to do."

"Thanks," Damion said, his tone sincere.

"Yeah, thank you." I nodded. "That means a lot." Even though knew we would likely never take him up on it. Without enough guards on board, we had nothing...again.

"So, they're alright?" Gray asked, his ocean-blue eyes sparkling with concern. "Elliot and Xavier?"

"For now." I had no idea when it would stop being true. I had planned on talking to Xavier once the guards agreed. Now, I would have no good news to give him, no real hope.

"And who..." Gray paused, pressing his lips together. "Who died?"

"Aukai," Damion said. There was loss buried deep under those two syllables.

"No," Gray said. He looked at Damion, his eyes wide and sympathetic. "I'm sorry."

"Thanks." Damion turned to the other guards. "I appreciate you volunteering, but I just don't think we have enough guards to attack. I'll let you know if we do decide to act, but for now, try not to panic anybody, alright?"

The guards agreed.

"Should we just go back to our shifts?" a girl asked.

"Yes," Damion said, dejected. "Shifts as usual."

The guards all started shuffling out, still murmuring among themselves.

"I guess I should go back to my shift," Gray said after a moment of uncomfortable silence. "But if you need anything, let me know."

I was expecting a wink. There wasn't one. "Yeah, we will," I said.

Gray turned with a little wave and walked back to his shift.

I looked down at Damion's watch. 11:27 p.m. "Oh," I said. "It's late."

"Is it?" Damion looked down at his watch. He arched his eyebrow. "Oh."

I sighed. "I'll tell the others about the guards."

"Yeah." Damion nodded. His shoulders slumped. "You should."

I thought to the others, telling them we didn't have enough guards to do anything. I bet Wayne was relieved. He barely seemed to want to fight at all. He only seemed to be fighting with us for Hamisi.

"What are we gonna do?" I asked my brother.

He shook his head. "I don't know."

We started to walk out of the training area, though neither of us knew exactly where we intended to go. We aimlessly and soberly walked through the halls in silence. I broke it.

"Do you wanna talk?" I asked. "About Aukai?"

Damion pretended to be confused. "Why?" He looked away from me. "I'm fine."

"Damion," I said, in a "who do you think you're kidding" voice. He looked at me, and I changed my tone to a softer one. "I know you guys were friends."

"It's fine," Damion said, looking ahead once more.

"You have the right to be sad, y'know." He never put his feelings first. He'd been like that when we were younger, but now that he was responsible for the whole Base, he was even more so.

"I'm not," he said. His voice was firm. "It sucks, but it happened. I'm fine."

I sighed. This wasn't going anywhere. I would have to try again later.

"Fine." I rolled my eyes. Why wouldn't he let *me* help *him* for once in his life?

"We should get some food," Damion said. We turned the corner leading to the dining area. "We haven't eaten since the battle."

"I'm alright." Knots of worry tightened in my stomach, and eating would only make that sickness real. "Maybe I'll just go train."

I was exhausted, but I needed to be doing something. It wasn't likely I would sleep anyway.

"You should really eat something," he said. I appreciated his concerned for me even, especially since he'd just lost a friend.

"Later," I said. "You go."

"Compromise," he told me. "Get some water."

"Fine," I grumbled. I followed him into the dining area, which had hardly anybody in it.

After drinking a bit of water, I separated from Damion and walked to the entirely empty training area.

I grabbed new knives from the rack. All except one of mine had been left at the Taker camp. I walked over to the target boards and stepped onto the squishy dark-blue mat. I took out one of the throwing knives—lightweight, with sharp silver edges.

I secured my fingers along the handle, lining up my middle finger with where the blade began. I lifted my hand over my shoulder, stepped, and brought my arm forward at high speed, sending the knife cutting through the air with the jerk of my wrist. The sound of it stabbing into the wooden target seemed to echo through the room. I took out another knife, repeating the action with great speed and force. I kept going until my belt ran out, and then I walked over to the target to snatch out my blades.

Throw after throw, I kept on going. I had already been exhausted from the battle, but I kept on attacking the target board. I was sweating through the shirt under my gear. Sometime during my throws, hot water began streaming from my eyes onto my cheeks. I threw the knives harder, sloppier. With each miss, my frustration increased, but I threw harder still.

The Takers have him. I threw another blade, whipping it across to the target. It hit the leg. I took another knife from my belt. *I can't do anything.* I threw, sending it deep into the other leg of the target. *It's all my fault. I thought it was over.* I sent yet another blade spiraling into a low position on the board. I quickly reached for another blade, but my belt was empty.

My shoulders slumped and my hands hung at my sides in defeat. No amount of horrible knife throwing was going to change the fact that Xavier was gone, and I couldn't help him. I could imagine the Takers at the target board all I wanted, but they remained somewhere, kilometres away, hurting my friends.

Xavier. He had been gone less than a day, and I already missed him with an ache.

If I could have gone back to the morning, I would have wrapped my arms around him tightly and never let him go. But I couldn't. I would probably never get to see his dark chocolate eyes or his contagious grin again. And I hadn't even talked to him much in the morning before the battle. I was too awkward, too worried, because when we'd kissed, I'd felt something new. I should have talked to him. Had I even hugged him before the battle? I couldn't remember.

He's always been there for me. And now, I'm just letting him down.

I moved with slow, numb movements and took out my knives from the target. I slipped them back into my belt. It was time I went to bed. I was so worn out I thought I might tip over any minute.

I walked back through the halls until I reached the sleeping quarters. I sat on the cot, my shoulders and arms sagging down. Too tired to move, I didn't want to reach all the way up onto my shelf for my pyjamas and change, but I forced myself to anyway.

The whole room smelled like old socks. Or maybe that was just me.

Ariana came into the quarters and sat down beside me on the cot. "I'm sorry the guards didn't take it well." She met my eyes, giving me a small smile. Her eyes were red and puffy from crying. "And I'm sorry about what I said, about you not trying. I know you're just trying to be, like, smart about all this."

"Thanks." I didn't want to be smart about it. I wanted to rush in there and save the day against all odds. I had briefly considered going in alone, but I was worried that the Takers wouldn't shoot to kill.

"Hey," Ariana said. She must have noticed how deflated I looked. "This might not be it. We could find something else."

Something else. There has to be something...

"Ah," I hissed. Ariana's calf had accidentally brushed mine. Pain, like a thousand tiny needles, sliced through my burned leg.

"Whoa." Ariana's eyes went wide. "What happened?"

I stared at her. "Oh, you know," I said, rolling my eyes. My tone was sharper than necessary. "Just burned it at the campfire roasting marshmallows. What d'you think?"

"Well, why didn't you tell Damion?" she asked, peering to see the burn. "Looks pretty bad."

"We were a bit busy. And it's fine."

She shook her head. "No," she said, with the authoritative tone of a mother. "You're gonna get that healed."

"Really?" I raised my eyebrows.

"Yeah." She folded her arms over her chest. "Don't you know that you could get a bagillion infections from an open burn like that? And why wouldn't you want it healed?"

"I forgot about it." I shrugged. "And I'm tired. I'm not gonna go look for my brother."

"Promise you'll get him to fix it up in the morning?" she asked, tilting her head slightly.

I sighed. There was no point in arguing. It *did* hurt.

"Yeah." I yawned. "Sure."

"Good," she said.

"Alright." I looked from the bed to her. "Well, I'm gonna sleep now before I pass out, so..."

"Right." Ariana shook her head and got up. How did she have so much energy? Maybe Ariana had found coffee somewhere in the kitchen.

Thalia was already out cold on the other side of the room, and hopefully the exhaustion would be enough to let me sleep.

"Night then," she said as she walked the few feet over to her own cot.

I lay down on my own, careful to prevent the scratchy blanket having any contact with my burn. "Night," I said. My head crashed down onto the pillow. I checked with my brother. At least he was fine.

I was exhausted, but I couldn't sleep.

How could I sleep? *Xavier might not get to sleep at all tonight. He's surrounded by people that want to hurt him.* Would tonight be Xavier's last? How long would the Takers keep him alive before they got impatient? His bed was empty, and he was probably strung up somewhere with pain pumping through his body.

I needed to know if he was alright. He was much farther that what I could easily reach with my mind, but I'd been able to communicate over larger distances before if I really pushed myself. And lately, it seemed like I was getting stronger.

Xavier? I called out to him.

Several heartbeats later, and with much apparent effort, his response came. *Yeah...*

He must have been in the pain-cuffs, which I remembered well. They made thinking a challenge, let alone thinking to someone else. *Alive.*

I took a deep breath. I closed my eyes to focus better. *Are you hurt?* I asked, though I knew what his answer would be.

Yeah.

This time, my breath caught in anticipation. *How bad?* Was he already as bad as I had been after the car ride?

S'bad, he replied. I didn't even know you could slur in telepathy. It must have been horrible if he couldn't focus on whole words. *Electricity.*

I pressed my lips together. Electricity was agonizing and took away all control. I knew. I couldn't bear the thought of Xavier going through that for the hours they had him. *Oh, god,* I thought to him. *Xavier, I'm so sorry.* If only it could have been me in his place.

They've...stopped now.

And how are you... I paused, looking for the right words. *Holding up?* My head had started to ache a bit, but I pressed on.

He was silent for a while. Just as I started to worry, he responded, *Honest? Crappy.*

My heart lurched. Xavier could take a lot, and if he was already doing badly... How long would he be able to take it? How long would Elliot?

Just keep holding on, okay? I told him.

But what was he holding on for? We had no chance of getting them out.

I will, Xavier thought.

There was no waver in his tone. He kept his promises, and he had promised me he wouldn't die. I had to hold onto that.

Xavier... I couldn't lie to him. *I'm trying, but...I don't know what to do.*

He was quiet again, this time for longer. *Don't...risk yourself.*

Weren't all of us at risk by not doing anything to stop the Takers? They would probably attack soon now that they saw us as a threat. Even if they didn't, they would still take everything from Earth, slowly killing us off. *I can't—I won't—leave you there.*

I became sure as I thought to him. I was going to do something, even if I didn't know what yet. *I will find another way. There has to be something else. Xavier, I...*

I had no idea how I was going to do it, but I wasn't going to sit back while the Takers continued to destroy everything I loved. *Promise,* I thought to him.

My dad had said to make my own happiness. Maybe the best I could hope for was knowing I'd done my best for the people I loved, that I'd fought for *their* happiness.

I couldn't let my hopelessness consume me because I still had people to fight for.

They're...looking...Base, Xavier thought to me, after several seconds had passed. *They'll find...eventually.*

Once they found us, they wouldn't need to keep Elliot and him alive. Depending on their progress, the Takers might decide they didn't need our friends even sooner.

We'll just have to think fast then, eh? I tried to sound confident, and I thought I did an alright job.

In reality, my hands shook against the fabric of my blanket. I had to do something. I had no idea what. But it had to be something quick. *Could you tell them we're somewhere else?* I asked, really straining now. *Maybe they'd leave you alone a bit, even send some of them looking, which would give us a better chance to—*

He cut me off. *No. Can't.*

What do you mean? I asked. *Did they... Are you too hurt to talk?*

He took a few seconds to respond. *No. I...I'm scared. They...find out... They'll kill me. I... No, I can't.*

I hated this. That he was there, afraid he would die. And I wasn't there to stop it. *It's okay,* I thought to him. *It's okay. We'll figure it out.*

Promise, he thought, giving me pause. *Don't...ask Elliot. They'll... kill us.*

I promise, I thought, feeling a pinprick in my temple. *Just keep hanging on, okay?* There was silence. *Xavier?* I thought, after a few moments with no reply.

I received nothing else.

If there was any hope of some sort of rescue, we would want the least amount of Takers there as possible. Lying about where the Base was might have been the perfect distraction, but a rescue would be for nothing if Elliot and Xavier were killed.

With my gaze staring up into the solid black paint that coated everything in sight, I thought about the battle, Xavier and

Elliot, being tortured by the Takers, and the guards' reactions to our proposal. About how everything had seemed hopeless afterwards.

Then I thought of Gray. He had offered to help.

He had X-ray vision.

An idea propelled me up off the bed into a sitting position.

I was a relatively stupid—and crazy—idea.

But it was an idea.

Chapter 29: Sentenced to Naptime

I swung my legs over the edge. I reached under the cot, grabbed my shoes, and brought them up onto the bed, not caring that they were slick with mud. I took the socks out and slipped them onto my cold feet. I pulled my shoes on next, yanking the laces as tight as they would go, then stood up.

I went over to Ariana's cot, careful that my steps weren't too loud. I gave her a gentle shake on the shoulder. "Ari," I whispered. "Ari, get up."

She responded with a deep, loud snore.

I should've known better. I shook her a little harder. "Ariana."

She snored again and pulled her beige blanket over her shoulder. The movement revealed fresh tear stains on her pillow. My heart sank. But it also made me that much more determined to make my idea work.

I shook my head. I should let her sleep. Besides, there was no waking up Ariana in the middle of the night when I could barely wake her up in the morning. I didn't want to wake the other girls either. I abandoned Ariana's cot and crept out of the sleeping quarters.

I rubbed my eyes at the bright light of the hallway, blinking rapidly until they adjusted. I strode at a brisk pace, nearly running, until I got to the office room.

I curled my fingers around the long silver handle, the metal cool against my skin. The door creaked open, and I slipped inside the dark room, taking great care to ensure the door closed without a sound. I fumbled along the wall for the light button. When I found it, I pressed my thumb in and flooded the room with light.

I opened the small cupboard at the back of the room and took out a couple sheets of paper and a pen. I sat at the table. My movements were furious and quick as I rushed to scribble down my ideas before I forgot anything. I even came up with some new ones.

I sat there all night, until my eyes strained to see the paper and my head threatened to fall down onto the table. I was *not* going to let Xavier down. We would get him and Elliot out alive and get the first RCC in the process.

I blinked, the tiredness almost overwhelming me, and stared at the paper. All my ideas were down. They were crazy, but they had a better chance of working than sitting at the Base doing nothing.

Morning, I thought to Ariana. It was probably late enough into the morning that I could wake her up now.

Ariana's thoughts grumbled at me. *Where are you?*

I rolled my eyes. She probably thought I had done something stupid without her. *Office,* I thought, sitting back in my chair and closing my dry eyes for a few seconds. *Tried to wake you up. Come.*

Ariana walked in a few moments later, looking right at the scattered papers. Her eyes widened. "Have you been here *all* night?" she asked, taking in my pyjamas and probably baggy eyes. "What is all this?" She picked up a paper, turning it over in her hands.

"A plan." I looked up at her, hopeful. "It's cranked, I know, but I think we should try it. We have to." As she examined the paper, I handed her the other two that went with it, then sat back. "Can't finish the drawing until we have the locations, but other than that, it's all done."

"I'm in, obviously," she said, putting the plans down. "But this couldn't've, like, waited till morning?"

"I didn't wanna forget what I thought of," I said, crossing my arms. "Besides, we can't waste any time."

"You look like something the hunters killed in the forest," she said as she shook her head.

I yawned and blinked my dry eyelids. "Thanks," I said sarcastically. "Love you too."

She laughed and shook her head again, bringing her long, black hair along for the ride. "You're wearing PJs and sneakers," she pointed out disapprovingly.

I looked down at my outfit, then back at her. "I didn't even notice," I admitted. A smile snuck onto my face. Guilt immediately creeped up on me, reminding me how urgent this was. "But really, there's no time to waste. I'm gonna call the others. And Gray, obviously."

Everyone arrived not much later with confused looks on their faces.

"What's all this about?" Hamisi asked, scratching the back of his head.

"News?" Damion asked as everyone took their seats—except Gray, who leaned against the wall. There was a certain well-masked defeat in his tone.

"An idea." I passed the papers up to him. If he wasn't letting me help with having lost Aukai, then at least I could give him hope for Xavier and Elliot. "It could work, if things go right."

"When do things go right?" Wayne asked under his breath. I ignored him.

Damion passed the papers to Hamisi and turned to me. "Did you make all of these this morning?" he asked, scrunching his eyebrows in confusion.

"Sorta," I said, shrugging. "Yeah."

Ariana rolled her eyes. Hamisi passed the papers to Wayne, telling him something I didn't catch.

"She was up all night," Ariana told Damion. She gestured to my pyjamas. "She didn't even change into her gear before, like, rushing out here."

Wayne passed the sheets to Gray without saying a word. Maybe Hamisi had asked him to be nice.

"Seriously?" Damion sighed. "Can't take you anywhere."

"I think they look fab on you." Gray smiled at me.

"Read," Damion ordered him, arms crossed.

"Aw, don't be jealous." Gray grinned, looking him up and down. "You look hot too. Love the whole brooding bad boy look."

Damion rolled his eyes and turned to me. "I think we can do it."

He was putting a wall up, trying not to get his hopes up. I understood. We'd been hopeful last time.

Gray slid the papers slowly across the table to Thalia.

Thalia looked over them, and there was some more whispering between Hamisi and Wayne.

"I'm for it," Thalia said, nodding. She slid the papers back into the center of the table.

"We're in," Wayne said plainly.

I already knew Ariana was in.

"Gray?" I asked. Gray's agreement would determine if we could do the plan at all.

"Course," Gray answered. "They're our friends." He said it that simply, like it was obvious. My respect for him grew tenfold.

Inside, I was bursting with eagerness. It was happening. We were going to get them back. It had only been a day, but I felt like it had been months. I missed Xavier terribly. When we got him back to the Base, I wasn't going to let myself be afraid about all those new feelings. Maybe it was risky, but if I never took any risks, I wouldn't really be living, even if we did survive. Besides, we were about to take much bigger risks.

"I'll check with Xavier and Elliot," I said. "Just give me a sec."

I leaned back in my chair and closed my eyes to focus. *Xavier?* I called to him.

A few seconds later, he replied, *Alive.*

We're coming for you. But I need to know... Will you be able to walk? It would be much harder to sneak them out if they couldn't. We would likely need them to run.

He hesitated, then thought, *Yeah. What's...plan?*

I filled him in on the details. It was a heavy strain on my mind, and I could tell the conversation was taking a lot out of him too. His words were jumbled and slow. He would need to save his energy for the rescue.

I'll talk to you soon, I thought to him. *Just hold on.*

"Xavier's alive and can walk." I told the room, then got in contact with Elliot. His response was somewhat the same. "Elliot too."

"So, what do we do now?" Ariana asked.

We wouldn't be able to leave for a few hours. Damion still had to get together the guards who had volunteered, and by the time we got all packed, it would probably be around noon.

"We—"

I was about to suggest we eat and train when Damion cut me off.

"You get some sleep," he said, looking directly at me. "It's a good plan, but you'll need your rest. We'll all eat and gear up before we go. We're as trained as we're gonna be."

"Yes, sir." I mock saluted him. I didn't feel tired any more though. If anything, I felt more alert. And who was he to sentence me to naptime?

But after Damion healed the burn on my leg, I did as I was told for once and went to bed. I didn't want to fight with him and Ariana about it. I'd thought anticipation would make it hard to sleep, but I was wrong. As soon as I did my checks and lay down, I was out cold.

Chapter 30: Mission Impossible

R enee, have you heard anything yet?" Ariana asked, biting down on her glossed lip. The worry was plain on her face. I'd been trying to get in contact with Xavier and Elliot for a while now. We were in the training area getting ready to leave.

"No," I said, shaking my head. "Nothing." My insides were knotted with fear. Would we get there only to find them gone?

"When was the last time you talked?" Ariana asked, her words picking up pace. "Because the last time you mentioned was, like, when we made the plan."

"Yeah," I said, downcast. I retightened my weapon belt just to keep my hands busy. It was heavier now with a Taker's gun hanging down from it. Hamisi had saved the one from our first attack, and I needed it for my part of the plan. Gray would be paired with me, and between the two of us, I was the better shot.

While we were waiting for the others to gear up, we'd thought it would be a good idea to contact Xavier and Elliot. Now I was full of anxiety. *What if we're too late?* Any doubts I'd had that this plan would work deflated, filling me with images of Xavier and Elliot dead and everyone else dying on the mission.

"Probably saving energy," Ariana said. I wasn't sure who she was trying to convince. Xavier and Elliot wouldn't leave us wondering like that unless they physically couldn't respond.

"We're ready," Damion called. He and everyone else jogged to meet us at the doors.

I took a deep breath. "Let's go."

Since we'd left later than we'd planned, we only ended up getting a quarter of the way there before dark. Having such a large group certainly didn't help with speed. We had to make camp for the night.

I hated it. How could we stay and rest when we didn't even know if our friends were alive. And if they were alive, something bad was probably happening to them every second we wasted. But as much as I wished we could just keep going until we got there, I knew we would need our strength. Walking for hours upon hours without a break would drain us.

As I lay there, alone with my thoughts and trying to sleep, the confidence I'd felt when we left started to peel away. *What if we're too late? What if something goes wrong and I lose Damion or Ariana?* This was *my* plan. If something happened...

I turned over onto my side and shut my eyes tighter. The plan *wasn't* going to work if I was too busy worrying and didn't get any sleep. I drifted off a little while later.

After breakfast the next morning, we got our packs ready and left. Everyone was quiet now.

It was several hours later, and the sky was liquid tar by the time we could see the Taker camp. We were lucky we had a guard with night vision to help guide us. We moved carefully, trying not to let the mud slurp under our feet as we approached the edge of the camp.

"Thalia, Gray," Damion whispered. "Which tents?"

"That one." Gray pointed to a tent in the center of the camp, confirming it was the one with the RCC. We'd had a feeling it would be in the center, but it sucked nonetheless. We would have to get past a lot of tents—a lot of Takers.

"Thalia?" I asked. Her ability to track people came in handy.

"That's Elliot." She pointed towards the back of the camp. There were only a few tents between it and the forest. She pointed to another. "That's Xavier." This one was a few to the left of the other.

We split into our groups but didn't leave for our positions yet.

"You guys ready?" Ariana asked.

"There's no turning back once we're in," Damion warned.

Everyone confirmed we were ready, even if we weren't really. Could anyone ever truly be ready for a mission like this one?

There looked to be around thirty Takers on guard, which meant their numbers had probably increased since the last battle. Each of our groups moved to strategic positions along the forest line, where we could see guarding Takers but they couldn't see us. Gray and I were on a diagonal from the RCC tent, Thalia opposite from us, Damion and Hamisi in between Xavier's and Elliot's tents, Ariana on the left of the camp, and Wayne on the right. The other guards had positions all around the camp, ready to take out the Takers in front of them too.

Now, I thought.

We all made our moves at once. I lifted the silenced gun and fired into a pair of Takers' heads. I ignored the rotten feeling in my stomach as they fell to the ground. *For Xavier and Elliot,* I repeated the mantra as I shot. The rest of my team used knives and swords.

We didn't wait to start the next phase. Speed was our only ally. Gray and I ran past the tents of the sleeping Takers to the one with the RCC inside.

Scan, I thought to Gray, and he nodded.

He peered into the tent with his X-ray vision. *Shoot fast. Three guards are awake.*

He pointed to one spot on the canvas tent and made sure my gun was angled correctly. I shot. He moved quickly to point at another spot. I shot. Another. I shot. *Good*, he thought. *The RCC Taker is in the very back.*

It didn't feel good. Nothing like the epic avenging kills I had completed on VirtReel's alien games.

I'll cover you outside, Gray thought.

I crept into the tent. I looked through my snoring enemies, and my dead enemies, and found the sleeping man with the RCC in his brain. I tiptoed across the tarp floor, wincing at every crinkle it made underneath my feet.

A woman turned over. I held my breath, staying still for a few seconds.

She didn't move again.

Finally, I'd made the rest of what seemed like an impossibly long journey, though it was only about ten feet. I crouched down beside the RCC man, leaning close enough to his ear that the others wouldn't hear me. The smell of fruity shampoo filled my nose.

"Don't make a sound," I whispered, summoning my mental strength. *"Get up quietly, and don't try to signal anyone for help."*

The man's dark eyes opened wide. He sat up. His mind pulled against mine. After a moment, he stood. The tarp crinkled under his weight. I rapidly scanned the room to make sure nobody had stirred from the sound. The man opened his mouth but pressed his hands against it. He mouthed some words that I couldn't decipher in the dark.

"*Follow me closely, and make no move toward the others.*" We left the tent, joining Gray outside.

The three of us began to head toward the line of trees.

We didn't get very far.

A shrill scream erupted from the front of the camp—right where we were heading. Takers had already started to spill out from their tents.

Chapter 31:
Murphy's Law

I smacked my feet down against the mud, putting them one after the other. *Meet at the back*, I thought to everybody. My heart was a hummingbird pecking into my chest. The Takers had already started in our direction—they'd obviously figured out our targets—and streams of red cut through the air. Some lasers whizzed over our heads, some blew chunks of mud up around our feet, and some managed to skim our jackets.

"*Keep running!*" I barked at the RCC Taker, who had begun to slow down beside us. He sped up but still failed to match us.

Taker tents surrounded us, forcing us to weave between them as we raced to the treeline. More and more Takers poured out of their tents toward the front of the camp, joining in on the chase. Too many to count. Definitely too many for the twenty-five of us to take on. It was escape or die.

Gray and I—and our captive—were almost to the back of the camp, not daring to look behind us at the oncoming Takers. We had to get past a few more rows of tents and then as far into the forest as possible. There weren't many Takers pouring out near the back yet. Most headed to the front. Damion and Hamisi should have freed Xavier and Elliot by now, which meant they too just needed to get past some tents at the back. We could all make it if the Takers on this side of the camp didn't wake up too soon.

"Almost there," Gray panted.

Dark outlines of trees grew closer and larger. Damion, Hamisi, Xavier, and Elliot were just getting out of their respective tents. They weren't far from Gray and me. They weren't moving fast either.

"We can make it," Ariana said, now sprinting alongside us with a couple other guards. Fierce determination was on her sweaty face. We were approaching the last row of tents.

I looked behind us, where our friends—now including Thalia and Wayne—struggled to move faster. Xavier had an arm slung over Damion for support, and Hamisi seemed to be helping Elliot walk telekinetically. Thalia and Wayne covered them from the behind.

An alarm wailed throughout the camp. It was loud enough to drown out all of the yelling, running, and shooting. Loud enough to wake the rest of Takers within the seconds it took for one of our guards to destroy it with electricity.

The Takers flooded out from all directions. There must have been almost fifty coming up behind us, and at least thirty poured out from the tents we had yet to pass.

"Faster!" I yelled. The RCC person ran with us, only a foot or so behind me.

A beam came straight for my head. I ducked. The red light flashed in my eyes as it barely missed me. I brought my head back up, blinking rapidly. I couldn't see properly.

I tried to keep running, but I slipped forward. My knees and hands met cold, muddy water, which splashed fat droplets onto my chin and face. A laser shot into the puddle I had fallen in, and I scrambled to pull myself up. Another beam flew by, singeing off some of my hair.

"Renee!" Ariana ran toward me. She dodged the lasers like it was rehearsed choreography. She gave me her hand and helped yank me out of the slippery mud puddle.

"Thanks," I breathed as we started running again. There was more fire every second. And now the fire wasn't just from behind. Takers were rushing at us from all directions. I lost sight of our friends.

Ariana threw up her force field, shielding those of us in the front.

"Take some shots." Gray gestured to the gun I had forgotten I had. The couple of other guards with us were already shooting, using guns they must have found during the fight. "Hurry."

I shot from the edge of the force field, and we kept trying to push through.

We reached the last row of tents. The forest was only about twenty feet away. We only had to make it past the thirty or so Takers who were shooting at us and avoid getting shot from behind or the sides. Easy.

I fired shot after shot, barely taking time to aim. Everyone on our side was behind us. The gun whirred with each shot, vibrating in my hand. Takers fell down in front of us, but their numbers remained thick. More and more shots poured in from all directions, a constant onslaught.

My heart pumped harder as we tried to dodge the growing fire and at the same time escape past the Takers in front. They were getting closer, pushing us back. Our only defense was Ariana's shield, which she struggled to maintain while we dodged deadly red beams.

We were forced to back up against a tent, taking the defensive. All hope of making it out had been crushed. Then steamrolled. We were just trying to not die as quickly now. I couldn't see signs of other guards' abilities being used. How many had already died?

Ariana kept her shield up, her fierce determination never fading. The five of us would hold out as long as we could. Hopefully our other friends had made it. I fired at the Takers. The shots, bolstered by some other guards with guns, were keeping the Takers at bay as they shot at Ariana's shield, trying to press forward. We were down to about fifteen Takers at the front, but more from behind had almost reached us. Once they did, it would be over. A shield couldn't ward off over all those people.

My gun whirred again as I tried to fire. Instead of a beam launching out of it, the green lights on the side flickered down, and the whirring fizzled out.

"Seriously?" I asked no one in particular.

I tried desperately to turn it back on. Nothing. It was dead. I threw it to the ground outside the force field. My shoulders dipped down.

The RCC person had been non-resistant since I first took him from his tent. There was hardly any mental pull and very little pain in my head. He must have noticed I wasn't thinking about him when the gun failed. He took the chance and pulled with all his willpower against my mind.

"Ah." I clutched my head, fighting to maintain a firm hold on him. Like a pet's leash, I wrapped the mental rope around and around my hand, keeping him with me as he tried to pull away. But the pain was inevitable as he struggled to break free. My vision grew blotchy and black around me, and my head felt filled with bricks. Sharp pain coursed through my temples. I fought to stay on my feet, to maintain my hold.

"Let. Me. Go," the man hissed. With every word came a fresh pound in my head. The leash was starting to unwrap itself.

The five of us here weren't going to make it out. The hope I held onto was for the others. With all the Takers focused on us, they could escape.

"I'm outta knives," Gray said. He sounded hopeless too. I had a couple, but all my focus had to be on holding that mental leash. It was burning my mind more and more.

"My gun's dead too," said one of the two guards with us, an older girl whose ability had something to do with poison.

The force field flickered. A laser beam flew past us before the force field went back up. The Takers at the back sounded nearer and nearer to our row of tents. Their shouts and footsteps rung loudly in my ears as I played a deadly game of mental tug of war with the RCC person. I ground my teeth together, desperate for the pain to stop. *I can't do this any more... Can't I just...let him go?* How many minutes did we have until they killed us all anyway? Three? Two?

One?

A hand landed on my back, helping me straighten up. Red beams flew out from behind the failing force field, shooting down the last of the Takers in front.

"Damion, no." I turned to look up at him. Tears pricked at my eyes. "You were supposed...to get away." The pain from holding the RCC person was making it hard to speak.

"We're all gonna," he said. "You have to get ready to run."

I tried to focus my vision and whipped my throbbing head back and forth, each turn feeling like my brain was slamming into my skull. *Soon...just gotta hold on...until we escape.*

"Where is...he?" I asked. Elliot was struggling to stand against the tent, eyes drooped, breathing heavy. But... "Where's Xavier?"

Whoosh. Two tents on the other side of the camp burst into flames. I got my answer.

"He'll meet us, I promise," Damion said, squeezing my hand. Another tent was engulfed in fire. "But this won't keep 'em back long, and he can't do it again. We have to go."

I couldn't leave Xavier. Not again. There was no telling if we would have any energy left after this.

The sharp pain in my head reminded me. "I don't have a choice, do I?" I looked over at the RCC person, whose teeth were clenched as he tried to out-will me. "I'm holding *him.*"

The others wouldn't make it if they dragged the man. But looking at Elliot made me wonder if Xavier would even be able to walk after setting the fire. A whole wall of flame now separated us from the Takers behind us. That would have taken a lot of energy under normal circumstances.

"You do." Damion was quiet for a second. He pressed his lips together before speaking. "If you...take him out now, somebody can take the RCC."

My new ability. I could destroy the man and go after Xavier.

"Take him out?" Thalia asked. She turned to Ariana. "What's he talking about?"

"I'll explain later," Ariana said, her voice nearing a whisper. "Or I guess you'll see."

"You'll...let me go after him?" I asked in disbelief.

"I'll go with you." Damion gave a nod. "But yeah."

"We need Damion here." Wayne shook his head. "Whatever you're planning to do, we have more people. Someone could get hurt."

"You'll be—" Damion started.

I hated to admit it, but Wayne was right. "He's right," I said. I breathed in and looked my brother square in the face. "You have to stay with them."

"And there's no time to argue about it," Hamisi told my brother. He turned to me, his tone urgent. "Whatever you're gonna do, do it now."

I pressed my hand to the RCC person's arm, keeping a firm hold as he tried to jerk away. Suddenly, I felt doubtful. I'd only managed a flower when practising. "I don't know if I can do this."

Damion gave me a hard look. A look that reminded me of what the Takers had just done. "Do it."

I swallowed and looked back to the Taker. I hardened my gaze and tightened my grip on his arm. Images of Xavier— beaten and bloody—flashed behind my eyes, replacing the scene in front of me. Ropes of awful memory wrapped around my heart, squeezing it and pumping my blood with the loathing I felt for the Takers. They had slaughtered our families. They had tortured me and sent us out here to die.

And that wasn't enough for them. They had come down to Earth, to suck up its resources and preserve their gluttonous lives. They'd taken Xavier and Elliot, and now Xavier could be... I didn't even know if he would be alive when I found him.

"Renee." A soft hand brushed my arm. Ariana. "It's done."

I hadn't realized I'd pressed my eyes shut. I blinked them open to find a pile of grey flakes on the ground. The pain in my head was already fading. A silvery-blue chip stood out amid the ash. Damion plucked it out. He tucked it into one of his pockets, deep inside his jacket.

"If you're going," he said, "you gotta go now."

I nodded. I gave a last look to my brother and friends. Hamisi, Wayne, and Thalia were all wide-eyed. I turned away, sprinting towards where the fire ended. The others ran in the opposite direction, into the safety of the forest.

I tried to shield my eyes against the dark smoke as I pushed closer to the flaming tents. I blinked against the stinging in my eyes and focused on a figure lying on the ground. *Xavier.*

I ran faster, the heat washing over me with new intensity as I grew closer to him. Sweat coated my skin, sticking my clothes to my body. I coughed as the smoky air was drawn into my lungs.

I knelt beside Xavier on the mud-crusted grass. He lay unconscious, half of his body still in the fire. Only his jeans hadn't been burned off, and they weren't good shape. The side near the fire had singed down to shorts length, and the side near me had not fared not much better. His chest and face were painted with dried blood, and his hair was slick with sweat.

"Xavier," I called. I tried to edge closer. The heat seared my face. "Xavier."

"Get the Soaker!" A Taker shouted from behind the wall of fire. Fresh panic crashed through me like a wave. I had to get us out of here before they put it out.

I grabbed Xavier's arm and held it firmly. Though his skin burned mine, I clenched my teeth together, refusing to pull my hand away. I tugged him backwards with all my strength, but I was forced to stop a few times and start again. Finally, I got him a couple feet away from the wall of fire. My hand was pink and stinging when I pulled it away.

"Xavier," I said again. "You *have* to wake up." He didn't stir. I shook him with my other hand but drew away quickly from the heat. "Xavier." I tried to shake him again. Nothing.

Water started to pour over the wall of fire, which grew smaller. "Please, Xavier." I wrapped my fingers around his, ignoring the pain. I squeezed his hand. "Let's go home."

His brown eyes slowly blinked open, unfocused, as if he were coming out of an anesthetic. He turned his head to the other side.

"Where...?" His voice was quiet, thick with tiredness. His eyes came to focus on me. His eyebrows dipped down in drowsy confusion. "Renee?"

The fire was low enough now that I could see the Takers, blurry figures from the smoke, behind it. "I'm sorry," I said. I put Xavier's arm around my shoulder and dragged him to his feet. "We have to go."

My shoulder and arm burned. He leaned heavily on me as we trudged away. My heart thudded harder and harder. The fire kept getting lower.

Eventually, Xavier seemed to wake up more. A small portion of his weight was lifted from my shoulder. We moved a fraction faster as the safe haven of the forest beckoned.

The fire was almost out behind us.

When we reached the first line of trees, our cluster of friends was waiting. I didn't have time to call them idiots. Hands lifted Xavier from me, and we made our retreat, weaving through the thick trees. The sounds from the camp grew distant.

We'd gotten almost a quarter of the way back and had entered a small clearing when Xavier collapsed against Damion. I helped to set him down and let his head rest on my lap. He had cooled down, well past normal, and his breathing was shallow.

"Is he okay?" Ariana asked, stepping closer. Her voice held a tremor. "Damion?"

"He's fine," Damion assured her. "Exhausted."

I didn't take my eyes off Xavier. We had him back. He would be alright. He had to be. "When will he wake up?" I asked.

"I don't know," Damion said. His voice grew quieter. "You didn't wake up for days."

"Days?" I repeated. Though I'd already known, I didn't want it to be true.

"I believe it," Elliot mumbled, and I glanced over at him. His dark figure was slumped against a tree.

"Where did the other guards go?" I asked, looking around.

"We told those two guards with us to run ahead," Damion said. "I don't know how many of the others made it out. I think some of them were able to run back into the forest when it got bad."

"I'll check." I closed my eyes and reached out with my mind. "I found nine of them..." I tried to keep contacting the others but came up short. "That's it."

"Was Caleb one of them?" Gray asked. "He's my little cousin." I hadn't heard from Caleb.

I tried again, just in case. "I'm sorry. He won't get back to me," I told Gray.

He glanced down and bowed his head.

"Maybe he's just knocked out," Ariana said to Gray, giving him a small smile. "One of the others could have brought him back."

"Yeah." Gray nodded. "Yeah, maybe you're right."

"I can't believe we actually did it," Thalia said, lifting the mood a bit.

I looked back down at Xavier and couldn't have agreed more. We'd managed to keep our promises. Maybe all of our struggles, everything we were fighting for, would eventually give way to the peace we wanted. Someday.

"We should get them back soon as we can," Hamisi said, looking over at Elliot, then Xavier. "They look like they need the rest."

After he healed my burns, Damion and I took hold of Xavier and lifted him off the ground. Hamisi suspended Elliot in the air. When he got tired, Ariana and Gray took a turn and lift him together. The walk back to the Base was careful. We had to stop a couple times to rest, but we made it.

We were home.

The group of other guards we had fought with opened the gates for us as we approached the burn marks on the ground. They all gave us hugs, with expressions ranging from excited to relieved to grave. Alexis, who had super-strength, took Xavier from Damion and me with ease, which we very much needed after the hours of walking. Though it did look quite funny to see her carrying his large frame in her thin one.

Gray's eyes lit up when he saw a boy a bit younger than us in the back of the group. He ran over and gave the boy a hug. I smiled. That must have been Caleb.

After everybody was done hugging and had settled down a little, Damion spoke to the group. "Thank you all. I know not everything went as planned, but we have the chip now. With any luck, the Takers will abandon this camp and move farther away. We still need to be on guard for now, but we're finally a step closer to being safe from them. We couldn't have done it without you."

With the help of Hamisi and Alexis, we laid Xavier and Elliot on cots in an empty sickroom.

"How was he?" I asked Damion. "When you found him?" I was trying to clean up Xavier's face a bit, and Ariana was doing the same for Elliot. Damion's healing hadn't erased all the blood.

Damion took a second to answer. "Not good," he said. He looked at me. "They were using ice water."

My eyes grew wide. "Oh god." That would have been horrible for anybody, but with the way the cold impacted Xavier, I didn't even want to imagine.

He was healed physically now, but would he be okay when he woke up? I tucked two blankets around him. The last thing he needed was to wake up cold. Hopefully the small bit of warmth would help re-energize him faster.

Damion left to go to the office and hide the RCC inside a small metal box in the cupboard. Only the people who had been in the battle with us would know where it was. Nobody went into the office except us, and we wanted it to be safe.

"Do you really think the Takers will leave their camp?" I asked Ariana. There had been so many more when we attacked this time. I'd started to have doubts.

"I know they will," Ariana reassured. She grinned at me. "We did it. We're safe."

I had to believe she was right. I let myself believe that we were. The Takers were going to leave, and we were safe, for the moment. I grinned back at Ariana.

"We did it," I echoed.

More than that, this victory made it seem like we could actually stop them from destroying us. Our struggle, our losses, wouldn't be in vain. The human race would survive.

For the first time since we'd arrived at the Base, I didn't need to check that everybody I loved was safe before I curled up next to Xavier and slept.

Dear Reader:

Thank you. Thank you for opening this book and letting me tell you this story. There was a time not long ago, where having somebody else holding a story I'd written felt like a dream. Believe me when I say that you, you holding this book, have brought a dream to life. For that, I could not be more grateful.

I would like to hear what you think of the book. What you liked, didn't like, what made you laugh or cry. Everything. Please email me: smpearceauthor@gmail.com, or contact me via social media with your thoughts.

I respond, I promise.

About The Author

Blogger, honor roll student, tutor, world's best big sister, and now young adult author. As a budding novelist, S.M. Pearce wrote the first draft of Outliers at the young age of thirteen. A proud Whovian, she shares a passion for creative writing and art, and aspires to a career in architecture.

Visit S.M. Pearce on Facebook and Twitter @smpearceauthor, and her blog: brainclutterblogs.

Acknowledgments

First off, I'd like to thank my parents, for supporting me, and helping me through this writing journey. For telling me that I can do anything I set my mind to, and always doing their best to give me the tools I need to succeed. For hearing me ramble for hours about new ideas, and always encouraging me to keep having them. I truly could not have done this without their love, support, and encouragement. I'd also like to thank my friend Bailey, for reading the roughest of rough scenes, and for her continued support and excitement for me as I wrote.

Next, I would like to give thanks to my amazing beta readers, Sarah and Isabella. They have helped me immensely in developing this story, and I couldn't appreciate their time and feedback more. Thank you both, for the help, and also the laughs.

Finally, I would like to give thanks to my wonderful editors, Anya Kagan and Erin Rhew, for their dedication to making this story the best it could be.